The
Colours
that
Blind

Also by Rutendo Tavengerwei

Hope Is Our Only Wing

The Colours that Blind

RUTENDO TAVENGERWEI

HOT
KEY
BOOKS

First published in Great Britain in 2020 by
HOT KEY BOOKS
80–81 Wimpole St, London W1G 9RE
www.hotkeybooks.com

Copyright © Rutendo Tavengerwei, 2020

A CIP catalogue record for this book is available from the British Library.

ISBN: 978-1-4714-0818-2
Also available as an ebook and in audio

1

For my aunt Synodia Tavengerwei,
who has a very kind heart.

This book is dedicated to the memory of
the Elim Vumba missionaries, whose story
has stayed with me ever since I heard it.

And to everyone who feels inadequate, you are enough.

PART ONE

the thing that happened

1

Tumi

I f sleep is meant to summon peace and rest, then why does mine hunt down dead memories and haul them back to me like a cat with prey?

It's the same every night. The scars are the first thing I see, and when I do, it feels as though it is happening again. They are always so vivid. Clawed onto a face. A man's face, a woman's face, sometimes no particular face. Burrowed deep in skin and smeared with charcoal.

Then that strong smell, flooding my nose and choking the breath out of me. It terrifies me, how real it feels.

I whisper a prayer, like I do every time I realise I have escaped my terrors and that it was the alarm ringing, not clucking chickens, that woke me.

It takes me a minute to put myself together. But it's OK. I've shaken all of that off now and it's time to go win a race.

Let's do this!

Stormzy's rippled rap is now blasting through the double bass of my headphones as I walk to the mirror fitted in the middle of my wardrobe. I stare blankly at my reflection.

My tie looks too tight, tucked into the nook of my shirt as though I'm about to hang.

It's ridiculous, given that I'll take it off in a bit, but today I need to look like a winner. And winners don't look as if they're trying too hard. I loosen it a little and step back, craning my neck to see if there's an angle where I like my reflection better. I take in a deep breath and my eyes lock with the brown ones of the pale figure in the mirror. My lip curls slightly. It's usually at this point that I remember why the horrors keep visiting me at night. I still look the same way. And that is the problem.

Focus, Tumi.

The track changes on my playlist and I click to bring it back to Stormzy. It's the nerves that have me all riled up like this. I can't afford to mess up today, and Stormzy's best for getting that confidence flowing in my veins. I start rapping along to the tune. I must keep my head in the game and not be distracted. For the rest of the team, failing is just a minor setback, but for me it's not an option. Winning this race is like breathing; it's something I have to do.

Focus, Tumi. Champion, that's all I must see. Not the paleness of my skin, but a champion! People love champions.

3

Mkoma's car honks outside. I steal a glance at my game face before peering through the window. We're still at the warning honk that he always gives to say that the car might just leave without me. But, knowing my brother, I have a few minutes before he really gets annoyed. I look at the calendar and mark the date. Three more weeks to go! Today will set it all in motion.

In a few days Coach Ngoni will choose the swim-team captain. The battle is between Bongani and me, and although almost everyone tells me that the coach will pick me, because I am clearly the better swimmer and Bongani's butterfly is weak as hell, little flies of doubt occasionally buzz around me.

The thing is, everyone at school adores Bongani and thinks he's cool. I'm up against a lot here. He is already captain of the tennis team and the track team, and there's been talk that he might be made prefect next year. And as if that's not enough, he plays piano sometimes during assemblies, making all the girls want to chat him up. The only good thing is that whenever Bongani plays, it's always renditions of Cardi B or Khalid, leaving old Mrs Roderbelt in horror at such 'improper behaviour and mischief'.

I mean, the kid's a real jack-of-all-trades and a master of ... well, none. So I guess, all things considered, he's cool or whatever, I mean, if that's the sort of thing you're into.

We're friends, but really it isn't a big deal. What matters is that I'm part of the team.

The car honks again. I peep through the window and see it now, Mkoma's black Discovery, out of the driveway, parked by the road, with the gate slid open behind it.

I will definitely be in trouble with Mkoma if I don't get out of the house immediately. As I pass the kitchen, I pop my lunchbox into my schoolbag, sling my gym bag across my shoulder, grab the pile of books by the kitchen counter and bang the door on my way out, racing to the car.

Mkoma is not always the most patient person. His eyes are already pasted on the rear-view mirror, giving me the pre-talk before the actual 'the clock doesn't take pity on anyone' speech. I pull the main gate shut behind me and glide into the car. His eyes fall on my headphones and I quickly slide them down as though they've suddenly become hot.

'What did I say about being late, Tumirai?' He presses down on the accelerator. I watch him shift his legs between the pedals, change gears with one hand and gently place his foot on the accelerator again. I close my eyes as the cylinders bow to the sound, and I imagine myself in the driver's seat. Just two more years and I'll be sixteen, shaving, and old enough to drive a car like it really ought to be driven.

'I'm sorry, Mkoma,' I say quietly, fidgeting with the pile of books the librarian allowed me to bring home and binge-read. This time I got books mostly to do with biology.

I figured the most important things I have to work on to improve my swimming are speed and endurance. And if I am going to devise an effective personal technique, if I am to be better than the rest of the team, I have to read as much as possible to understand my body and activate my core.

I glance at my phone and my eyes linger on the date. It's almost as though it's haunting me. In three weeks, I must have read all these books and applied my new knowledge as quickly as I can, so I can be the fastest at the national trials. Coach says there are only ever two new recruits picked at any try-out, out of the hundreds that pitch up. But he says if we're lucky they might pick our team for the relays because there's a bit more room there. The whole team is hoping we all get picked, but secretly we're preparing for the individual events just in case.

Normally Mkoma fusses about how the chlorine is especially bad for my skin and that swimming means more visits to the dermatologist and expensive creams, blah blah . . . But for my birthday, Mkoma gave me a blank cheque, anything I wanted! So I asked him to drive me to Bulawayo for the national swimming try-outs.

I sit waiting for my brother's iconic line.

'You need to be more serious, Tumirai, about life, about school, because, you know – the clock doesn't take pity on anyone.'

And there it is. There's the line.

I smile and look out of the window.

'You only get very little time for a shot at so many great things in this world. And you must understand this now: people like us cannot afford to be mediocre. They won't give you a chance out there unless you work harder than anyone else and take it!'

'Yes, Mkoma.'

I almost know this speech by heart now. People like us are looked down upon simply because of where we come from; people like us are presumed incompetent before we do or say anything; people like us have our countries robbed and are mocked for experiencing poverty as the resulting consequence; people like us are told to hold in our grievances and move on because we suffer from paranoia; people like us are people of colour, or no colour in my case.

Mkoma has told me again and again about the injustices the world has committed against 'us' – in this country, in the world. Among the many things that changed Mkoma, being overseas was one of them. He came back hardened and angry. I think that happens when you see your life pass you by and you're forced to accept it as though it was part of your plan all along. Also, I don't think it was very easy for him over there. He often talks about how *they* jealously guarded all the good opportunities for themselves, while also stealing the good ones back home too. The 'revolving wheel of injustice', as he calls it.

Mkoma must have realised I had drifted off again. He glances at me, his eyes searching my face to make sure I'm listening.

'Seat belt.'

His voice is always stern when he's serious. Right now, it ripples with frustration that I was late yet again. But it's really not my fault. Waking up early is for some people, people like Mkoma. But I clearly missed out on that gene.

When I finally glance at him, his face is serious and his focus steady on the road with his eyebrows slightly bunched up. He has something on his mind. Typical. I have memories of Mkoma when he used to be carefree and when his laughs simply would not stay in his belly. But that was before the thing that happened ...

'Saru will fetch you in the afternoon after she's gotten Noku from nursery school. Don't go home by yourself.'

Mkoma reminds me the same way he does every morning, with his right eyebrow raised and his voice stern. I sigh. I hate that he treats me as though I'm just a kid. The other boys in my class either drive themselves back home already or walk, but I still have to be picked up from school like a little child.

'You have your sunscreen?' Mkoma just needs a dress and he would make such a perfect mother, honestly.

'Yes,' I mumble as I try to balance my books and my gym bag.

I always try to remind myself not to get upset at him. Somewhere deep down I know he means well, and I imagine it can't be easy trying to play father to a soon-to-be-fifteen-year-old brother. So I always try to exercise my best patience with him. But also I think this crankiness has something to do with the fact that the coffee pot was empty this morning.

'Tumirai,' he calls after me as I reach to close the door.

'Haa, Mkoma, I'm going to be late now.' I don't mean to, but now irritation oozes out of me.

'Don't forget.'

Mkoma's eyes are sincere and his lips crack into a tiny smile. His hand reaches out for a fist bump. A smile creeps up on me. I love this part.

'I never forget.'

2

There is an electric teenage energy that fills the air on the last day of school. Even Mrs Roderbelt, who usually does a stellar job at hushing students just by the sound of her heels in the corridor, has given up and is now just standing by the pedestrian gate watching all the chit-chatter.

Her green pleated skirt dances in the wind the same way her flowy blonde hair does. Her white blouse hangs slightly from the belt where it is tucked in. She now seems to have detained a few boys by the gate, talking on and on about something that evidently bores them. I think she should have joined Parliament instead. She would have loved it there, with all that endless talking.

'Isn't that right, Tumzy?'

I turn and glance at Musa, who is sitting on a green bench close to me with his arm hanging lazily around some girl from the lower form to whom he is no doubt feeding lies. I raise my chin at him in agreement.

Musa is one of my few real friends. In the earlier forms, he struggled a little with his maths and geography ... and chemistry; well, with everything really, so the teachers were not always patient with him. Mrs Roderbelt always used to complain that he was too slow for her A class, but too fast for the B class. It must have been quite an awkward position for Musa to be in. I thought I knew how he felt, so I moved and sat next to him to help when he got stuck.

My eyes wander around the parking lot, looking to see if Saru has parked somewhere, but I can't see her. Saru is Mkoma's ... well, I don't quite know what she is to him, to be honest. All I know is that she has a kid, Noku, with him, and that we're family.

Kids are laughing and chatting. So much excitement for a few days of holidays. Because we all know that in a week most of us will be back here, seated behind those wooden desks for holiday school. Mkoma says holiday school became a thing after 2008, when the teachers were striking and every child needed a tutor. That was the year my father disappeared.

After everything calmed down, people never figured out what to do with their kids, I suppose. For my class, holiday school isn't exactly compulsory, because I'm in the third form and exams are almost a whole year away. But with mid-term exams coming up in a few months, we still need to be ready. Mrs Roderbelt has made it abundantly clear that she will not tolerate anything less than perfection in her chemistry class, because otherwise it will tarnish her perfect record. She said this with a sharp eye on Musa.

Two girls from the sixth form pass me by the bench at the pick-up point, smiling. 'You killed it today in the pool, mrungu,' one of them says. A group of boys start chanting 'Mrungu! Mrungu!' as soon as they see me, ruffling my hair and shoving me playfully as they pass. There's a wide grin plastered on my face.

The school is a mad scene, with cars constantly riding in, picking kids up and sending them into the holidays. The prefects don't seem to fuss about us walking on the lawn today. It's almost as though school is a prison and we're all leaving it. Bongani and Liam toss a rugby ball on the other side of the car park. They turn towards me and nod, now walking in my direction. I glance at Musa, who is still preoccupied with the girl, now sitting a little closer to her than before.

'Yo, *blud*,' Bongani says, turning to Liam. They've been friends for as long as I've known them, probably longer, so they're close enough to call each other 'blud'.

'Your kind killed it in the pool today, didn't he? He was a beast in there. Did you see how long he was underwater after that dive?' he asks as though I wasn't there. I don't know why people do that.

'Flip, boy, you ain't white! What were you doing showing up like that?' Liam laughs. He always makes those rejecting jokes whenever Bongani implies I'm white, but I think he means it. I don't know that it hurts me, because he's right, I'm not white like him.

'Look at his white-boned genius self!' Bongani says, now turning to me. They both chuckle and fake-punch me in the stomach. Laughing with them sickens me, but I join in, the same mistake I've been stuck with since my first day at St Catherine's High when Bongani had said I couldn't be black because my skin was clearly white, almost as though he got to decide. Now, that does sting. He reminds me of my Bamkuru and his philosophies about how I look. And although I want nothing to do with Bamkuru ever again, I'm not so dumb as to let Bongani or any of the other kids think I'm not cool enough to take a stupid nickname.

The thing is, at St Catherine's almost everyone comes from a well-off family, so to stand out you're either athletic, swagged up or a school embarrassment. Nobody cares about a kid who gets all the answers right.

And that's why swimming is my drug of choice.

When I first joined the school, I had never felt so misplaced and lost, which is strange because St Catherine's is quite diverse, with black kids and white kids, a few mixed kids and even Meng Sue and Chang Li, the Chinese students.

But I am the first kid with albinism ever to have come here. Some of the other kids told me they had never been that close to 'someone like me' before.

It doesn't really surprise me. Back when we used to do things Bamkuru's way, I was at the school for the blind. Almost every student there had albinism. Although admittedly most of us just had bad eyesight, we could hardly be called blind. I didn't necessarily enjoy being at the school for the blind, but at least there I was just a kid: not too pale to be black or too black to be white.

'Looks like you might just take the captainship from me, mrungu!'

My stomach twists as he says it, but I smile. Problem is, everyone at school calls me by that name now so it's too late to make a fuss. And although every time I hear it my stomach turns, I still pull my lips into a smile.

'Is that quaking I hear, Bongani?' Coach passes by in his St Catherine's tracksuit and cap, smirking. Liam and I hiss behind Bongani, throwing little jabs at him to show he's been had. The coach must have overheard our conversation.

I grin as I watch the displeasure on Bongani's face. The swimming games today were lit! I'd won two of the solo races, leaving Bongani the runner-up at least a good four seconds behind, and on top of that I'd made a beautiful finish for the team relay. The whole school had chanted my name at the end of the event – but only that same name I let Bongani impose on me. I suppose it's quite exhilarating when people know your name, even if it's not your real one.

There's always such a fuss when I'm in a tournament. In those few moments, although people are in their own house teams, all of St Catherine's seems to come together, chanting our war cry and cheering as I plough up and down the pool as fast as I possibly can. It's the way of the blazer, as we like to say.

Although I love the support, like I said, most of the kids don't actually know me. Some of them sort of do, of course, but only from glimpses of the life that I allow them to see on Instagram. But that's the thing, that's why I need swimming. Because it keeps me alive and relevant, it covers my skin, makes me one of them. And those few hours at the swim meets are my most treasured moments. It's always butterflies and racing blood, a feeling I wish I could catch, trap in a bottle and sprinkle in the sky.

Tonia, the girl who sits in the corner in class, walks past me to her father's car, laughing hysterically with her friends. She always wears her wavy hair in a neatly pulled-back bun and purses her lips slightly before she smiles. Three years in the same class and only this afternoon after the swimming tournament did she slide into my Instagram DMs: 'Fam you were slayin out there' with a heart-face emoji!

Every afternoon at three twenty sharp Saru's red VW

Polo swerves into the car park with Noku tucked into a car seat in the back. She always leans across, opens the door and allows me to slide into the passenger seat, before waving to the prefects on duty and driving off. It's routine. But today she's late. I look nervously at my wristwatch.

Musa's mother pulls up and beckons for him to get into the car. He jumps up, pushing the girl under his arm aside.

I still get goosebumps every time I see Musa's mother, and not the good kind. Once Musa asked me to his house on a Saturday, thinking that he stood a chance with me at *FIFA*. I remember it clearly. He had the controller in his hand, pressing the green button, any button, spewing pleas for me to take it easy on him. We heard the front door click as it closed. His mother, all merry, almost sang Musa's name on her way to his room. But as soon as she opened the door, her forehead zigzagged in lines and her eyebrows lowered. Her voice quivered as she shouted at Musa, upset that he would bring a stranger to her house. But I was hardly a stranger. She had met me at least four times already. Her rants seemed to be about more than Musa not asking for permission to invite me over. I left there as soon as I could, and Musa has never invited me back.

His mother lowers the passenger window and stares at us. I rub my arms even though I have a blazer on.

'Yo, Tumi-boy, I'll check you later, boss. Don't forget we have team practice on Tuesday.'

He pounds his fist on mine. Unlike the others, Musa never calls me 'mrungu', so although he comes up with a new lame nickname for me every day, I don't mind it.

His mother ignites the engine again. I wave at her. She almost smiles at me.

3

I stand close to the wall, peering through so I can match Saru and Mkoma's voices with their expressions. I have never heard Mkoma and Saru fighting so openly before. Saru's voice seems much calmer than Mkoma's, which bounces off the walls and makes his lips tremble when he speaks.

'You couldn't have told me before?'

'Emergencies don't exactly leave time for you to plan, do they? That's why they're emergencies. You're acting like I planned this.' They're both quiet for a while and my eyes bounce between the two of them, hungry for the drama.

'The doctors say she'll be flown to South Africa first thing tomorrow morning. I need to go with her.'

Mkoma breathes deeply, his eyes fixed on Saru, whose leg is now gently tapping. I don't think she realises yet though. Mkoma scratches his head and chews on his bottom lip. I can tell he is looking for the right thing to say. Whenever

Saru's leg bounces like that, it's a sure sign that the anger is creeping slowly into her system.

'Can you not take Noku with you then?'

Saru heaves a sigh. She is still calm, but her voice now has a hint of frustration in it.

'You remember, don't you, that Noku's passport is still off being renewed? And it'll take at least another week or two, which means I can't possibly take her with me, can I? And even if I could, what about Tumi? Who will stay with him?'

'You know very well that I can't miss my flights, Saru. I have to go in for work. I have two flights tomorrow. What are we supposed to do now?'

I purse my lips and watch.

Mkoma better check himself. That leg really be bouncing now.

'I told you, the kids can both stay with my aunt in Marondera. I won't even be gone that long.'

Mkoma scratches his head, gets up from the sofa where he is sitting and paces up and down. I glance at Noku, walking towards me with one hand holding her doll as though saving it from a tragic fall, the other rubbing her crusty eyes. She certainly looks like she enjoyed that nap.

'I can't let Tumi go to a stranger's house, Saru, you know that. If anything happened to him ...'

'Oh, I see how it is! So basically you're saying I am so

irresponsible that I'd send Noku to a stranger, right?'

The anger has set in now. It might just get real in here . . .

Mkoma looks at her as though he wants to say yes, but seeing the look on her face he decides against it. He scratches his head again. They now both look visibly irritated, frustrated, troubled . . . there's no one right word to describe it. Mkoma walks over to Saru and cups her cheeks in his hands. She tries to suppress a smile and pushes him away, but playfully.

'C'mon, Saru, you know that's not what I mean. After what happened with Bamkuru, I'm only saying I have to be careful where I let Tumi go.'

Saru rolls her eyes at him as he strokes her hand. This right here sums up their whole situation-ship. 'It's complicated' doesn't even begin to explain this weirdness.

A thought crosses my mind. This is my big chance.

'I can take care of Noku.'

I have it all figured out. It's easy. If I stay with Noku, Mkoma will have no choice but to see that I'm no longer a child and he'll stop treating me like one. And also, it will mean I can avoid missing any of my swim practice.

Mkoma looks at me, his face blank. 'Tumi, please. Shouldn't you be doing your homework or something?'

His voice is tired and hints at irritation.

'Mkoma, I can do this.'

'How exactly, when you're still afraid of the dark,

Tumirai? I don't think taking care of anyone is something that's on your list of strengths right now.' He buries his face in his hands in frustration.

There is honestly no need to say such things in front of people!

Noku sniggers by my side, looking up at me as though she somehow expects me to join in. I bunch my eyebrows and narrow my eyes at her. Mkoma says men aren't afraid of the dark; that's why he sleeps with his lights off. I get that. And I'm not really afraid of the dark, but ever since I left Bamkuru's I've had to sleep with the lights on because the dark hurts my eyes. And besides, sometimes the night hides terrible things that can creep up and take you.

Saru looks at me and smiles softly, as if saying to ignore Mkoma.

'I think I'll just take them to Ambuya's house in Vumba.' The words spill out of Mkoma's mouth. I don't think he intended them to.

I stand there frozen and watching Mkoma, waiting for him to take them back.

I haven't forgotten the conversation I heard between Mkoma and Saru a long while back, when Saru used to sleep over more. They were sitting on the couch in the middle of the lounge. At first I heard echoes of their conversation from the corridor where I was, before I heard Saru mention my name: '... does Tumirai know?'

Mkoma had replied in a quiet voice, 'You don't tell a boy his age that his Ambuya watched people die. He won't understand . . . She will tell him herself when the time is right. In any case, it is really her story to tell.'

I had shuddered at the thought, and scars had been all I could see. Even though Saru and Mkoma had changed the subject, and even though I had tiptoed back to my room and left my light on when I got into my bed, all I could think about was Ambuya watching people die, perhaps even killing them too. All I could see for days in my terrors were the scars.

Come to think of it, I actually haven't seen Ambuya since . . . the thing that happened. She phoned once or twice, but we didn't speak for long. And even before that, we were never close. It wasn't like how it was with her and Mkoma, who Ambuya had practically raised, because he went to a high school there in Vumba and visited her often. The few times I had seen her was when Bamkuru had taken my cousins and me to the village to visit.

After my father disappeared, Bamkuru insisted that a young boy like me needed to be around cousins his age, and Ambuya hadn't fussed about it. Though I wish someone *had* fussed about it, given all of Bamkuru's weird cultural misconceptions and superstitions about my albinism. But I know Mkoma, who was only a seventeen-year-old heading off to a new country for the first time by himself, couldn't take me with him. Although I know it's selfish, sometimes I wish he had stayed with me, because then maybe some things would not have happened the way they did.

Back then, Bamkuru had a store near Ambuya's house, and when he needed to restock, that meant a trip for all of us. We didn't go often but the few times we did, it had always been for one night. Once or twice I had heard Ambuya hissing at Bamkuru about something behind closed doors. But all the other memories I can see now are of her laughing with him, her head pulled back and the veins showing through the wrinkles in her neck. A dark and jagged scar follows her jawline, zigzagging along it as though someone did a rush job of sewing together torn skin. My own scars, accumulated from all the times I grazed my knees while playing chitsvambe outside, aren't nearly so darkly stained. She looks like the people they talk about who snatch unsuspecting albino boys, shove them into a truck and take them across the border to be sold somewhere nobody knows, before the police discover them. Those aren't made-up stories, you know. Those things happen.

And anyone who laughs that much with Bamkuru deserves to be in a prison cell just like he is!

'She's been complaining for a while that she never sees us.' Mkoma interrupts my daydreaming.

My jaw drops. *He really is serious about this!*

'I'll drive down on Friday with the kids, spend the day there on Saturday and drive back early Sunday, get some rest and fly out Monday. It's perfect.'

Nah, fam. It is not perfect.

I can tell a bad idea from a mile away, and this is one of those really good bad ideas. I wait for Saru to say something, to talk some sense into my brother, but she just stands there and nods. Am I the only one to see that this has trouble painted all over it?

'I can't go,' I blurt.

Everyone looks at me.

I stand there nervously, aware that Mkoma might get upset, but I have to do something. I can't say anything bad about Ambuya without proof. She sold half her furniture, ground nuts into peanut butter with her bare hands and, from the way Mkoma tells it, sold both kidneys, half her heart and her liver to get enough money to send him to university in America. She is almost his mother and he's very protective of her. But I know it's all a front.

There has to be another option, someone else who can take care of us. Besides, Ambuya doesn't have Netflix or much network, let alone a pool.

Mkoma stands there uncharacteristically quiet for a while, then asks, 'Why?'

'Musa and I have to practise for the Zim swim-team selection. And also Mrs Roderbelt said she wants everyone present for her chemistry class when holiday classes start next week.'

I stand looking at him, fingers and toes firmly crossed and hoping he will find these two reasons compelling enough to cancel his trip.

'Tumi, but Ambuya's place is so much fun. We can play in that big yard, and chase chickens, and eat lots of guavas. I want to go, Daddy!'

Why is Noku in this conversation?

I look at her with a tinge of resentment as she stares up at Mkoma with her big brown eyes. There are so many reasons why I don't like her right now. Apart from the obvious, she also always calls me by my first name as though we're the same age, instead of saying 'Bamnini' out of respect, like she's supposed to, because technically I'm her uncle. You don't hear me calling Mkoma by his first name. I call him 'Mkoma' for a reason. No wonder he still thinks I'm a child if even Noku can't respect me.

'You will pack your bags tomorrow.' Mkoma's voice is very calm.

He lifts the grinning Noku, who seems fully aware of what she has just done.

4

Next morning I am in Mkoma's bedroom looking for an extra bag to pack. Mkoma has stepped out to fuel the car and run a few errands before we leave. Noku is somewhere in the house. Maybe I should be watching her, but I can hear the soundtrack to *Princess Sofia* playing and I'm sure she's safely in front of the TV. Besides, I'm a little frustrated because I can't find a bag small enough for this trip, which I'm hoping will be short. All the bags in Mkoma's room are either too big or ones he uses for work.

I wonder if I can use that as an excuse.

I dismiss the thought as soon as it settles in my mind. As if Mkoma would ever buy that. I sigh as I swing the wardrobe door open again. I didn't look properly before, but the truth is I really didn't want to. My eyes lift up to the very top of the wardrobe. Mkoma's backpack is lying there, waiting for me.

As I pull it down by the strap, a box tumbles to the floor together with the bag, hitting me on the head and scattering its contents everywhere. I stand there for a while, eyes scanning the bunch of fat letters, all addressed to Mkoma's old address in America. I kneel on the floor, sweep the letters together with my hands and put the whole pile back in the box. They are numbered, as though they should be read in sequence, and I riffle through, but I can't seem to find the first one.

I can hear the gate sliding open now and I peer outside just in time to see Mkoma driving into the yard. I dash back to the box and quickly go through the letters. I shove the envelope marked '2' into my pocket and my hands shuffle through the rest, still looking for the first letter. I know I shouldn't be doing this, but I'm curious.

The sound of the car engine dies down and I can now hear Noku's excited voice cheering about something Mkoma has brought her. My eyes suddenly spot a letter by itself, almost under Mkoma's bed. It's marked with a 1! Footsteps are advancing towards the bedroom, so I toss the box up where it was before, grab the letter from by the bed and shove it into the backpack. All this just as Mkoma walks in.

'What are you doing in here?'

Be cool, be cool.

Ever since Noku and I accidentally knocked over his camera, Mkoma doesn't like us in his room. By Noku and me, I really mean Noku though. I was obviously being well behaved, not snooping in his room at all.

My heart is throbbing and I know my face looks guilty. I don't know if he saw me. I lift the bag to show him, hoping he won't ask any more awkward questions.

'You still haven't packed? We're behind schedule, my friend. Chop-chop.'

I nod, trying to hide my relief as I exit the room. I'm a little excited. I wonder if there are secrets in those letters. Maybe they're from Saru. I hurry to stuff the backpack with all the clothes from my bottom shelf, throwing a pair of running sneakers in there too, so I'll have time to read through one of these mysterious letters. I peer into the corridor to see where Mkoma is, and bump right into him. My hand lingers behind my back, hiding the letter.

'Are you ready?'

'Almost. Umm, I just need to use the bathroom before we go though,' I lie, trying to buy an extra minute to read. He nods and heads into Noku's bedroom to carry her bags to the car. I slip into the toilet, lock the door and my eyes scan quickly through the words on the paper.

My mzukuru,

I was so pleased to receive your letter that I showed it to everyone here in the village. But also so sad to hear you're missing home. Of course we miss you too, but you must be strong and continue to work hard and focus on your

*studies there. Your father would have been so proud. We're
all well here and eager for when you return.*

*The question you asked is a grave one, one you have
asked me multiple times but I have not been ready to
answer it. Thinking about it now, I don't quite know
that I am ready to tell it yet. You see, mzukuru, the past
is a difficult thing, especially when you have to recount
and remember where the wounds formed. But for you,
mzukuru, I will try. I have slipped in this envelope a
few pages from the diary I kept as a young girl all
those years back. The young man at the post office
said I could not send the whole book to you. He said
I had to pay more money if I wanted to do that, and
what ridiculous amounts he told me, mzukuru. I was
not sure if he was trying to take advantage of an old
maid like me, so I tore out the first few pages for you to
read for now, and I will send more with my next letter.
Perhaps it is better that way – you know my memory is
not sharp now anyway. I do so dearly hope that these
pages will keep you company while you are there, so far
from us. And I hope this anger you feel, that you spoke
of, will wane somewhat as you read this. I know they
are only words on paper, but it is my prayer that you
will see that you are not alone, not even in your misery
about your life changing and your dreams becoming
increasingly slippery. And who knows – perhaps sharing*

this part of me might also do me some good.

*I hope you are eating well, my mzukuru. I will ask
the young man at the post office if I can send you some
peanut butter, straight from your Ambuya's kitchen. In
the meantime, read this part of me and know that I carry
you always in my spirit.*

With love always,
Your Ambuya

Mkoma's voice barges in, calling me to the car, and my
underarms sting as though I've already been caught.

*Ambuya wrote the letters? Why are they numbered?
What does she mean, Mkoma asked a grave question?*

I step out of the bathroom, slide both letters into a book
I'm carrying with me, balance my poorly packed backpack
on one shoulder and my gym bag on the other and march
to the car, trying as best I can not to show that I'm hiding
something.

5

Ambuya's story

16 March 1975

I am wondering now as I sit here writing in my old bedroom hut back in the village that I thought I would never come back to, I am wondering – on the day that your life spins on its head and trouble marches to interrupt your normal, do the winds whisper warnings, or the birds call for your attention to alert you to it? Because if so, I must certainly be deaf.

Today was one of those days where you pray the light in from wherever it can come. I feel as though I dragged all the minutes to nightfall and have used up all the strength I had. And yet it is only the first day of many.

I tried not to break down and weep this afternoon as I stood by the stove in Bas Roger's farmhouse stirring something. I can't remember the fancy name the Missus said now, but it was one of those soups that Amai mentioned that the Missus likes to have on Sundays. It was my first day working at the farmhouse today. Two years of nurse training at the Andrew Fleming Hospital in Salisbury and I am now responsible for scrubbing floors, feeding hungry stomachs and washing dirty laundry.

I know I should not grieve so much. It's not Amai's fault, the arthritis. Yet I can almost still hear the ripping as I tore the seal from the envelope three days ago. The shock and pain of it all feels fresh, almost as though it is right now that those words are spilling from Baba's letter. *Come back home*, it said, *you are needed*. Short, precise and life-changing. Befitting of Baba.

And so I'm here, while my peers are finishing off the last few months of the training. It is part of growing up, I imagine. Though I wish someone had warned me about it, because I never would have done it.

I remember exactly what I was doing today before trouble marched in. I had stepped away from the stove and was standing by the window in the Missus's kitchen, craning my neck to see if I could spot Baba. What vain hope, because all that's visible from that window is a vast forest of shrubbery. It reminds me now of the time I heard Baba say that when Bas Rogers's grandfather was first given the land, they had made a boy ride a horse till it was tired, to mark where the farm ended. But do horses actually ever tire? I wonder.

And as I stood there, I lost myself in the view of that shrubbery, thinking of the striped dress I'd worn in

Salisbury – the modest long one that I used to wear when the girls and I would go dancing – and how it had not cheered my spirits. And how even though my hair stood proud, I still felt as though the core had been carved out of my soul.

That was when I noticed the clouds beginning to gather and the wind starting to whistle.

The entire day had been warm, but now there was a cool breeze pushing through the window. I used to think I'd outgrow it, but I still love how playful the wind becomes when it introduces the rains. And how the smell of the earth floats to your nostrils in its excitement to muddy up. I closed my eyes and smiled, allowing the wind to sift its fingers through my afro.

'Rosie!' The Missus's voice made me jump, and I rushed to the stove to wipe the froth that had begun to spill from the pot. I had completely forgotten about the soup!

'It's Thandiwe, madam.'

'Oh, you Africans and your difficult names. How am I meant to remember that? When you're here, your name is Rosie and you must answer to it.'

The Missus has a nephew who grew up right there in the farmhouse, although I have not seen him in years. Is he 'African' too? I have always wondered.

Some time in the past that I can barely remember now, 'African' was only a fact. Africa was simply a geographical location that I was born and grew up in, so of course I was –

am – African. But somehow when the Missus said it today – whenever *they* say it – it feels like something to be ashamed of. Surely it is some kind of crime to take away someone's sense of belonging like that. To push someone to reject themselves.

But even though my throat tightened, I looked down and continued to wipe the stove as quickly as I could so she wouldn't see that some soup had spilled.

The Missus grabbed the rag out of my hand. 'Don't you see you are spoiling the stove, you silly girl? Your first day here and you're doing everything wrong. Your mother ought to come begging on her knees for this.'

'Sorry, madam.'

'Argh, and you've over-boiled the broccoli, Rosie! It's not supposed to look brown like this. What kind of soup will this be?'

'Sorry, madam.'

'Do you speak any more words maybe? Goodness! You need to learn English. How am I to talk to you if your vocabulary is limited to two words? One would think you'd be smarter. Didn't your mother say you were training as a nurse? Don't they teach English in those African schools of yours?'

I looked down again, this time shuffling my fingers and trying to keep the tears in. I did know English. I wondered if she knew that I had never had a choice. English had been forced down my throat like medicine. Without it I would never have been accepted in any school, let alone been allowed to train as a nurse.

'Useless! Simply useless,' she had gone on, before taking the pot off the stove and throwing the soup down the sink. I blinked in shock. Just yesterday I had slept on a barely full stomach because there was not enough to share between the eight of us at home. Comrades are dying, fathers are leaving to join the war, and Amai keeps taking in more children because she has a kind heart. And here the Missus throws soup down the drain!

The strong sound of an engine hummed in the background. You could always tell when Bas Rogers was on his way, simply from the purring of his car a mile away. He had kept the old thing for a long time, perhaps even since before I started school. And on Sundays, as far back as I could remember, he always went out to play cards with his friends in the city.

'Go to the front and see if Mr Rogers brought anything home with him from the city. And tomorrow, please do something about that hair! It looks like an overgrown shrub.'

'Yes, madam.'

I held in the little flutter of anger in my chest. It can never come out. We need this job, all eight of us. And Farai needs to continue at school. Otherwise the cycle will continue. He will end up working on the tea estate, just as Baba does.

I could hear the sound of the wind as it grew stronger, bossing around old pictures of the Missus and Bas Rogers on their wedding day. I dashed through the living room on my way out, adjusting the windows before all the frames fell down from the mantel. The anger of the wind banged the last open window closed, and I quickly pushed down the latch.

There was a storm coming. Even the curtains to the house fluttered nervously, trying to convince the wind to take it easy. The leaves played around, threatening to move away. I stood outside on the veranda, watching the car as it finally drove through the gate. I uncomfortably wiped the storm dust off my eyes.

The car slowed to a halt in front of the house. The clouds tore over. The thunder slid in. I could see Bas Rogers, his face a web of wrinkles, delicately woven by time. My eyes immediately went to the passenger door as it pushed open against the force of the wind, now bringing little sputters of rain. A man got out of the car, one hand carrying a small bag, the other one running through his hair. My heart leaped as he closed the door. The storm was here!

6

Tumi

I am having a hard time imagining Ambuya any younger. Of course I know she wasn't born old, but somehow I don't quite think I realised it. I have so many questions, and growing reservations about going to Ambuya's. I stare at the remaining pages of her diary that were in the letter, wondering what this is all about. Why has Mkoma never mentioned it?

I watch him in the rear-view for a minute. Should I ask him? His brow is furrowed again. Maybe I should keep it to myself for now. He might not be very pleased with me for having gone through his things the way I did.

I glance at Noku, sitting next to me in the back of the car, singing with excitement. I wonder whether Mkoma would take me back with him if I somehow managed to fake my own death, or something more believable like insanity. But knowing Mkoma, he'd probably scare any madness out of me with that deep look of his that feels like he's boring right into you with his eyes. Or he'd drive my fake corpse straight to the morgue, just to teach me a lesson.

My eyes drift to Mkoma, driving on, with his face serious and his brow thick and folded. I have no idea what he's worrying about this time. I look out the window and wonder whether I stole Mkoma's life from him, whether he would have been much happier if he hadn't had to grow up so fast. I miss the way he used to laugh when he pulled pranks on me. Yes, Mkoma used to pull pranks, and cackle away like a hyena. But I have no right to think like this.

Perhaps this is why Ambuya wrote him letters. Perhaps those letters are why he's so blind to who she really is.

My stomach grumbles. Noku catches on and whimpers. The most decent thing she's done in a while. 'Daddy, I'm hungry.'

She pokes her head between the two front seats towards Mkoma. I bet all that singing is what made her hungry. I'm bobbing my head, shuffling between Drake and Takura on Spotify and enjoying the bass. My eyes meet Mkoma's in the rear-view and his settle on my headphones. He says they turn me into some kind of zombie. I think the real reason he minds is because lately I've been sharing my playlists with Noku. And a few weeks back she made a little boy at her crèche cry after chasing him at break-time, screaming, 'Neo, do you love me?'

Needless to say, Mkoma hasn't been very keen on my headphones since then.

In the car, Noku has been composing songs for the whole hour we've been on the road, and most of them have the same tune, if you can call it a tune. About an hour ago Mkoma switched on the radio to drown her out, but that didn't stop her at all. She still sang along, with mostly made-up lyrics, consisting of words that the *Oxford English Dictionary* still needs to be informed about.

'Noku, get back in your seat, please.'

'What are you chewing, Daddy?'

I turn the volume down to hear this.

'I'm not chewing anything, Noku. Now, back in your seat, please.'

'But your mouth is moving.'

Mkoma sighs while I hold back my laughter. The thinking lines haven't disappeared from his face yet.

'Noku, do you really think that I would eat something by myself and not share it with you guys?'

She pauses and stares at him with her nose scrunched up. 'Yes, I do,' she says eventually, with absolute certainty.

My hand flies to my mouth, suppressing the muffled laughter that threatens to ripple out of me. Mkoma turns his head to look at her, his face half surprised and half lighting up with laughter. He chuckles through his nose and shakes his head.

It's because of that one time Mkoma had chicken nuggets at work and left the takeaway box in his car for Noku to find.

That's all it had taken for him to lose her trust when it came to food.

I look ahead through the windscreen. There are barrels in the road and a boom-gate up ahead. The police are back in the roads again. At first after we got a new president last year there weren't a lot of roadblocks. Mkoma had been so excited that day. He had woken up early and, with his flag wrapped across his T-shirt, headed to Unity Square for the march.

He kept saying that all his life he had never been able to answer the question: 'Who was your last president?' And after the 'not-a-coup', we couldn't keep him from asking Noku, any chance he got, who the former president of Zimbabwe was. But now he scowls and protests if you remind him of his once so-jubilant self, rejecting any association with the president, almost like Chance the Rapper does with Trump.

'Noku, back in your seat!' Mkoma's voice bellows again.

'It's not fair.' She scowls, complaining that her hunger is more important than being buckled in. Mkoma watches her through the rear-view mirror, making sure she's strapped in. His eyes shift to me. Without being told, I make sure Noku's strap is secured.

'Some people are so mean! Daddy, why are we going through a famine in this car?'

I look at her little sulking face and let out a giggle. Mkoma, who in this case is obviously 'some people', can't help it too.

'I'm jumping out of the car, Daddy!'

'No, no, Noku. Settle down. Tumirai, make sure she doesn't undo her buckle.' He looks at her through the rear-view, his face now serious. 'And besides, there are things out there that can eat you . . .'

Mkoma slows the car down. I look at him in the mirror and can see him as he watches one of the police officers standing by the boom-gate. His face doesn't register fear, only annoyance. As the police officers come into focus, my muscles tense. My lungs jam up and I can't breathe. Mkoma brings the car to a halt in front of the boom. I am gasping to breathe.

'Good afternoon, officer. Is there a problem?' Mkoma starts.

My hand goes to my hip and I remember the pain, the screams, the scratching. The whole image of that night settles in my mind in troubling detail. My throat closes up.

I catch a glimpse of the officer handing Mkoma back his licence and waving him through. The car starts moving again.

'What vultures! Aren't police there to protect us? Instead all they do is make us feel uneasy, as if we've all done something wrong. Busy there inventing fake crimes and filling quotas for taking our money and our rights. We're not blind.' Mkoma shakes his head and mumbles to himself, still peeping back at the police through the mirror.

It takes me a moment to relax.

My stomach grumbles again. Mkoma looks at me through his mirror, and then shifts his eyes to Noku, who is now visibly sulking with her hands crossed over her chest.

'Why don't we stop at the Halfway House and get some pies?'

Noku smiles.

7

Ambuya dances the way she always does when a car belonging to one of her children or grandchildren pulls onto the homestead. Her grey dreadlocks sway back and forth. Mkoma drives slowly towards the shade of the mango tree, a big grin on his face, while Ambuya trails by the side of the car, next to his window, singing and dancing. I try and imagine her the way the diary entries describe – big afro, flowing dress, younger.

Nah! No way she was ever younger than this.

A big farmhouse stands on one side of the yard, with two huts right beside it, almost like having three houses there. Ambuya uses one of the huts as a silo for maize after the harvest season, and the other as a kitchen because it was built to accommodate cooking fires. So when she needs to cook delicacies that would use up too much electricity, she uses that kitchen instead of the stove in the main house. Today seems to be one of those days. But Ambuya enjoys food cooked on the fire anyway, so any excuse to use the flames is a good one for her. Listen, for this I'm not complaining.

I can smell the mouth-watering smell of matumbu, a fine dish of cow intestines that she serves with sadza and spicy vegetables. I lick my lips, well aware that I'm going to be doing some tongue-chewing tonight from all that goodness.

'Eeeeeh Chineke God-oo!' Noku shouts, hands on her head, mimicking all those Nollywood actresses she's been watching lately on TV.

'How could you have wanted to miss this-oo?'

Her big wide eyes dart about wildly, taking in all the animals roaming around Ambuya's small yard, sending a clear message that they own the place.

The kindergarten teacher recently asked Saru if Noku's father is Nigerian because of all of the dramatic expressions that Noku comes out with, using her best Nigerian accent. But Nollywood movies are Saru's Achilles heel, so all those expressions that Noku uses are not going anywhere any time soon.

There are things that I enjoy about being at Ambuya's. Like how the moon always seems to come out early and stare down the last rays of the sun. And how clearly you can see the stars twinkling without competing with all those city lights, almost as though they are greeting you. But I'm still not safe here, and I have to show Mkoma before it's too late.

As soon as the car stops, Ambuya pulls open Mkoma's

door and engulfs him in a long embrace, singing his totem in the process. She turns to me, but I quickly look away. I remember the scars, but this time they look even darker. Befitting of someone who watches people die.

Once when I asked Bamkuru where Ambuya got her scars, he took off his belt and gave me five good ones on the soles of my feet for being disrespectful. Though it still made no sense to me, he said that it was not our culture for children to ask such questions. Bamkuru is like that – he has all these things he believes because of culture. And I think some of them are a bit messed up. All I got out of Mkoma was that Ambuya had gotten the scars on her face from doing something brave. But I knew that it was the kind of lie that you tell children to calm their fears.

My eyes accidentally trace the scars once more before I drag them away. Mkoma says it's rude to stare, so I'm trying not to. I hold tight to my seat belt, which is still firmly done up.

'Mzukuru wangu.'

My eyes are glued to Ambuya as she dances her way towards my door.

I hear the screams that tore out of me when I was taken from my warm bed and shoved in that white van in the pitch of night, with Bamkuru's voice somewhere in the background.

The door opens. My palms moisten.

'Ah, you look as though you've just seen a ghost, Tumirai. Give your Ambuya a hug.'

My body tenses as she unbuckles my seat belt.

'Ambuya, what about me?' Noku says, stomping on my feet to jump into the old woman's arms. I breathe in relief.

'Ambuya, Daddy tried to starve us. My stomach was grumbling so much I thought there was a cow in my belly.' She pouts, eyeing Mkoma and sending them both into fits of laughter.

'Don't worry, my mzukuru, your Ambuya has prepared some delicious food for you.'

Ambuya's eyes shift to me, smiling heartily, with Noku balanced effortlessly on her hip despite how heavy she is. Laughter floats in the compound. A young boy leads the goats and cattle into their kraals at the edge of the compound, close to the big bowing tree that seems to have more branches and leaves than it can hold. I remember playing under there, enjoying the shade and the whispers of the tree. Bamkuru had once told us that the bowing tree slumped like that because it held so many people's secrets and they were too heavy for it. He said that if you went under it, you could hear it whispering the secrets through the wind, trying to give some of them away.

Mkoma unloads the groceries from the boot while two other boys who have emerged from nowhere pick them and take them to the main house.

'Tumirai, get out of the car so that I can see how much you've grown.'

I had almost forgotten that I am still in the car. A strange feeling bubbles inside me as I get ready to be stared at. Ambuya reaches for my hand and my heart explodes, causing my lungs to go stiff. Mkoma gives me a sharp eye. I slide out of the seat and force a smile.

'How are you, Ambuya?'

'Ah ah ah, look at you, almost a full-grown man now, mzukuru, with that thick voice breaking nicely like that.' She nudges me as though we are friends. Although I don't want to, I can't help but smile.

'Very soon you'll be a strong man with all those pretty girls hoping you'll chase after them, huh, Tumirai?' she says, winking at me.

I look down, slightly embarrassed.

'Now, everyone, let's go inside. You must all be hungry.'

I look at Noku, waiting for her to talk about our little stop at the Halfway House, but that was a whole three and a half hours ago, and by the silence I figure she must be hungry again. We eat and then sit around the fire in the round hut, licking our fingers. The flickers of the flame illuminate the kitchen and dance across people's faces. The room is full. There's a boy – Ranga – one of the people who helped carry the groceries earlier. He's almost my age, and I heard Mkoma say that Ambuya has become mother to him because his parents died. There is also a much older cousin who has been having trouble finding a job in the city but will be getting a ride to town with Mkoma when he leaves, an aunt and her daughter who came from next door to greet Ambuya's grandchildren, and an old man who doesn't say much but who catches my eye because of a huge tattoo of a knife on his bicep. Ambuya's home almost seems like a centre for wanderers.

'So your Ambuya tells me you're doing a great job flying big aeroplanes around the world,' the old man says to Mkoma, his voice soft.

Mkoma smiles and starts telling his best stories from work. The room goes quiet as we all drink in his voice and swallow his hilarious tales. His mood right now is a whole vibe.

Mkoma has that thing about him. When he starts talking, when he doesn't have thinking lines furrowing his forehead, everyone draws in and listens attentively. Sometimes even if he's only blubbering on about whatever, like that he's hungry, people still want to hear. I smile. I should own up to it – I'm proud to be his younger brother. I like this side of him.

Tonight he isn't the strict Mkoma, or the worried one either. He seems more carefree. Perhaps having Ambuya there makes him feel like a child. Or maybe it's the way an evening fire lifts the veil of storytelling, giving the tellers confidence and allowing the rest of us into new worlds.

8

Next morning I'm staring outside through the window in the big lounge in Ambuya's main house. I can see the winding twist of the river snaking downhill, tempting me to come take a dip. I sigh and step back from the window. I should be in the gym right now, or better yet doing lengths in the pool.

There's an old couch next to where I'm standing, and a vinyl deck in the corner. The TV in the front of the room is one of those old ones that looks like it has an occiput.

I roll my eyes at the sound of laughter outside. Mkoma is talking to someone and I can hear Noku begging for more of those juicy guavas from the tree. My stomach growls. I'd really like one right now, but I'm not going out there. I'm staying in here long enough for Mkoma to see that I'm not on board with his scheme of leaving me behind in this forgotten part of the world.

Just a little while ago, I was complaining that my workout

app isn't updating my routines, and he said I had to chill. His words exactly. 'You're taking this too seriously, Tumi, you need to chill. Even if you don't make it into the team, what's important is that everyone knows the effort you've been putting in.' I'm not even going into how irritated I am just thinking of him saying that. And to stab a bleeding wound, Noku echoed, 'Yes, "A for effort" – isn't that right, Daddy?'

A for effort?

Sounds almost blasphemous.

Where at the Olympics do they give medals for effort? Where Sway?

Nah, I should be improving my endurance right now, not stuck in this time capsule of a place. I'm not working this hard for some imaginary A for effort, while Bongani and Liam waltz into the Zim team just like that. I'm going for gold. Unlike the rest of them, I need to get in. So don't talk to me about A for effort. I need to win!

I step back from the window and collapse into the sofa next to Ambuya's vinyl deck. I point the remote at the TV and mess around with the controls. There's a little bit of feedback coming from it but no sound, and anyway there's only one channel, the boring one.

On the mantel there are a few pictures of my father standing in a classroom, probably at the Oakwood Mission School in Chinhoyi, where he used to teach before he disappeared. Next to those are pictures of Mkoma, back when he used to smile more, of my grandfather when he was alive, and of Bamkuru. How does Mkoma not see that this is shady? After what Bamkuru did, Ambuya still displays him like he's some hero.

I scowl and move my eyes to the side. There's a poem hanging above the other sofa, opposite me, with a picture stuck in a corner of the frame. I stand to get a better view. It's a young woman with a big afro and some white guy beside her. I spend a while looking at it. It looks a bit like Ambuya but I can't be sure.

I head towards the bedroom as soon as my phone starts ringing. It's probably Musa. I have been avoiding him all day because I don't know how to tell him I'm not around to train. And frankly I don't want to hear the disappointment in his voice. I halt in the corridor and feel my eyebrows almost touching as I frown.

Ambuya looks at me and smiles. The jagged scar stretches with her skin as her cheeks spread.

What was she doing in my room? Where is Mkoma when you need him?

'I've just brought back the clothes you were wearing last night. They were soaked in smoke after sitting in the kitchen hut, but they smell all fresh now. It's a good thing I washed them.'

I nod quietly, trying to erase the frown.

Why is she randomly explaining? I didn't say anything. Only guilty people do that.

I watch as she begins to walk away. Then she stops and turns towards me.

'Oh, and Tumirai – I found this in your pocket . . . '

My heart freezes at the sight of the envelope. The second letter. I must have left it in my pocket yesterday.

'Where did you get it?' Her voice is more serious now. 'Did your brother give you his letters?'

I don't answer. She smiles, but only with her eyes this time.

'I don't think your brother would appreciate you taking his things, my boy. I won't say anything to him, but perhaps you should keep it safe till you can put it back where you found it.'

My dear mzukuru,

It is always so good to hear from you. Your letters give me so much joy. When I received this one, I went and told all our neighbours how well you did last semester. They are all so proud. My friend Mrs Moyo promised to slaughter a chicken for you as soon as you come back. You have always been so smart, mzukuru, something you get from your father, no doubt.

I am glad that you felt you could see me in those torn diary pages I sent you. I am sending more with this letter and I hope that my young thoughts will continue to comfort you every time you think of home. Especially in those moments when you are tempted to think you cannot overcome the harshness you say you are facing there in that foreign land.

You know, mzukuru, each time I think of the terrible things we suffered in the past, and how hard we fought, I think of you. And I smile because I know that it was all worth it, every single fight. Because look how proud you have made me, mzukuru, making so much of yourself in a world where the odds are stacked against you. What more could I wish for? So though you might feel like it, don't give up, mzukuru, because it has never been in our blood to do so.

Your Ambuya

PS The boy at the post office wouldn't let me post the peanut butter I promised you. Something about it not being allowed. I am sure he doesn't know what he's talking about. But don't worry, mzukuru. For you, I will find a way.

PPS Never forget how much I love you.

9

Ambuya's story

16 March 1975

When I saw him standing there in the pouring rain, my stomach caught a whirlwind. It felt as though my brain had completely forgotten to remember him. It was like seeing the dead.

'Thandie, you're back?'

I wanted to scream at him when he said it. I wanted to run as fast as I could, to cry. All I thought was, I wasn't the only one who left.

Bas Rogers struggled to get out of the car. He must have had one too many beers, like he always did when he played cards with his friends in the city on a Sunday afternoon. I dashed to his side of the car, trying to keep my eyes only on the bas. But oh, how mischievous young eyes can be. As they slid to Matthew, I could see his brown hair dancing wildly in the wind. Things that had absolutely gotten no consent from me fluttered everywhere in my stomach. He closed the driver's door and came to help me with Bas Rogers.

'Oh yes, girlie, your mother did say you would come in her place.'

'Yes, bas.'

'You remember my nephew Matthew, don't you? Nice young fella. He's going to be an engineer soon, aren't you, Matthew?'

Bas Rogers seemed cheerful. He must have won at his game of cards, and the alcohol had definitely sent some joy his way. His eyes darted between Matthew and me as if he already knew we were hiding something. I nodded back at him, this time making sure to keep my eyes where they should be.

It reminded me of when we were younger. Amai had actually raised Matthew, while the Missus supervised. But unlike in the village where everyone is your uncle or aunt because you've known them since you were born, the Rogerses and us are not family or anything close to that.

As I held the bas's right hand and helped him out of the car, Matthew stood there watching me. I could not see his face because my eyes were where they should be, but I could feel his gaze boring right through me.

'Matthew will be here for a while. It's good to get another set of eyes to help manage the farm. He's decided he's not better than us. That he's not too good to help us around the farm even if he has a degree, haven't you, Matthew?'

I raised my head and looked at Matthew, who avoided my stare. It was typical of the bas, even on a day when he was in a cheery mood.

'We picked up a few things from the market. They're in the back – go grab them, girlie.'

'Yes, bas.' I nodded and, as soon as the bas was standing, I dashed to the back of the truck. The wind had grown stronger and the rain was starting to spit harder. Bas Rogers had bought two sacks of rice and what I suspected was meat, neatly wrapped in newspapers. Oh, the smell of meat. I don't know when last I ate meat. With the war and everything, it is truly a luxury.

I held the back door with the weight of my back, fighting the rain as it recklessly poured down on me. And then the thought came charging at me as though it had been catapulted. My hair! It would most definitely shrink now. Showers of water flooded through it, flowing past my face into my very wet dress.

'I didn't know you were back. I wanted to write ...'

The air thickened. I gasped as the rain poured past my nose.

'You're really not going to talk to me, Thandie? Not that I don't understand, because I do.'

'I'm here to work, Matthew. I'd appreciate it if you didn't make that impossible.'

I kept my voice as soft as I could, because even though

my insides boiled with all sorts of emotion, I had not forgotten that the land and hence all the power was not ours yet. I lifted a heavy sack of rice from the boot of the car and balanced it on my head. As I reached for the wrapped-up meat, he grabbed my arm.

'I really am sorry, you know. I shouldn't have ... I wanted to ... I'm just really sorry for everything.'

His bluish-grey eyes were sincere, almost as though he would cry, but I pulled my arm free and walked towards the house.

'What are you doing, you silly girl? Taking a bath? Now the rice is all soggy. Whatever shall I do with you?'

The Missus stood right by the door, safe from the wild spit of the heavens. I breathed in deeply and held my tongue. Matthew appeared behind me with the other sack of rice and the rest of the meat, just as drenched as I was.

'And where do you think you are going, dripping with water like that? You'll have to go home and change. Matthew will take the food in.'

Matthew said nothing. Maybe because it wasn't his place to, or maybe because he considered it rude to speak against his aunt. Or perhaps to him it was normal for someone like me to be treated that way. I will never know for sure what he thought in that moment, but I do remember that he said nothing.

10

19 March 1975

I cannot sleep though the night is thick. Amai will not be pleased that I am still burning the candle away, but I cannot stop my heart from pounding wildly like a ceremonial drum.

Trouble marched into our yard today. I saw it with my two eyes, standing next to my brother, differently jointed metals of a bayonet slung loosely on its shoulder like an accessory.

'They call him Bullet because he never misses a shot,' Farai my brother had said. And I shivered. I still am now. Because although the gunman is as young as I am, his stare left me thinking that wherever in the bush he hides, he must chew up the bones of war and violence for sport, spitting them out like mere pith.

So when Amai was wailing and rocking because Farai said he was leaving to join the comrades, I followed the stone-faced man outside where Amai could not hear and begged him to let me cook for the comrades instead.

'Allow my brother to finish school. Let me serve you in the meantime,' I almost cried. I'm thinking of his snarl now, and the shivers I felt spreading all over me.

'We will be watching you,' is what he said. 'Don't think we don't see you cosying with the white man.'

Heavens tell me, what have I done?

I think I might have just opened the door to my nightmares. Because now they are all roaring at once and showing me their teeth.

11

22 March 1975

I haven't been able to write for some days now. I am nervous all the time and I fear that these nerves might just become my new normal. This country is in the thick of guns and bullets. I have heard on the bas's radiogram stories of comrades dying in Nyanga, and in other reserves. The white man telling these stories says the security forces have the situation contained and are protecting the people. I wonder then, who are *the* people? Do they include us?

I am anxious lately that someone will find out about my association with the comrades. I pray that no one ever finds this book, because if they do, I will have written my own death. But I feel as though this page is the only place I can truly be myself. The only place where I can write the things I am afraid to say.

These last few days, I have had to discreetly cook a meal of sadza and chicken for a group of hungry grown men, wait for one of the war boys picked from the village to fetch me and take me to whatever location the comrades are at. It isn't a daily thing because they always creep up and down the area, past the border just a little way away and into Mozambique where they train. But I have to always be ready in case word comes that they are around. I have to always be careful, because no matter how much the village fears the comrades and might even support them, no one can be trusted. It feels as though I am now in the business of stocking anxiety.

Today, the Missus and Bas Rogers sipped some tea together with Teacher Edwards, the missionary I've heard so much about; Miss Judy, a niece of one of the Missus's friends; and two men whom I suspected were officials from the Rhodesian Security Forces. There was an older man they called general and a younger man with sharp eyes and a slow lazy blink whom I did not at first recognise.

Strange things have always happened at Bas Rogers's farm, for as long as I can remember. Lately this general, who is a middle-aged plump man with a tired and sagging belly, turns up at the house often, in a white Alfasud. He sits out by the veranda with the bas, sipping a glass of sherry and speaking in low tones. I am worried he will read the uneasiness on my face and see that I am trying to glean useful information for the comrades.

Back when I was very young, I remember another old

man who used to visit the bas, talking to him by the trees in a dusty Peugeot, a map laid between them. Baba had once said he suspected that the bas secretly worked with the security forces, allowing them to hide their weapons in his house and plotting routes to catch the comrades – the 'African terrorists'. I agree with Baba – with all the people that the bas hosts, he can't only be a farmer.

The day blazed this afternoon, disassociating itself from the usual coolness of Vumba. What puzzles me is that in this heat the white man still has his tea, dabbing at the sweat on his brow yet voluntarily swallowing all that hot water!

My eyes glided to the younger official and stayed there as memories reeled in, dancing around the surprise I felt. I could never have forgotten him, even if I wanted to. Phillip! The thought felt almost as daunting as the one I had of Matthew, because it brought back the unwelcome feelings of rage and shame. I stood there recounting to myself all those weekends and holidays Phillip had spent at the farmhouse with Matthew.

'Oh, Judy, I love your new hair. You always look so trendy. That nephew of mine must come and see you for himself,' the Missus had said.

'Oh, thank you,' the young woman had simpered. 'I saw it in one of those magazines and knew I had to have it!'

I had had to stop myself from frowning. Her hair was a big puffy blonde show that looked almost like mine, but somehow hers was acceptable, and I was to remember that this was not a zoo.

'Rosie! What are you standing there gawping at Judy for?'

I awoke from my daydream, realising all eyes were now on me because of that question. I looked down and shuffled back into the house in the direction of the kitchen.

I looked at my reflection in the silver metal rims of the Missus's pot as I waited for the water to boil on the stove. I tucked in a few standing hairs along my hairline and patted them down into my neatly flattened cornrows. The last time the Missus had made such a fuss about my afro. Although I had plaited the cornrows loosely, they would at least buy me peace for a few days.

I slid the plate of scones I had baked earlier onto the tray and marched to the veranda where they laughed and dabbed their sweat, stealing one last glance at my hair as I passed the small mirror in her corridor. The radiogram was playing in the background, and puffs of cigarette smoke spiralled up from the bas and the two officials. The Missus sat there fanning herself, a glass of icy water by her legs. Ian Smith was being interviewed again. I've heard him before saying exactly what he was saying today. The bas stood up and marched into the house, turned the knob of the radiogram until the sound carried itself outside and returned to his seat. They all fell silent and listened as the

American interviewer asked him questions.

'Once upon a time, Prime Minister, you said you'll
never see black rule in this country in your lifetime.
Do you still stand by that?'

'Yes, I believe that that was a fair comment. I think
that if we ever got to a stage of having black rule
then our policy would have failed. Now, I have heard
many experts say that the constitution we produced
here is one of the most complicated ones that the
world has ever seen. Now, how can you ask a mass
of people who don't understand what even a simple
constitution is whether they approve of a complicated
one and whether they think it's the right one or not
for their country? This is the predicament we find
ourselves in.'

'Well, that's the problem of all democracies,
Mr Smith. Democracy, as I understand it, is not a
political intelligence test, thank God, otherwise we
would all be run by professors from universities, but it
is a means of saying no. Don't you think in Rhodesia,
like in any other country, most of the people who vote,
vote on the basis of whether they think well of you
and whether they think you can lead them well?'

The general curled his lip and tapped at his cigarette with

a serious expression. I think he's a little younger than Baba, although his face is already starting to sag, He straightened up in his chair, tapped the butt of his cigarette and shot me a glance as he intervened.

'These journalists don't understand what we're trying to do here. What they don't see is how ungrateful and greedy these blacks are. We have given them all this land in the reserves and in the townships without them earning it, and still they complain. What else do they need? Why is no one talking about how the whites are being killed?'

I kept my eyes from him as he went on.

'And these terrorists are only becoming more relentless, aren't they? This is why we called you here, Edwards. It's time for you and your mission friends to move away. Go back home, or to Umtali, anywhere but here. The locals don't even want you here.'

Teacher Edwards, sitting in what seemed like a hovering cloud of smoke coming from the general, smiled. I kept my lip from curling. Missionaries! Baba always talks of how the Bible led the gun here. Yet Amai is still smitten by them, always going on about how supportive they are and singing the praises of Teacher Edwards and the others every time she goes to Sunday service. The way she speaks of them, it is almost as though they are not like the rest of the land hoarders.

'With all due respect, sir, I believe we still have work to

do here. I'm assured we're planting a seed.'

In my heart I scoffed. What arrogance! Even the general and the bas looked at each other and laughed.

Bas Rogers spoke. 'Oh, these young eager boys. What seed would that be, Edwards?'

I too was interested in finding out what seed he thought he was planting. I watched the teacher out of the corner of my eye as he fidgeted in his seat, somehow isolated like a young kudu surrounded by a herd of lions. But even so, he calmly took a sip of his tea, almost seeming in control of himself.

'I don't know that we can treat people the way we do in this country, denying them fairness while expecting things to stay in our favour. The mission school is important, sir, a benefit for both our government and the locals themselves, if you will, a way of balancing the scales. Locals need education and medical facilities, things they're being deprived of. They're people just like y—' He reconsidered. 'My point is, if we keep isolating the locals, we run the risk of weakening the potential of this country that we all claim to love.'

There was a small silence while the general chewed on the teacher's words.

'It almost sounds convincing when you say it,' he said eventually, pulling a whiff of smoke from his cigarette and blowing it right out. 'Tell me then, what happens if this cause of yours, this umm, this ... what did you call it?'

'Planting a seed,' the bas helped, leering and sipping on his tea.

'Yes, yes, this seed planting. Tell me what happens if it then claims from you more than just your time and effort, eh? What will you do then, Edwards?'

The teacher swallowed and gave a faint smile. 'If it does ... then so be it.'

The general smirked, relaxing into his chair with the cigarette still held in between his fingers. 'Be careful there, Edwards. I hear this God of yours is in the business of testing people.'

Silence.

I trotted back into the house and carefully poured the boiling water into the little white teapot that the Missus liked before marching back to the veranda, where the men were still talking.

'Aye, Rogers, I meant to tell you. We have this security system now that we're giving to all the whites. It's a kind of an alert that links your house to our police camp in Umtali. I personally haven't seen anything like it ...'

The general paused again, blowing out a puff of smoke. He glanced at me with his cup of tea in his hand.

'You never know, do you? What these terrorists are up to, what they can do. You never know who they are or who they're working with.'

At that very moment, my eyes met his. And just as quickly, my right hand lost control of the teapot I had in my hand, allowing it to tip recklessly, dumping hot water into Bas Rogers's lap. We both yelped. I guess him because of the pain he had just endured, and me for the shock and the pain to come.

'You stupid, stupid girl!'

All of them, every single one, turned their eyes on me. My heart rocked wildly. I watched the bas blazing with anger, as he whisked me to my feet with his hand on my neck. He pinned me to the wall, his fingers tight against my throat. Everything went quiet and still, and in my ears I could hear the clear sound of Amai singing peacefully. It was almost as though she was an angel singing me home. My vision slowly crept away from me before suddenly returning as I collapsed into the arms of Teacher Edwards, panting desperately for air.

'I told you these blacks are trouble,' the general said, sipping his tea as though he had not just seen a woman almost killed in front of him.

As Teacher Edwards helped me to stand, I tried calming my racing heart and trembling hands. Bas Rogers now sat back in his chair, speaking as though nothing had just happened. I wondered for a second if my brain had just played a trick on me. Had I made it up and lived the horror of it in my head? Because apart from my shaking hands, everything seemed as it should be. In the corner, Phillip puffed on a cigarette, staring into the distance, his face registering no hint of a care. The Missus continued with her fanning, an old magazine open on her lap. Just another day at the farm.

Then, as though vouching for the reality of the moment, Teacher Edwards enquired after me, reminding me of what had just happened. My eyes drifted to Bas Rogers and the red skin on his right leg where the hot water had scalded him, now being dabbed with ice wrapped in a towel.

I looked down, filled with shame for some reason, and walked back in the house.

12

26 March 1975

I saw him again today. Matthew. He found me when no one was looking, when I was by the sink scrubbing pots.

'Thandie,' he said and my heart stood still while I fought to keep myself from turning to him. His voice came closer.

'C'mon, I know you can hear me. You can't ignore me forever.'

I hesitated, eventually gave in, and turned. His hands were muddy as though he had been handling dirt.

'Matthew,' I said, only to acknowledge his presence.

'Can we talk?' he hissed, peeping quickly behind him. We both know why he whispered. I think I almost understand it, but somehow it still angers me when I think about it, that talking to me has to be a secret he keeps. I turned back to the pots in the sink, giving my back to him.

'Thandie, listen, I know the way things were when I left

was not ideal, and it's mostly my fault. I promise, if I could change it I would.'

I paused with my hands sunk in the water.

'Mostly your fault?' I echoed.

'All my fault. I meant ... it was all my fault. And there's not a single day I haven't thought about it.'

'Not a single day, you say?' I asked turning again to face him. He smiled as he stood by the doorway looking at me, and all the memories came flooding back.

'OK, so maybe I skipped a few days here and there, but there were a lot of single days I thought about it.' He walked towards me and stopped by the kitchen table, grinning from ear to ear. I had almost forgotten how he smiles with his eyes, making their almost greyish-blue colour dance. I'd forgotten how his cheeks and the tips of his ears always flush a slight pink as his lips stretch into a smile. I'd forgotten how his smile could make you feel better, like some kind of medicine. All I'd remembered was how he left, and how I'd felt the day I found out. It had erased everything else.

'I'm glad to finally see that beautiful smile of yours. I'd missed it.'

I snapped back to the present and turned back to my dishes. I started scrubbing the pot in the sink, trying to undo the memories, to shoo away the past.

My voice went low and quiet. 'So how was your trip to England?'

I could hear the wooden kitchen table creaking. I think he must have sat down or leaned heavily on it, but I said nothing.

'You believe me though, don't you? I know I shouldn't have left the way I did. I should have ... I'm sorry, Thandie.'

I frowned. I was unsure what I hated more – the fact that he had unapologetically erased everything of that night or the fact that I didn't want him to. I stood there trying to iron out the stubborn creases in my mind. My head was a volcano spilling wildly with unexplained and mixed emotions, all difficult to understand. The cold touch of a strong coarse-palmed hand pulled at my elbow. I jumped as nerves sent alarm bells ringing through me. Not from Matthew's touch itself, but because the last coarse hand that had touched me had been firmly pressed against my throat, the other day. He took a small step back from me, confusion criss-crossing his features.

'I really am sorry, Thandie. I *really* am. You must know that.'

He looked down with what looked like remorse splashed across his whole demeanour.

'I don't know what else to say. But I genuine—'

I moved closer to where he stood, leaned on the table beside him and nudged him with my elbow playfully. 'I know. Now let's put all that silliness behind us. Tell me about all the mischief you caused there in England.'

Footsteps suddenly sounded in the corridor, heading our

way and capsizing our little moment. I slowly moved back to the sink while watching Matthew out of the corner of my eye walking swiftly to the other side of the kitchen, wearing a different face.

The Missus walked in. 'Won't you join us, darling? What are you doing in here?'

Her eyes focused only on him, almost erasing me from the room. I looked down and returned to scrubbing the pot in the sink.

'I was just telling . . . girlie here . . . umm, to make a cup of tea for me. Two sugars, no cream, please.'

I glanced at him and nodded.

'Yes, bas.'

I am still stuck with the picture of his back as he walked away, following his aunt from the kitchen. And as though he knew the war that had exploded in my head, he paused, turned and mouthed a silent apology. I remember the little ball of fiery anger that fluttered in my stomach. But I also remember the smile I gave him as though it were custom. And as I stood there watching his frame disappear into the corridor, I thought again of that day all those years back. There are questions I can't shake that bubble up in my mind. Can things be so easily swept away and all ills and complexities forgotten? Or do we try to conjure up false truths that console us? False truths that at least leave us feeling that our humanity isn't so damning?

13

28 March 1975

Amai has been very unimpressed with me the whole day. She says I spent a good half of the morning looking dazed and uninterested, as though my head was filled to the brim with useless daydreams.

I went to the church service at the mission with her. In truth, she forced me, but I think only because Baba was not there. And as I sat there in the pews, all I kept thinking of while the man preached was the last day I had seen Matthew before he left.

Twice Amai nudged me because I did not sing along to the hymns. But that was because for some reason I couldn't stop thinking about that day.

It was a Tuesday, and I had been reading with Matthew like we did at times. He lay his head lazily on the skeleton of a truck that had been blown up by a landmine some weeks before that, listening to me as I read aloud. His arms had been raised, his hands forming a pillow behind his head. The wind softly blew on the trees around us, causing the air to rise with the tempting scent of freshly dampened mud. Occasional drips left by the morning rain teased at me from the leaves above us. And as I turned the page to the next, my eyes lingered on the text of the next poem, and my displeasure with the words on that paper bought my silence.

It was his right eye that peeped first, wondering what had stolen my voice. And on seeing my bunched eyebrows, he sat up and looked at me.

'What's wrong?'

I looked at him, eyebrows still bunched up, and returned to the page. He reached out and gently pulled the book out of my grip. I watched as his eyes traced the poem before they lifted up and looked at me. I can almost hear it now as though for all these years my ears have trapped his thick voice, bold and alive enough to intimidate a roaring lion. I watched his lips as the words slid off his tongue.

'Who said love was fire? I know that love is ash. It is the thing which remains when the fire is spent. The holy essence of experience ...'

He looked at me and smiled.

'Too many big words?' he joked.

I was too taken with thought to laugh.

'You look like it bothers you.'

'It doesn't bother me.'

He smiled again and turned the page to another poem. I forget now, but it must have been the one that had something to do with a spear.

Matthew's voice rose as he began to read again. But thoughts were still darting through my head.

'How can love be ash instead of fire though, Matthew? Fire brings everything alive. Fire is full of the touch of breath, it is the very meaning of life. Isn't that what love should be?'

He was silent for a while, his eyes softly touching the frame of my face as though it held some sort of salvation.

Eventually he said, 'Because ash is the only thing that survives the burn of the heat. It's the only thing that lasts when everything else dies down. It withstands everything.'

A momentary silence followed. Then my heart erupted as he bent slightly forward with his hands lightly tagging at my chin. I trembled slightly as he reached for my cheek and leaned in towards me. Mayhem ensued in my chest and I drew back, fidgeting nervously.

'Matthew,' I let out. A burning fire sat in my chest and my stomach felt as though it contained boiled rocks. But I could never beguile myself into thinking that I had the right of passage into this world. A world where this, what Matthew was doing, could happen. A world where we would not be punished for proposing something different. The world has not yet prepared itself, even now. It has not yet learned how to unchain itself from things that bind, from the colours that blind.

'I'm sorry, I thought … It's only that I thought …'

I frowned. Treason! Only the previous week, one of the villagers had been found lynched from a tree because she had given birth to a white man's child. Another week prior, a young boy was burned because his madam said she felt uncomfortable about the way he looked at her.

'Thandiwe, say something,' he had said, his hand reaching out for mine. I stood and stepped back and stared at him blankly. I too was at a loss. I too was afraid of the things the world had not yet accepted. And I think this is why I could not hear the preacher at the mission today. I think it is because I am still afraid.

14

Tumi

The rain whimpers as it touches the roof. Somewhere in the depth of sleep I can hear the wind still whistling outside, making my window rattle gently.

I can almost feel them, my nightmares. Waiting to glide in, riding on the back of the wind and bringing to life things meant to be forgotten. And although I know I am sleeping, I already feel them pulling me in, and it is starting to feel as though it is happening again ...

Two figures are towering over my bed, staring down at me just like they did that night. Scars! My eyes scurry around the room. Before I can sit up, one of the men grabs my shoulders while the other grabs my legs. For a brief second everything goes still and I can see clearly: my desk in the corner of the room; the duvet discarded in a pile on the floor; Bamkuru and Maiguru's closed bedroom door adjacent to mine; a man with vivid scars on his forehead and right cheek; my body swinging with no sign of a fight in the hands of the two men, and the screams stuck in my head that can't come out, lodged between confusion and fear. Then as though with an interruption from gravity, I come back to myself. The minute my brain wakes, my throat burns a thousand fires as I push out every scream I can. I wriggle and try writhing my body out of the grip of the two men while they hurry along the corridor.

Who are they? What's happening? I can't breathe! HELP!

Out of the corner of my eye I catch Bamkuru's wife Maiguru. Her frame shows as she stands just outside her door, her silk headscarf still intact and her hands tying the pale pink nightgown she had thrown on. She looks surprised to see them. The man holding my feet immediately lets go and scurries towards her. I struggle to get up, but before I can kick out or run, the other man's hand has already made it around my neck, partly strangling me. Everything goes silent. Pictures from one of the books I picked up from the library earlier whizz through my brain. In the few seconds that the man has put pressure around my neck, he has cut air circulation to my brain and massively slowed down the normal flow of blood. I try to shake him off. My brain is already starting to fail, switching off my sense of hearing. I try to push him off, but I am losing energy. My vision grows blurry as his grip tightens. Tears slowly trail the curves of my cheeks as I watch the other man's boot ram Maiguru in the stomach again and again, and blood oozes out of her nose.

Where's Bamkuru?

I keep trying to wriggle. I can see a shadow of a third person in the background. My spirits lift slightly as I tell myself help has come, but before I can turn to see who it is, a cloth is over my nose, stinging my eyes and filling my lungs with chloroform. My eyes flutter. Maiguru's eyes flutter too. My eyes give up on me . . .

My hearing comes back to me first, more because, regardless of how much I blink, the darkness won't be shaken. For some reason I can hear rattling. The thick smell of fresh cabbages fills my nose, but I can definitely tell that I'm not in a field. There's a swerving bump that sends me sliding sideways and what sounds like clucking chickens protesting. Where am I?

I lie still, listening and trying to figure out what's happening. My nose still stings from the chloroform and my throat is burning. My heart shudders as I realise that I'm in a car, a pick-up truck.

Where are they taking me? Wait till Bamkuru finds out. He'll save me.

I have to run! I try to scream but this time my screams are blocked by a gag in my mouth. My hands won't move, and my legs too are unable to come out of the bind they are in. Tears begin to flood my eyes. I'm so afraid, I can almost touch the fear. I try to move my head but there is no space. The truck dives into something – a pothole, I think. The chickens cluck again, and my heart cries. I have to get out! We hit another bump. The road definitely isn't tarred so I know we've left the city, but it solves nothing because then we could be anywhere! Some grainy-stringed material rubs my feet and my cheek. A sack? Oh good grief, I'm in a sack. My poor heart! The engine suddenly stops. I open my eyes wide, hoping that maybe I can see something through the little spaces in the sack, but the dark stands guard. I really am not ready to die yet!

'Good evening, gentlemen.' It's a voice I don't recognise, and it seems slightly far from where I am.

'Licence and registration, please.'

The police! I try to push out a cry. A dog barks and the chickens join in, covering my muffled screams. C'mon!

'What do you have back there?' I can hear footsteps approaching, and sniffing close to what I think is the window where I'm curled up in a sack. The police must definitely have a dog. But still, my screams lie under the clucking of the chickens, which now seem agitated by the barking dog.

'We are just transporting some chickens and cabbages for a local food stall up there, officer.' I know that voice. My heart stops beating, I hold my breath.

'Open up. Let's see what's back there.' Another voice. There must be two officers then. They could save me!

'Is something wrong, officer?'

Bamkuru? Bamkuru! I'm overtaken by immense confusion. He must be trying to save me!

'Hey, mdara, open up!' A third voice, this time female. There are three officers! Maybe I do have a chance.

The door creaks as it swings open. I writhe for them to see movement as the chickens cluck louder. A light darts in the truck, bringing my eyes to life. Sacks packed with cabbages are everywhere around me, and positioned in front to adequately hide me are cages of chickens. I have no chance! My heart sinks as I realise I might never see Mkoma again.

'OK, close it,' one of the officers goes. Well, that definitely doesn't sound like a chance! Tears gush out of me as the memory of Mkoma laughing plays in my mind. I have to do something! I whisper a little prayer for a miracle as I heave my folded body sideways, pushing it roughly against the wall of the truck.

'What was that?' the female officer says, opening the door again. This is the real reason God sent us women!

My hip hurts, but I don't care. I throw myself around again.

'Hey! Hey! Stop him!'

I'm not sure what's happening outside, but I can now

hear the sound of feet scurrying everywhere, with the barks
of a dog trailing away after whoever's feet those are. I push
myself against the wall again, until I'm sure I've broken a
bone or something. The torch moves and hovers over me.

'There's something moving back there!'

My eyes open and I can feel my heart racing wildly. I try to
blink it all away.

It's just a dream, it's just a dream . . .

The rain is humming softly. My throat is still burning
and I am trembling. I breathe in deeply to calm my nerves.
I haven't relived that nightmare for a while now, yet it feels
as though the thing has just happened. My pyjama shirt is
stuck to my skin with sweat. I glance at the other bed. Noku
is still lying there peacefully, though I'm not sure whether
she's asleep. I turn to the other side and I can almost hear
the fear hiss out through me.

What the hell?!

Ambuya! She is there, hovering suspiciously over me in
the dark, staring at me as though ready to shove me in a van
with chickens.

'm not safe here! I have to find a way out. I stand on the veranda of the main house, watching Noku as she struggles to fit her doll's dress onto the little kitten in the yard. So early in the morning and she's already brimming with energy. I yawn, rubbing the sleep from my eyes. A proud rooster moves about the yard, head held high, completely unaware that it will be dinner soon. Ranga stands by the goat pen with his foot resting on the wooden bars as he watches the goats move out. He whips the cattle out of the kraal, steering them to the pasturelands. I stretch and walk down towards the edge of the veranda. The ground is still damp from last night. Shivers spread down my spine as I remember. Noku is now holding the kitten by its neck, forcing the tiny dress over the poor thing's head. The kitten mews in supposed protest, trying to free itself from her and reminding me of my screams from last night. I must tell Mkoma. I must tell someone!

The kitten finally stops playing nice, extends its claws and scratches her.

'Ouch! Why you go scratch me now? Ah, ah! Come wear your dress, biko!' She follows it as it darts out of sight.

I hold back my laughter. I see why her teachers are convinced there's some Nigerian blood in her. If I didn't know better, I'd agree with them.

Ambuya appears from the kitchen hut. I freeze.

'Tumi, there you are! How did you sleep, mzukuru?' She walks towards me and I can hear the violent trudging of my heart.

Something's up! She better stop trying to act brand-new with me. I'm wide awake, sis!

'Why don't you go and clear those branches that fell from the bowing tree last night? The rain was so powerful, wasn't it?'

I head to the tree, watching her out of the corner of my eye. To my far right is that river again. I so badly want to take a dip! But even when I was younger we were never allowed to swim there. Ambuya always told us that the current was so strong it had swallowed a lot of people.

I glance back over at Ambuya, who is now humming in the kitchen hut, sweeping. Ranga has already left for the pastures with the animals. Noku has disappeared after the poor little kitten. It's just Ambuya and me now. I need a way out. I might not have much time.

I push the wheelbarrow by the wall of the main house towards the tree and kneel almost hidden under the drooping branches, piling up the ones that had fallen.

'Be careful there, Tumi. You don't want to disappear under those big branches.'

What's that supposed to mean?

The sun is now confidently above us. I quickly pick up all the fallen branches from the bowing tree before I disappear, like Ambuya said. Then I sit on the veranda watching a millipede creep past with its hundred legs. They always come out after rain. I pick up a stick and poke it, making it immediately coil up. The first time I saw that I was only four. And between fear and fascination, I was motivated by my intense curiosity to find out why millipedes curl when they are touched, whether something happened to them in the past. Mkoma took out a couple of books for me from his school library and together we spent that whole day reading about millipedes, including that they curl up when they feel threatened and unsafe.

At first I found that remarkable and rare, but looking at it now, I imagine everyone does that. Mkoma had definitely curled up after the night I was taken, and so had I. As soon as he had been told the news, he got on the next flight back and never went back overseas. I never thanked him for that. Perhaps I should.

My phone suddenly vibrates and I look at it nervously.

Yo son! It's tick tock over here bruh. You still in this or what?

Just a few more days until coach will choose the captain. Just slightly over two weeks and we'll be trying out for the national swimming team. Musa's right – we're running out of time.

The coach went out on such a limb to even get us a chance to try out for the national team. I've got to find a way to get back home so I can train. If I don't get on the swim team, I'll lose everything. The kids at school will start seeing the paleness of my skin again, and whenever that is all people can see, bad things happen.

The phone in the main house starts to ring. I check to see if anyone is closer than I am before darting inside, hoping it's Mkoma.

'Hello?'

I hold the phone in my hand, unable to answer back.

I knew this. I knew!

'Hello? Amai?'

My eyes bulge out and my heart beats wildly. Ambuya comes in from outside, the bottom of her shirt partly covered in soot, and the smell of smoke which she has absorbed from cleaning the kitchen hut very evident. I hand her the phone, heart still hammering.

She takes it and immediately turns to me, her sharp eye

suggesting that I move away. She walks into her bedroom and closes the door. I reach out for one of the empty water glasses on the table, silently follow her and press the glass on the door so I can hear better. It's a trick I learned from a book.

Why is Bamkuru calling Ambuya? Haven't I said it? Anyone who laughs with Bamkuru like that deserves to be in a prison cell just like he is.

'They're letting you out?' I hear Ambuya say, her voice puzzled.

Only three years, for taking a little boy?

I breathe in.

Only three years for shoving me in a sack and trying to sell me at the border to men who intended to make me part of their rituals because I look different?

I grit my teeth.

How is three years enough punishment for such hatred?

I press harder into the glass, my ear painfully trying to hear more. Ambuya is speaking in hushed tones and hisses. I pick up something she says. My breath leaves me and I immediately step back from the door, my heart in my hands. Before I know it, my feet are sprinting through the neighbouring estate, my body brushing roughly against shrubs of tea. My lungs ache for air and my feet run for safety. As soon as I can see the little township laid out in front of me, my eyes search for the police office. I trot there, gasping for breath. When I burst in, the four people inside immediately look at me. I stand there, panting, sweat pasted all over my face.

'Help me! My grandmother is trying to have me kidnapped.'

16

I watch the man's lips move as he speaks, but my ears have forgotten how to function and I can barely hear anything. I glare at him with my mind playing over and over again the dream I'd had the other night, how Ambuya hovered in my room, the call. The call!

Bamkuru's voice was just as deep and threatening as it had been the whole time I had lived with him. As deep and threatening as it had been that night when I thought he would save me and he didn't.

The man asks a question.

'Did you hear what I said?'

I open my mouth but I can't speak. He looks at his other officers and sighs. The man is tall with a round belly. I wonder if they eat doughnuts in this police station like they show on TV. I wonder if that's what's packed in there, donuts. He looks at the other officers and shrugs. The officers are not convinced. Almost unbothered actually.

One of them is sitting slumped in a chair, swaying sideways while scrolling on his phone.

'Listen, your brother will be here soon, but for now we're just going to call your Ambuya to tell her you're safe.'

They don't believe I'm in danger! Why doesn't anyone see it? I have to do something!

I bite my bottom lip for a moment. Although I can hear my heart warning me not to, I have to do this.

'She had a knife.'

They all look at me, brows furrowed. I urge myself to go on.

'In the night, she came into my room with –' I swallow – 'with a knife, and ... and ... when she saw that I saw it, the knife ... when she saw, she ...'

'You didn't say this in your initial statement,' one of the officers says, his face slightly horrified.

I swallow again and try to stop my heart from freaking out.

'She had a knife, and when I saw her, she quickly went out of the room. She would have used it if not for ... It's true.'

The slumping officer sits up and scans me, his eyebrows bunched.

'Are you sure?'

I nod silently.

He looks at his other officers, then back at me.

'All right . . . tell us again from the beginning. What happened? Why do you think she's trying to have you kidnapped?'

I look away. I have only spoken twice about the thing that happened. Once when the police found me in the back of the truck, and the second time when Mkoma asked. I've relived it in my head plenty of times, but that's because it stays there. It doesn't creep out as words and become real. By the time I have finished speaking, my stomach is cramping and I can hear my heart through the drumming in my ears, as if it's just happened again.

'Sit down, young man. You're shaking.'

I stare at my hands before glancing back at the officers, who are now speaking in hushed voices with concerned looks on their faces.

'. . . can't go back there till we know for sure. Doesn't matter that we know her. He's only a child.'

They're buying it – they now understand the gravity of the situation! It was wrong but it was worth it.

I curl up on the cold bench in the room, trying to warm myself. The sun has retired and fewer people are roaming outside. I tell myself I won't leave the station, not until Mkoma comes. My eyes close and I slowly drift into sleep.

17

'Tumirai! Are you all right?' Mkoma's voice barges in before he does. My heart strums. I sit up, shivering. He comes directly to the bench and his eyes search my face, those same furrow lines etched on his forehead. Guilt parades through my mind because I know that I've caused them.

'What happened?' He reaches out to touch me. I tremble and look down. His eyes drift to the other officers now standing close to us.

'Mkoma, can we go home now?'

I whisper because although it makes no sense at all, I'm afraid someone will hear me.

'Officer, I'm Tumirai's brother. What has happened?'

'What has happened is very unusual, Mr Mpofu. The boy, as you can see –' he turns as though to convince Mkoma that this is worth his attention – 'as you can see, he's a little scared. He thinks his grandmother is trying to kidnap him because he heard her talking to his uncle over the phone. Something about his uncle being released from prison where he was sent for trying to take him before?'

The officer is watching Mkoma's devastated face. Mkoma looks at me and nods.

'But I don't understand what this has to do with Ambuya, Tumirai. Why would you think she is trying to kidnap you? Just because Bamkuru called her?' His eyes are sad, and the furrows run across his forehead.

'Am I missing something here, officers? I know my brother is still tormented by what happened back then, and he's right to be concerned about that bastard coming out. But what does this have to do with my grandmother?'

I can tell Mkoma is trying to be calm, but apart from the confusion, there is a hint of anger in his voice. The officer exhales. His eyes are on me now, and his other two colleagues are watching this whole exchange carefully.

'Tumirai?'

Mkoma looks at me, trying to understand. I keep my eyes down.

'Mr Mpofu, the boy says yesterday he woke up to find the old woman standing over him with a knife in her hand. When she saw that he had seen her, she ran out of the room.'

My heart is thudding hard. When the officer says it, it almost sounds true. But again, lies do sound true, don't they? Isn't that why we believe them?

'Tumirai, is this true?'

I hesitate.

'Is it true what they're saying?' he asks again. His voice is soft and tender, almost as though it might just break into little pieces if he speaks any louder.

'Mr Mpofu, I understand this must be very difficult for you, but I have to ask, is there any reason to believe that the boy might be ... perhaps mistaken?'

Mkoma looks at me.

'My grandmother raised me, and I cannot imagine her doing anything like this. But then again, my brother has no reason to lie. He genuinely looks terrified.'

He pauses and wipes his face with both his hands as though someone has just splashed invisible water in his face. My hands are trembling again.

He sighs. 'I really don't know. What must we do, officer?'

'I think the best thing to do now is for you to take the boy somewhere safe. We will investigate further into this, but we cannot just arrest her without sufficient evidence, especially given that she has no prior history of any worrying conduct,' one of the officers explains. There is silence for a while.

'But I suggest that you take the boy far from your grandmother for now, at least till we get to the bottom of this. If what your brother alleges is true, this is not a light matter at all.'

Mkoma wipes his eyes and nods, his face serious.

'Officers, you have been very helpful. Thank you,' he says as we leave, his voice flat.

Mkoma and I sit in the car, driving back to Ambuya's. I can hardly see his face because of the dark, but it's impossible to miss his hand as it wipes his eyes. It breaks my heart that this is breaking his.

'I hope Noku is still awake,' he says quietly. I don't know how to answer so I only nod.

Maybe I should tell him the truth.

'It would just be easier if she's awake so that we don't spend too much time.'

But Ambuya cannot be trusted. I'm doing the right thing.

Mkoma reaches and presses my shoulder.

'Everything is going to be all right.'

I look down.

Finally I can see the mango tree in Ambuya's yard as the car approaches. My heart thunders. The car drives in slowly. The compound is quiet and lifeless – no lingering animals, no loitering cousins, no dancing Ambuya.

As the headlights shine into the yard, Ambuya comes out of the main house, tightening the dhuku on her head. She walks towards the car as it comes to a halt and peers in.

'Oh, thank God you're both all right. I've been so worried. I couldn't sleep. The police called to tell me what happened and said it's best if I don't come to the station. How is he?'

If she is innocent, wouldn't she have come anyway? I was wrong to lie, but I know she's planning something!

'He's all right, Ambuya. Just a little shaken.'

Mkoma steps out of the car, his voice now stuck in his throat. He stands by the door for a while before holding his hand on his forehead.

'It must have been that phone call from your uncle. It's ridiculous but he said they're letting him out. Tumirai answered the phone. But I didn't know about it before then. I told him not to call again.'

'Why are they letting him out so soon? Have they forgotten what he did?'

Mkoma almost yells this, and although it makes me feel warm inside that he cares, I have no right to because I've caused those lines on his forehead. I keep my eyes away from Ambuya. Noku comes out of the house in her pyjamas, her face painted with lines she must definitely have formed while lying on something creased.

Ambuya rubs her arm. 'Noku mzukuru, go back inside and wear something warm.'

Mkoma looks down at her little sleepy body.

'What's wrong, Daddy? You said you had work. Why are you back?'

Mkoma lifts Noku and kisses her on the forehead. My eyes drift to them.

'Daddy, your eyes are red. Have you been crying?'

I look away.

'Is it because of the nightmares Tumi has been getting?'

Mkoma turns to me again and then to Ambuya.

'He's been screaming in his sleep since you left.' Her voice is low and sad. 'I think it's about that night.'

'Daddy, last night Tumi was screaming so loud. I was so scared I had to go and wake Ambuya up. He was shaking and then ... and then, Ambuya woke him up and stayed till we both fell asleep.'

'Noku, my dear, why don't you go inside now?' Ambuya urges again, her voice very calm and collected.

But Noku sticks to Mkoma like glue, pouting and flashing those big brown eyes. He can't resist nodding to Ambuya that it's all right.

'Is that when you had the knife, Ambuya?'

'What knife?' Both Noku and Ambuya say it together. I catch the puzzled look on Ambuya's face.

'Tumirai, didn't you say you woke up with Ambuya hovering over you with a knife?'

Mkoma's eyes narrow as he puts Noku down. The lines on his forehead are different now. They're dancing between anger and confusion. Ambuya frowns and I just stare at my feet, unable to speak.

'Tumirai! You better answer me when I'm speaking to you or God help me –'

'Noku, go inside, mzukuru,' Ambuya insists again, trying to keep her voice soft, probably predicting the ugliness about to happen.

Noku tries to argue but one stare from Mkoma sends her sulking her way inside with occasional head turns to see if any of the grown-ups will change their minds.

'Tumirai!' Mkoma almost shouts, his eyes bloodshot and bulging. I step back a little, shaking slightly.

'Simmer down, mzukuru.' Ambuya reaches out to him, trying to calm him down.

'Tumirai ...' Mkoma breathes.

'You said when you woke up Ambuya had a knife. Was that true?'

As I swallow down the block in my throat I can hear the sound of hell breaking loose.

18

How can they let Bamkuru go after what he did? Doesn't anyone care that he'll come back to finish the job?

I've only seen Bamkuru once in prison. Right after the thing that happened, Saru thought it was a good idea for me to confront him so that maybe the nightmares would go away. I think it was something they taught her at university or some wise-for-nothing idea she got off a blog or somewhere. I hadn't wanted to go, but I'd been so desperate for the nightmares to stop that I agreed. Of course Mkoma wasn't at home, because he would have flipped out at the idea.

I cried myself to sleep for the rest of that week, but never told Saru or Mkoma.

That day they brought Bamkuru to the visitors' table Saru and I sat at, waiting for him. There were so many prisoners around us talking to their loved ones, all kinds of prisoners, even ones with scars on their bodies just like on the man who took me that night – and just like Ambuya's.

Thing is, Bamkuru is definitely not my loved one, but when I saw him I still sat up straight and pulled the corners of my cardigan into my palms so he would not see so much of my skin. He walked in, his face half annoyed as though we had dragged him from some lit party or something.

He wore khaki overalls, not orange like they show on *Orange Is the New Black*. He sat across the table and leaned into the chair, staring at me as though he was staring at a pile of something appalling like vomit. I remember my heart snapping at the lack of remorse in his eyes.

Most of what he and Saru talked about that day went over my head. I could not get over the expression on his face when he looked at me. I can still see the curl of his lips just before we left, little sharp spears spewing from his mouth as he said: 'We should have burned you at birth like people did in the past.'

Nobody can ever understand how I felt that day, not even Mkoma. Bamkuru had been the closest to a father I had ever had. And all he saw was my skin. It had been more important to him than the blood we shared. I prayed for him in that moment because only God knows what I'll do to him if I ever see him again.

'Tumi!'

I snap back to the present. I shift on my feet and look down to avoid Mkoma's eyes.

Maybe I shouldn't have gone with the knife angle. That might have been dumb.

'Tumirai! Is it true?'

'No.' It blurts out before I get a chance to change it.

Mkoma leans towards me as though he hasn't heard me well. I know I shouldn't have lied, but just because I added a little spice doesn't mean it couldn't have happened! It doesn't change the fact that Ambuya still talked to Bamkuru! And laughed!

'I meant, I thought she had a knife.' My voice trails off as my lies fail to deceive even me.

'You said what now?'

'I might have added that bit abo—'

Mkoma smiles and claps. My heart doesn't know what to do. I can't tell if it's beating fast or if it's just left me on my own. I read a quote by Mark Twain once that went something like, 'Tell the truth and you won't have to remember anything.' If I met him now, I'd want to tell him that I'd definitely be remembering this, that's for sure.

Mkoma wipes his mouth as though he's just eaten something greasy.

'Mfana, do you know I had to miss work for this? Or maybe you've forgotten? I'm just asking. Do you know this?' He laughs quietly. Not because there's anything funny, but because when rage doesn't know where else to go, it comes out this way.

'Ho-kay. Ho-kay.' He nods to himself. Whenever Mkoma adds an 'h' to the word 'OK', it always feels as though he's saying, 'Be afraid! Be very afraid ...' the way they do in horror movies. I glance at Ambuya, who seems as shocked as I am at this unexpected performance.

'Do. You. Know. Who. This. Is?' he enunciates, clapping between every word and pointing at Ambuya at the end of his sentence.

He's missing the point! It's not about whether there was or wasn't a knife. She spoke to Bamkuru. She asked me about that night! Why doesn't he get it?

My throat closes up, making it impossible to swallow. I've never seen Mkoma this mad before.

'Hey, mfana! Answer me when I'm talking to you! Do you know who this is?'

'Ambuya?'

I'm not even sure if that's the correct answer or what exactly he wants me to say! It feels like one of those multiple-choice questions that Mrs Roderbelt sometimes gives us.

Mkoma laughs again. 'Oh, so you know? Ho-kay! So you think she's one of your little friends that you can play games with, huh? I see. Do you have any idea what you've done?'

Should I say yes? Because now even I don't really know what I've done.

'Calm down, mzukuru! I'm sure Tumirai knows that what he did is wrong. This anger isn't helping anyone.'

I'm so glad that Ambuya has intervened. She's now literally standing between us. I wonder if Mkoma would have leaped at me otherwise. He stands there with his hands crossed uncomfortably high across his chest and tucked in his armpits.

But what I had done, although it seems wrong now, had been completely necessary. Apart from the knife, I had exaggerated only a little. I have to get out of here to save myself before Bamkuru finds me. And also so that I can join the team and not die in their eyes because I bailed. Why doesn't anyone understand?

I look at Mkoma and wonder. I know he knows what it means for people to put your worth on your skin like some kind of price tag. All his rantings about the prejudice he faced abroad make that perfectly clear. But then again, I can't help but think that eventually he was able to come back home. And although some things changed when he did, home was always waiting there for him. He came back to a place where people loved him and accepted him, no questions asked. No one looks at him like he's some animal in a zoo.

Where is home for me? Where do you go when your own home rejects you? When family spits at your blood ties and wishes you'd been burned at birth? Mkoma can never understand that.

'Get in the car,' he hisses. It's messed up, but I'm actually looking to Ambuya for help. I don't think it's safe to go with

Mkoma. I mean, I'm not trying to die or anything!

'It's late, mzukuru, and it's not good to travel in this state of anger. Why don't you sleep over tonight and travel tomorrow when it's light out and you have calmed down?'

'I have to fly out early tomorrow, Ambuya. I'm not going to miss it for this nonsense!'

He tries to remain as calm as possible except that his lip almost curls the way Bamkuru's did that day. I wonder if I've crossed that line, the one you can't ever uncross.

'OK ... but I don't think you should take the boy with you.'

I want to disagree with her, but I actually feel safer with Ambuya right now.

'He's clearly still dealing with what happened. With your uncle almost out, it is safer here where your Bamkuru won't come because he knows he's not welcome.'

Mkoma scratches his head for a while. I'm not sure whether to hope that he agrees or not. Without a word he slides into his car seat and slams the door. I take a small step forward. This is when he usually says it. That I ought not to forget, and I always remind him that I'll never forget how much he loves me. No matter how upset he is with me, he always says it. He lowers his window and looks me right in the eye, his face cloudy with tears and his voice broken with pain.

'I am very disappointed in you, Tumirai.'

PART TWO

*The colours
that blind*

19

Tumi

There's something about guilt and anger when mixed. Mkoma's words play over in my head as the guilt slithers in like a garden snake in the summer. And when I think of Ambuya laughing with Bamkuru, speaking to him casually on the phone, the rage crawls and stings my body like red termites.

I can almost hear Mrs Roderbelt's shrill voice telling us not to mix explosive chemicals in her lab lest we blow up the whole school. The way I feel now makes me feel like I've done just that.

Three days, and Ambuya hasn't said anything. No shouting, no reprimanding, only *good mornings* and *goodnights*, as though nothing happened. They say silence is golden, but hers is a shade of black that sends chills down my spine. If anything, that should tell you that something about her doesn't add up. Which is precisely why I still stand by what I did. Perhaps I shouldn't have added that little bit of spice, but what Mkoma doesn't seem to appreciate is that if I hadn't, those police officers never would have taken me seriously. It's weird, but for some reason everyone seems to be blindfolded like Sandra Bullock in that *Bird Box* movie, afraid to open their eyes to see the real Ambuya. If this were a fairy tale, I'd be the knight who breaks the damn spell!

The morning is dark and steady, with only birds calling each other from distant trees. My eyes hurt with tiredness. It is the same tiredness that refuses to roll me over into dreams that don't invite the past to barge in with telephone calls, scars and the smell of cabbages. I glance at my phone and scroll down Instagram. The picture Bongani tagged me in yesterday, of him at practice with a bunch of other guys from the team, is still there. I don't know why it bothers me that Musa is in the picture, smiling, but it does. Somehow it feels like betrayal. My eyes run across the caption under the picture again and I scowl.

Call me fishbae because I be outchea fishing!
#Zimteamloading #StCatherinesteam

That has to be one of the lamest things I've ever read in my life. I don't know why there's hundreds of likes.

But even as I think that, I am also terrified that I've been cut out. That they won't have a reason to rope me in now.

Flip! If anyone is going to be fishbae, it has to be me! I need this!

I stretch and get ready to do my drills. I won't let all this chaos keep me from making the cut at the national try-outs. I have to stay focused, keep training as best I can. I plant my feet firmly into the ground and start.

A hundred squats with makeshift dumbbells for spinal strength and thigh muscle, thirty seconds to rest.

Ten laps around the yard for leanness and to help my heart adjust to paced breathing, a minute to rest.

Two gulps of water. Guilt from the other night.

Fifty pull-ups for forearm strength and core stability, two minutes of panting.

Thirty jumping lunges, exhaustion! So much exhaustion.

I stand there panting, my body bent and my hands resting on my knees. I have a love-hate relationship with training. This part of my life is the hate part. It's also harder to train alone. I normally train with Musa when the team isn't training together. Without him, I feel as though I'm doing all of it wrong. And besides, it means nothing if I can't be in the water. All the research I'm putting into this, all the training, all the books I've read – it all seems pointless. I need someone to observe and report that all this muscle training is improving my technique, but of course neither Musa, the coach nor the team is here. I stare to the far right and wonder if I should just go down to the river. No one is awake yet, and Ambuya will never know.

As I slide the bricks off the makeshift pole and hold it in my hand, fear creeps in, painted with Bamkuru's face.

'Tumi!' I hear, and flinch as a hand touches my shoulder.

'Whoa, man! Watch it!'

Ranga dodges the pole in my hand as it swings wildly. I can see his confused face right in front of me now.

'What's going on? Why are you attacking me?'

I relax my grip on the pole and wipe my brow.

I could have hurt him! What is happening to me?

'I'm sorry, man.' I shake my head slightly when I say it, in the hope that the nightmares will fall out through my ear.

'You've been acting so strange since that night your brother was shouting outside. What's going on? What was that about anyway?'

I'm very disappointed in you, Tumirai.

There's clearly too much space in my head storing unwanted things. All my nightmares are coming at once.

'Hey.' Ranga nudges at me again, realising that I've drifted off. 'What's going on with you?'

I shrug because honestly I don't know either. He looks at me for a second longer then shakes his head and walks away, an afro comb stuck into his big hair.

Ambuya descends from the veranda, holding the pillar at the edge for balance. She turns to me and smiles as though I've just walked in with the sun. It's a genuine smile. I can see from the way the wrinkles form, the corners of her eyes stretch, and the way the guilt slides so easily into my gut.

'Mzukuru, come inside,' she says, beckoning me into the house with her free hand. My eyes search for Ranga, for a witness, but he's already following the cattle heading for the pastures. I can't tell if Ambuya's still upset and I'm afraid to find out.

I stand by Ambuya's bedroom door, right next to the lounge, and hope she'll send me after Ranga to herd the cattle or even outside to help Noku terrorise the cat. Now that the silence has been broken, I fear she'll say something I don't want to hear.

I watch her carefully as she sits on a chair next to her bed with her back towards me, holding what looks like an old letter in her hand.

'Come in and sit down, mzukuru.'

It's almost as though she has eyes at the back of her head. Her voice is quiet again. I hesitate a little before walking in and sitting on the furthest end of the bed. She looks at me and smiles again.

'Your brother called early this morning. To find out how you are.'

I look at my feet. It's both the awkwardness and the shame.

'What you did was a very terrible thing, Tumirai. Very unkind. I hope you know that.'

I nod, but I don't think I'd go as far as saying it was 'very terrible'. It was maybe messed up, but 'very terrible' is a bit much.

'I'm trying to make some order in here. Sometimes when there's clutter, you have to start throwing away some of your old things otherwise you'll be stuck in dirt. Don't you agree?'

I don't say anything. How would I know about storing junk?

'I'd like you to help me clean up in here today. Why don't you take down those boxes on top of the wardrobe and let's start with those, shall we?'

I bite down my uninterest and reach up for the boxes. The dust that cascades around me as I lay them on the floor is a clear sign that they have not been touched in a long time.

Ambuya's room is a mess, with things scattered everywhere. She stops wiping for a second and puts down the cloth in her hand. 'Tell me, mzukuru ...'

My heart starts beating and I hope she won't ask about what I did. It's already mad awkward the way things are.

'... why did you take those letters, especially without your brother knowing? What were you looking for?'

So not my lie about the knife. And she doesn't sound angry. I might be wrong, but I think she's genuinely interested in finding out. I'd almost forgotten that she knew about the letters. I bite my lip and shrug.

'Just curious,' I mumble. All this is high-level, take-me-the-heck-out-of-here-now kind of awkward. I'm not sure what to say to her. I avoid her gaze, but I can feel her watching me.

'What did it say where you stopped?'

I look at her and shrug.

'Don't know.'

I mean, how am I supposed to know that if the person who wrote it doesn't even remember? It's not like I crammed it.

She keeps staring at me, and I can't really tell what she's thinking. I feel my track-bottom pockets for the second letter, pull it out and quietly hand it over to her to read for herself. Whatever she wants, just to make this go away. She looks at the envelope for a while as though she is surprised that the writing is hers, before pulling out the letter and reading all the pages including the ones supposedly from her diary. I watch her as she smiles, reading them.

'I haven't spoken about this in a long while, although I have dreamed of it almost every other day for years.'

My eyes pop at the thought of recurring nightmares.

'I still shudder at it all, but I am so afraid to relive it. It felt easier to send parts of my diary to your brother. Easier than having to recount it.' Her eyes stay with me for a while before she picks up a heap of clothes from the other side of the bed and begins to fold them.

'When your brother asked ...' She pauses. 'He wouldn't stop asking me about the past. But he felt alone, and so convinced that the hate he felt there, so far away, that it was only him that felt it. I wanted to be there with him, even if I couldn't go there. To show him that there was a time that I ...'

There is silence for a while. I'm not sure if I should be contributing to this monologue of hers, but the awkwardness has fried me ready, so I only nod, to show that I'm paying attention. I've been told before that it's the politest thing to do when adults are speaking to you and you don't know what to say.

'I think it'd do you some good to hear the rest of the story ... from me. Perhaps then you will see ...' She stops again and looks at me, smiling softly and stretching again the web of wrinkles around her eyes. Her eyes look a bit sad even though she is smiling.

'Would you like me to tell it to you? You might be surprised how much we have in common, you and me.'

I hesitate but nod reluctantly.

She sits down beside me with a sigh. 'My memory is not as good as it used to be though, mzukuru. I remember some things vividly, but not all of them.'

I look at her blankly.

'But my father used to say that a good storyteller knows

how to build bridges where there are lost pieces. And for you, mzukuru, that is what I will now do.'

I don't have anything in common with her, I know I don't. And now that the story is to be voluntarily told to me, I don't want to hear it.

20

Ambuya's story

I t must have been the beginning of April 1975 because the harvest was just starting and I remember Amai sitting outside sorting the groundnuts. Baba sat next to her, stroking his dog's fur. The sun was already going down and a slight chilly breeze from the mountains was biting at us.

'You came back early again today. Was there trouble from the Missus?' Baba asked, still stroking his dog. That dog probably got the most of Baba's raw affection, perhaps because he never left his side. He was a faithful brown Rhodesian Ridgeback with a patch of black around his eye that he had been born with.

'No, Baba. But I met the missionary teacher on my way home today. He said he and his wife might stop over here sometime tonight.'

'Is that so? Oh, how good of them! We shall be expecting them then,' Amai said pleasantly, still shelling the groundnuts.

Baba and I looked at each other, recognising each other's annoyance at her fondness for the missionaries.

'What business does he have here? To remind us that his kind has their thumb over us?'

'Baba Thandiwe,' Amai hushed him.

I understood Baba. I shared the same rage against the missionary teachers. You see, mzukuru, during those days, an African child could only go to school after passing the admissions test. A test in itself has no ill to it, you might think. But to this day, I wonder what the logic was in that particular admissions test. What were they testing by assessing whether the African child could stretch his hand over his head and try to reach for his right ear with his left hand? How did the length of his hand measure his readiness for an education? And you see, mzukuru, it was not debatable. If they asked you to touch your ear and you failed, they would send you back home. 'Come back next year,' they would say. And when the next year came around, the admissions test would change again. 'Now older than six years? Too old to start school with the others.'

Most of the children whose fathers fought in the woods, some of them children Amai had taken in, were unable to go to school because they were not ready. Their little hands had not grown long enough to stretch over their heads and touch their ears. And both Baba and I thought, How dare the missionary teacher tell us he will come to visit us when his kind did such things!

Amai ignored our reluctance and tried to make sure we were prepared to receive the visitors.

'Thandiwe, stop daydreaming and start preparing supper. If Teacher Edwards and his wife are coming, we should try to have some food ready before they get here.'

'Don't they have food at their house? Busy eating the little we have here when they have rooms stocked with food there at that school! Iwe, Mai Thandiwe, you must stop barking every time the white man whistles!' Baba intervened.

Amai's voice softened. 'It is just one meal.'

Baba looked away, lip curling in annoyance.

'We already have so many mouths to feed here with all these children, and now we must tend to already-fed ones too?'

'What will all this hatred give you though, Baba Thandiwe? Do you feel any better because you have hated a man for his skin? Has anything changed because of it? Have we won the war now?'

'I will not be disrespected in my own house! It is that white man you must tell this nonsense, not me!'

Silence.

'These Sunday services of yours are allowing them to brainwash you. Praying to a God you cannot see while they loot our land and kill our children.'

Amai continued almost as though she had not heard him.

'I suppose we could have something a little tasty tonight maybe, Thandiwe? Why don't we kill one of the chickens?'

'Kill one of the chickens? Amai, we only have three left and we need them for the eggs. Will we kill a chicken every time a white man passes by this house?' I only said it because Baba had begun it all.

'Hold your tongue and know your place, child! You will not speak to your mother like that! What has come over you?' Baba was now even more annoyed at me than at Amai.

We sat in silence for a while, before Baba grunted and called one of the children to carry his chair to the bowing tree. I imagine he wanted to get away from the bickering. I would have liked to have done the same.

'Must I cook the whole chicken then, Amai?' I asked.

'It is not as though we can kill a whole cow for them, is it? We might as well eat the chickens instead of us rearing them and the comrades eating all of them. Don't think I don't remember what you agreed to do.' Amai's voice brimmed with irritation.

'If the comrades find out that we're feeding white –' I stopped before I said anything else, because there's a look from an African mother that can calculate how much longer you have to live if you continue along that road.

The sun had retired by the time I got the fire going. The

chicken sizzled over the flames, next to the pot of sadza. Amai hummed as she sat next to me, and under the bowing tree the children now sat around Baba, who narrated one of his old folk tales, making gestures and luring them into a world of suspense and intrigue. My brother Farai emerged from nowhere and walked towards us with a serious look on his face.

'Good afternoon, Amai,' he said, then looked around again.

'Thandie, they're waiting for you.' His voice was quiet and cautious.

My eyes slid to Amai and then to the pots on the fire. Amai shook her head and immediately stood up. I could see the look of disappointment she carried on her face. And if I'm honest, I struggled too because I had not eaten chicken in months. And although I had not liked the idea of cooking for the missionary teacher and his wife, I had been looking forward to ripping the juicy flesh off the chicken bones.

'Are you happy now, Thandiwe? Do you feel like a hero? Because what you really wanted to do anyway was cook for those comra—'

'Amai!' Farai cautioned her, turning around to see if anyone had caught on. There were two things. We could die if it was found that we were cooking for the comrades. And we could be killed if the comrades found out we were reluctant to do so. But if there was anyone to be angry with, surely it was Farai. If not for him, we might not have been in this mess to begin with.

Amai breathed out slowly and tightened the zambiya around her waist.

'Farai, bring the clay pot in the kitchen with the thick milk we got from the cow this morning. You must run to the mission immediately to tell Teacher Edwards he cannot come tonight. Thandiwe, you will need to hurry up so that the children can eat and there will be no movement at this house when you leave. Nobody can know what you two are doing!'

Amai stood watching me quickly start on another pot of sadza for the children. She sighed and pressed my shoulder to try to reassure me that even though she was unhappy about all this, she was still my mother, there when she was needed.

21

When Farai and I started off to serve the comrades hiding in the trees, the sun had begun to rot and turn into darkness. My heart shivered uncontrollably because, regardless of having done it before, my spirit still quaked every time I walked into those trees at night. Each time we left with a secret pot, I would look back at the homestead and it would seem to me as though it was a dancing ground of ghosts. I remember how dead it looked – robbed of sound and everyone already asleep with all the doors locked. It was safer that way.

'Are you ready?'

I imagine I nodded at Farai and talked courage into my system. Because no matter how brave, mzukuru, no one ever gets acquainted with fear to that degree.

I quickly wrapped my head in a dhuku, balanced the pot of chicken – which had cooled down a little – on the top of my head and held some plates in my hands. Farai held the heaving steaming pot of sadza.

'Let's go.'

He seemed calm, Farai. Fearless in fact. Yet all I could think of was what would become of us if someone saw us.

'We should move faster. The food must be hot when we get there.' Farai's voice was full of authority as though he was already a comrade himself. I nodded again. But as we walked past the bowing tree and towards the river, Farai suddenly stopped. I turned behind me, catching both my panicked heart and the sliding pot on my head just in time. Baba's dog barked loudly from somewhere in the yard. I moved closer to Farai, my heart tearing in shreds. We both stood still at the sound of footsteps heading towards us. Then, like horror slowly rolling towards us, the night brought around a familiar voice.

'Tisvikewo! Is anyone home?'

Farai looked at me with his forehead creased, and my heart pounded wildly against my chest. I watched him as he quickly placed the pot of sadza behind the bulging root of the bowing tree and stood in front of me hoping that, between him and the darkness of the night, I would be covered.

'VaGuhwa! We were not expecting you. Amai and Baba have already gone to sleep.'

We should have been expecting him though. With

the poor conditions in the reserves and the comrades demanding the little food that we had in the village, most of the villagers had begun to sleep hungry most nights. So VaGuhwa's visits were becoming more and more aligned to our dinner.

'Gone to sleep? So early?' he asked, walking closer towards us, peering to see what we were carrying. He wore his old brown suit like he always did. I had once heard Baba say it had been a gift from a white man he had once worked for in Chiredzi when he was still strong enough to work. Now he wore it daily though it was old and worn out.

Several rumours about VaGuhwa's life moved around the village. Ones I would not be surprised to hear that he spread himself. Some said he had been a comrade once before, during the same time as Baba, but had been too acquainted with the bottle so the comrades had asked him to go back home. Some said he had worked for a white man whose son had then pushed him off the farm when the father died. And some simply said he was a man who liked to tell stories, especially untrue ones.

I watched as his eyes trailed to my head. Although the night had been painted by darkness, my stomach turned and I knew he had seen the pot.

'And where are you two going if your parents are already sleeping?'

Farai and I looked nervously at each other. The plan

had been to make it to the comrades unseen, especially by VaGuhwa.

'I came to see your mother,' he said, then turned around to see if anyone was listening. He lowered his voice, came a little closer and continued. 'I heard that Rogers's boy is back, the nephew. I forget the name now. I even saw him today, can you imagine? Tearing about on that noisy motorcycle of his. And you know, people are talking. They say that you are now working at the Rogerses' farm now, Thandiwe. Is it true?' His eyes stayed with the pot on my head.

'Oh, it's a shame you just missed Amai then. She and Baba retired to bed just recently. Perhaps you can come back tomorrow when she is up?'

'Mmmm,' he answered, almost as though he were not paying attention to Farai. His eyes had now found the pot my brother had hidden behind the root of the bowing tree. He paused for a while, watching our uneasy selves, then pulled something out of his pocket and handed it to me.

'I picked this up today at the bottle store. I don't know – you are the educated ones who can read.'

My eyes traced the letters on the poster that read: 'REWARDS. REPORT QUICKLY.' Selling out one comrade could earn you 2,500 pounds. Selling out a whole platoon could earn you enough to afford to move out of these rural reserves to the African section of the city. And I began to worry that this man who had nothing and no one, and loved to pass on whispers, would not hesitate to volunteer information to the security forces for a pint of beer and a few eats.

'What does it say?'

Farai glanced at me uneasily. We both knew VaGuhwa could read.

'I can't see clearly. It's quite dark,' I said.

'Mmmm.'

'VaGuhwa, Thandiwe and I really must go. We will tell Amai you came looking for her.'

'Of course,' he said, as he walked away with his poster, turning only once to wave at us. A gesture that stole conversation from us and left us alone with our thoughts the rest of the walk to where the comrades hid.

22

A week after seeing VaGuhwa, I sat outside in the early morning, worried. I had seen the look in Farai's eye the previous day when he had spoken of him, and I feared what would happen to the old man if Farai told the comrades he thought he was a sell-out. There was something about this war that was already beginning to change Farai. Twice that week he had snuck back into the house in the early hours of the morning before Amai woke up. I had not confronted him about it but I had known he must have been with the comrades.

As I sat with a book balanced on my knees, the bushes close by wiggled and Baba's dog immediately perked up, ears in the air and tail high. His eyes stayed glued in the direction of the trees nearby. I got ready to run. The bushes moved again and I am sure my heart shook violently. All I could think of was how no one would find me if I was taken. Then the dog barked. I jumped as he snarled, moving in the direction of the wiggling trees. Something suddenly emerged out of the greenery. I grabbed my candle and retreated.

'Thandie, it's me!'

I turned and my eyes widened.

'Matthew? What on earth are you doing here?'

'If I didn't know better, I'd almost think you're not keen on seeing me.'

I must have stared at him, baffled.

'But I do know better.' His smirk was picked up by the ray of moonlight shining over us. 'So come with me. I want to show you something.'

'Matthew, if the comrades, or even worse, your aunt and uncle ... if they find out you're here ...'

'I'll bring you right back before anyone has even woken up, I promise.'

I stared at him, ignoring all the voices in my head, and followed him.

We walked through the trees towards the river in silence, surrounded by trees and wrapped in the dark of the early morning. Matthew walked in front with a torch in his hand, constantly looking behind to me, to make sure I was all right. I limped slightly as the pebbles on the ground pricked my feet.

'You've hidden your hair again today. I like it when it's out.'

I refastened my dhuku, quickly tucking away any protruding hair.

'Well, this keeps things out of it.'

I paused in horror at what I had just said, silently praying he would not now think that I somehow bred lice.

You're laughing now, mzukuru, because you realise the absurdity of what I had said.

'I mean, things don't get in so easily.' I tried to redeem myself. But I heard myself say that too. He turned back, a smirk pulling up the right corner of his mouth, and the tips of his ears lit up slightly.

'Maybe I should also try it sometime. With the bike, my hair catches all sorts of things.'

I giggled.

'Look at that! If your cheeks ever flushed you'd be blushing. I don't remember you being this shy.'

'Well, then stop trying to embarrass me,' I said, but I was smiling.

The tips of his ears shed a little of their glow. His eyes suddenly glided to my feet as he aimed the light of the torch there and his forehead furrowed.

'You're going to get yourself hurt,' he said, stopping. 'Here, wear these.'

He pulled off his shoes with their thick rubber soles and handed them to me. The last good pair I had had, although slightly oversized, I'd given to one of the children to wear to school. And I'd sold all the pairs I had worn at nursing school.

'Oh no, I couldn't. I'm all right like this.'

'You're going to need these if we're going to make it to the top,' he said, pointing to a hill only a little way from the river where we now were.

'The top? Are you going to kill me and bury me where no one will look?'

He grinned and shrugged. I looked at my feet again and then back at him.

'What about you? Won't you hurt your feet?'

'I have farm feet now. My uncle would be so pleased.'

I think I laughed.

In no time we had reached the top of the hill and sat looking down at the river and glimpses of the village and farm below. The sun slowly woke up, treading the sky with footprints of a rich and mesmerising trail of orange and red. Beyond us rose the neck of a tall mountain whose top fogged gently.

'It's so beautiful, Matthew. I can't believe I have never been up here.'

'The first time I saw this I thought to myself, God must really be some kind of a master painter who puts real heart into his art.'

He paused and looked at me, his face serious.

'I found this place a few weeks ago, and when I did, I thought of you.'

The last time his face had been like that had ended with me escaping the scene and him fleeing to England. I fidgeted nervously.

'It's such a humbling view. It makes you reflect.'

I narrowed my eyes, failing to connect the dots. I had no idea what he was trying to say.

'When I went back to England I met my father for the first time. I haven't told anyone. My aunt would be upset if she found out, but I had to find my father. It was you I used to talk to about things like this.'

Matthew had always longed to meet his father, and I think I understand why. Because a young man does need his father. His mother had been in a mental hospital since she got pregnant with him, and his father had left them. The Missus, Matthew's aunt, and Bas Rogers had taken him in when he was born. So Bas Rogers was the only version of a father Matthew had ever known. From what Amai told me, the Rogerses had not been able to have their own children. Over all the years Matthew and I had been friends, he would occasionally bring up the idea of trying to find his father.

'Bastard didn't even feel bad for what he did, can you imagine? He even asked me to buy him a beer, like I owe him something.'

He paused.

'My uncle must never find out about this though, Thandie.'

He looked at me, his face serious and his voice quiet. I wondered how cosy he thought I was with the bas that I would tell him.

'You know what the most disturbing part of it all is? I don't look a thing like him. Not the eyes, the nose, nothing. Not even the hair colour.'

'Are you all right?' I asked him.

He shrugged and, not knowing what else to do, I squeezed his shoulder.

'Did you go and see her?' He had always wanted to visit his mother, and had not been able to for years.

He looked at me and pulled something out of his pocket.

'She gave me this. Said it was her mother's.' A slight discomfort came over me as my eyes settled on the ruby ring he held between his thumb and his index finger. All the while his eyes stayed with me, and I cannot tell you what I feared in that moment, because even I am not sure.

I squeezed his hand and leaned my head on his shoulder. We sat in silence for a while.

'Do you hear that?'

I listened a little closer. A faint music rose and reached out to us. The sound of the ngoma pounding grew louder and with it rose war songs. The comrades must have been close by, having a pungwe, a night connecting with the locals, dancing, talking and eating. I remembered that Farai had left the house a bit late in the night and I had not heard him coming back.

'We must leave now,' I said, panicked.

Matthew immediately got up and held out his hand to me. I looked at him, confused.

'Let's dance,' he said, wriggling in a way that I'm sure he thought was dancing.

'Matthew, we must go before they see us. The comrades are close.'

The man would not stop wriggling, completely disrespectful to the rhythm of the beating drums. I could not help but snigger.

'What do you know about dancing?'

'Ahhh! What are you talking about? I'm a farm-boy! I know everything about dancing,' he said, his laughter booming and making my eyes pop out. I almost forgot about the comrades, laughing away as though we were surrounded by peace. He pulled me up and twirled me around in the beat of the ngoma, his hands vibrating from the rippling of laughter from within him. When he really laughed, his laugh always caught you by surprise. It was loud and chaotic, and he seemed to creep up and dive into it.

23

A week or so passed before we finally saw Teacher Edwards.

'Tisvikewo. Knock, knock!' A voice accompanied footsteps from outside.

Baba immediately stepped out of the kitchen hut, Amai right behind.

'Ah, Teacher Edwards, I'm so happy you've come to visit us. I am so sorry about the other night, but we got word that it was not safe to be about. Please, sit down.'

I peered out through the door before I headed out to greet them. As soon as my eyes scanned the faces of our visitors, my heart stood still, afraid to move.

'How are you, Matthew, my boy? I've been meaning to pass through the house and give you some roundnuts. You always used to trouble me for those when you were younger. Look at you, all grown up.'

My eyes danced between Amai and Matthew, who only

smiled when he saw me. He sat on the ground between Teacher Edwards and Tawana.

'Tawana,' was all I could manage. He stood up and swallowed me into his big embrace. A few years back, Amai had taken him in when his father had died, shot by the security forces. He had spent a year with us, before his grandmother had sent for him from another village.

'It's good to see you again, Thandie. All grown and even more beautiful now.' He tried to do it discreetly but I caught a teasing look in Matthew's direction, whose cheeks slightly reddened.

'Teacher Edwards, you know my oldest, Thandiwe?' In the same breath Amai diverted the conversation to me. 'Thandiwe, get the men some chairs and something to drink.'

'No, no, please don't worry yourself. We won't be staying long. We're fine here,' Teacher Edwards interfered.

'Have you managed to convince Matthew to join our services, Teacher Edwards?' We all looked at Matthew, who now sat there embarrassed and not knowing where to put his eyes.

'Answer for yourself, Matthew.' Teacher Edwards laughed.

'I'll drop in sometime.' His eyes glided to me.

'And, Tawana, how is your new job at the mission?' Baba tried to join the conversation even though I could tell he was unhappy about this visit.

'It is going well, Baba. I've been received very well.'

'But they don't let you stay in the big houses? They keep those for the white teachers, don't they?' Baba could not help himself, but at Amai's displeased look he mumbled a faint apology.

'Amai-Thandie – we have something rather important we wish to discuss with you.' Teacher Edwards's face had become more serious and he had changed from English to Shona. I remember how shocked I had been the first time I had heard him speak in Shona, and fluently too. Only the accent gave him away.

My eyes drifted to Matthew, whose face was also serious as he listened to Teacher Edwards speak. He glanced at me and quickly gave a wink and a tiny grin before nodding at Teacher Edwards, as though he had been listening all along.

'We're here about Farai.'

I picked up on the twitch in Baba's eyes this time, perhaps because I almost shared it.

'Oh, what has he done now? That boy wants to kill me with stress in this house.'

'I'm just a little concerned that he might be getting himself into trouble. You see, Tawana here caught him and a couple of other boys in the school's storage room, looting some of our foodstuffs meant for the boarding house. Now, of course I'm not saying the boys were taking the food to the comrades, but ...'

'Then what exactly are you saying?' Baba intervened, his voice slightly raised to match his eyebrow.

Teacher Edwards cleared his throat and smiled softly. 'Mr Shumba, I'm honestly not here to stir trouble ...'

'Is this why you brought this white man here, Tawana? Because it sounds a lot like you're all here to accuse my son of –'

'Baba Thandiwe, please!' Amai pleaded with Baba.

'You better have this white man gone by the time I come back, busy here accusing my boy of theft! Have we finished the issue of all the land you stole? Have we?'

Tension rose like dust at this point, and Amai kept her head down. Matthew looked alarmed and Teacher Edwards's face had blotches of pink as though he had been stung by something. Only Tawana seemed calm. Perhaps because he knew Baba.

'I will not have any of this in my house, Mai Thandiwe. I will not have it!' Baba said to Amai as he got up and left, mumbling to himself.

'I'm sorry about my husband, Teacher Edwards. The stress of the war is getting to all of us.'

'We shouldn't stay longer. It will be disrespectful to your husband if we do, and we are not trying to upset anyone,' Teacher Edwards said.

'As I imagine you must know, Amai Thandie, I would never think it my place to interfere if the boy has decided he feels inclined to play a part in collaborating with the freedom fighters. That's not why I'm here. I'm only concerned that if indeed assisting the comrades is what led him to do this, it puts us in a difficult position, because the comrades will need more and the boarding house will become a source for them. And we cannot afford to lose any resources because we are taking care of a lot of students who need to be fed.'

'I understand what you're saying, Teacher Edwards. Baba and I will see if we can talk some sense into the boy. We are hoping that he can get his O level certificate and be a teacher, you see.'

Tawana cleared his throat and looked at Amai with soft eyes.

'Yes, well ... err ... about that as well, Amai, I'm told Farai has not been in class for the past two weeks. I don't know if you were aware ...'

'He has not been to class? Did you know about this, Thandiwe?'

I shook my head, although I had suspected it, with the way he had been cosying up to the comrades.

Amai sighed and looked away for a while. 'Leave it all to me. I will talk to his father and we will see what to do.'

'I'm terribly sorry, Amai Thandie, for such an intrusion this early in the morning. We had better get going now before the other teachers wonder where we are.'

The men stood up to leave and Amai got to her feet as a sign of respect.

'Thank you for coming to visit. You must come back again, with Nurse Edwards next time.'

'Of course, yes. I had almost forgotten that she sent us to bring you a few things. We heard about the additional two children you took in just last week. You're doing God's work.'

I looked away. If we were doing God's work, then whose work were the rest of them doing, shooting our fathers and brothers in the woods?

Teacher Edwards handed over a bag to Amai and squeezed her hand. I could see the top of a bottle of cooking oil and what looked like mealie meal.

'Never tire of doing good,' he said as he let go of her hand. I still didn't trust him, but as I stood there I couldn't help thinking to myself that, for the first time, there was no black or white, only people . . . Perhaps this was the way it ought to be.

24

I t was a Sunday in the warm month of April 1975, the day the Christians celebrated the resurrection of their Lord. Amai had already left for the mission to attend the church service, something about communion. All the children had gone with her. Baba had gone to visit some friends at the next village, an excuse to stop Amai from asking him to join her. Farai was somewhere, hopefully still alive. We had not seen him for at least a week. But Baba had said not to worry, he was a man fighting for the cause.

I remember wiping that long table outside on the Rogerses' veranda. The Missus had said there were friends coming over for lunch to celebrate the religious holiday. I laid the mats in front of each seat, ten places to be exact.

'Judy will be coming to see Matthew, so make sure to place them next to each other,' the Missus had emphasised before the family had left for the service in Umtali, where they could have a service away from the mission folk, who allowed everyone to mix and dine together in spite of the segregation laws. To my surprise, the bas had gone along to church too, missing his card game. It was probably the only time I had seen the bas go to church. The rest of the time the Missus went alone.

The breeze blew lightly at the gum trees lining the driveway and I marvelled at the sight of the tea plants stretching out across the estate. No wonder men from the city came to buy bags of the bas's tea. It was lush and green, 'good crop', as he called it. And no wonder trucks of it always left the estate full. Baba had said the bas's tea was in demand. Something about a special process that the bas used when he dried the leaves. Once Baba had brought some of the dried leaves and had brewed a cup for us. I hated to admit it, but I had started to enjoy the delicious taste from the moment the aroma had floated out of the brewing pot.

My eyes drifted to the table. The Missus had china so pretty it could mesmerise you. Fine porcelain plates, white with pink and yellow flowers at the rim, sparkling crystal water glasses, shiny polished silverware and, in the middle, to harmonise all that beauty, a vase with sunflowers that Bas Rogers had picked for her that morning. All things Amai could never have. I wondered if one day freedom would come for my people. If it was even legal to dream of having a house of my own where I could pick sunflowers from the back yard and lay out china for a Sunday meal. And as I cosied with my daydreams, the sound of a motorcycle floated in, sending the dust up in a panic. Matthew!

The motorcycle came to a rest and Matthew waved.

'Where's everyone?'

'On their way, I'm sure. Your uncle and aunt went to attend the Sunday service in Umtali.'

'My uncle went too? Well, I'll be damned.'

He walked onto the veranda with his feet dusty and bare. He walked to the table as I laid out the bowls of hot steaming stew. The Missus had insisted that I have everything including the food out on the table at noon on the dot. 'We wouldn't want you pouring hot water over anyone like last time, now, would we? Best have everything ready before my guests arrive,' she had said.

He leaned towards the bowl of chicken and lifted the lid. We both licked our lips. I hadn't had chicken in weeks and he hadn't had chicken in hours, I suppose. I understood that it was more important to feed the comrades, to feed the cause and hurry the race to freedom. So I didn't complain, at least not always.

Matthew reached out to steal a piece and I immediately slapped his hand.

'Oh, c'mon. It smells so good. It's torture to wait for everyone else.'

He teased, reaching again for the bowl. We tussled over the lid, laughing. For a brief moment, the different worlds that Matthew and I lived in didn't exist. It was only us. What could go wrong? I thought.

'What's happening here?'

We both froze and fell silent. My heart began to beat like festival drums and I slowly placed the lid on the table and stepped back. Bas Rogers stood there with Baba on one side, a sack balanced across his shoulders, and Phillip on the other. It was the shock of seeing Baba there that shook me the most. I had thought he was with his friends in the village. I feared him at that point, feared what he had seen, what he must have thought.

'Good afternoon, bas.'

'Uncle, good afternoon. Cousin Phillip! They've let you come and visit us at last!'

Matthew moved from my side and walked confidently to his cousin, who engulfed him in a hearty embrace. They enjoyed a short laugh as I shifted on my feet, unsure whether to retreat into the house or not.

'I have missed you, Matthew! Uncle here said you had driven to the city when I visited the last time! And it's a good thing I'm here, eh? You're still up to your old tricks, I see,' he said, shoving him playfully.

Matthew stole a glance at me and smiled at his cousin, a little colour filling his cheeks and ears. 'You should have written to say you were coming! I would have come to meet you.'

'Oh, not to worry, cousin! I'm already here, aren't I?' he said, ruffling Matthew's hair playfully.

'We have a lot to catch up on – at least you have a lot to tell me about! I'm here for a while, you see. They've sent me here because they say the terrorists are crawling up and down into Mozambique. Uncle here has been kind enough to allow me to stay here where I can get some home cooking, instead of eating slop on the base with the other soldiers!'

I kept my eyes fixed on the ground, afraid that if I raised them, all the truth of my involvement would seep out.

'Yes, at least there's one of you boys who doesn't think he's too good to serve this country,' Bas Rogers said, walking onto the veranda, his brow raised and his lip curled in disgust. His eyes danced between me and Matthew.

'Come show me where to put my bags, Matthew,' Phillip said heading into the house.

'You can use your old room, Phillip. I'd like a word with your cousin here.'

Phillip and Matthew exchanged looks before Phillip walked into the house with his bag. My eyes glided to Baba, who still stood there holding the sack.

'Matthew, what was going on here? I leave the house for a bloody second and you lot are busy playing around here! Your aunt will not be pleased about this.'

I craned my neck to see if the Missus was close by, but could not see her. The bas walked towards me, his breathing heavy from what sounded like anger and disgust both meshed together. I stepped back, remembering how tightly his hand had been wrapped around my throat the other day.

'Bas!'

We all turned to Baba.

'Err, bas. What shall I do with this sack? Should I take it to the shed?'

I imagine Baba was trying to help. He wanted to distract the bas for my sake.

'Get out of my sight, boy! Lazy bastard! Must you be told what to do every bloody time? Wasting good money on you.'

Baba stood there for a moment longer, watching the bas as he came closer to me on the other side of the table.

'You're lucky I'm feeling merciful today, girlie, it being the day Our Lord rose and all. You'd best get yourself out of here before I forget just how merciful I'm feeling,' he said.

I watched Baba linger there a little before walking off, mumbling to himself.

'But you . . . !' The bas now turned to Matthew with his finger pointed at him. He stopped himself and shot a glance at me. I scampered away and stood in the corridor out of sight, my back pressed against the wall and my ears reaching out in their direction.

'Where were you this morning? Got your aunt in a real bloody mood, you did! Made me attend service with her because she couldn't find you!'

'Uncle, I told you I was going to attend church at the mission today.'

Matthew's voice was quieter than usual, almost as if he knew it was not what he was meant to say.

'Bloody hell! This nonsense has to stop, Matthew!'

Bas Rogers's voice boomed so loudly I jumped.

'Since you've been back you spend less time here than with those damn missionaries, busy lying to each other and fraternising with the Africans! Now you listen to me carefully, boy. The only religious teaching you ought to be listening to is what Rhodes said about not associating with these animals. Not filling your head with that nonsense the missionaries preach. You hear?'

'But, Uncle, I was . . .'

'You were what? Will you now tell me that you're going to join them in the trees too and become one of the terrorists, eh, Matthew? Is that it?'

Terrorists. That word again. I still wonder even now as I tell you, mzukuru, that when people were all killing each other, both black and white, then why were only the Africans terrorists?

Matthew said nothing.

'You know what the chaps at the station call you and your missionary friends now, Matthew? Bloody *kaffir-boeties* – that's what they're calling you! Such an embarrassment to the family.'

Kaffir-boetie? The only time I'd heard anyone use that term was when Baba told us stories of how we lost our land. He had said it was an Afrikaans term from across the border that was given to any white man that cosied with the blacks. A way of shaming him.

'Why do you insist on making a mockery of this family? Why can't you be more like Phillip, eh?'

I didn't need to see Matthew's face to know that it had been a fatal blow right into his gut, not to mention mine.

25

Tumi

Morning is here again and I am walking with Ranga and a herd of excitable cattle deep into the foggy valley, through the lush banana plantations towards the green of pasture. We're both quiet, but my mind is loud, mulling over Ambuya's story and trying to find clues. There has to be something that will slip as she's telling her story, thinking she can teach me some great truth. There has to be something that will lead her to confess that she's plotting with Bamkuru, that she was somehow involved with the thing that happened. There has to be something about those scars, something that even Mkoma is yet to discover.

'We need to move a bit faster – soon it'll start to get hot,' Ranga says, following the cattle, who seem more accustomed to manoeuvring through this rugged terrain than I am. As amusing as they are, with their puffing and occasional dashes from Ranga's whip, the only reason I came along is because Ambuya sent me. But I'd far rather be training.

We reach a part where the ground is still damp from the rain last night and the river hisses, close to us. It doesn't look as dangerous as Ambuya says.

'Do you think I could take a quick dip? Can the cattle not graze somewhere here?'

Ranga looks at me and swings his whip.

'Ambuya says you're very good at this swimming thing.'

Swimming thing?

My right eyebrow lifts. Ranga sees it and immediately tries to correct himself. There's this thing about my face – it's a terrible ally and sometimes it leaks information about emotions I'm not even aware I have.

'I mean, I like swimming too, I guess. I've even watched recordings of Kirsty Coventry on multiple occasions scoop up awards for us at the Olympics. She's a real fish, that one! But swimming is more of a white people's sport, don't you think? I'm more of a football guy myself.'

He dribbles a fake ball with his foot and heads it past an imaginary goal post. I smile as I remember Mkoma's many reactions during the World Cup. The teams he supported always seemed to disappoint him regardless of his shouting and coaching from the sofa.

'Did you watch the game against Liverpool last week?' he asks me.

'Part of it. I heard it was five-nil.'

'Man, I try sticking with them but they keep doing this losing thing. I don't even know why I was surprised about it, because they've taken us there before. It seems now they've just dumped us here.'

I laugh and shake my head.

'That's why you should try swimming.'

'And die in the water? No, mfana. Besides, I'm too dense to float.'

He's funny.

'Tell me about it though, this swimming. Are you any good?'

Am I any good? Fam, I might as well have fins the way I move in the water!

'What's it like?' he adds.

I can't help but think he sounds like Mkoma when he tries to sound interested in the secret lives Noku claims that her dolls have.

What's there to tell?

'Well, I don't know where to start.'

'OK, tell me, why swimming? You could have chosen anything, but you chose that. Why?'

I look at him and smile. I can hear the war cries at St Catherine's chanting in my ears. But he's right – perhaps they would still chant at something else.

'Well, there's something about water that I don't know how to explain. If you fight it or tense up, it swallows you.

But if you let go, it carries you. It teaches you to loosen up and let go.'

I think I have complicated things and might have gone a bit too deep on him. He scratches his head and I can see a hint of uninterest seeping into his eyes. It happens, especially when people don't understand something. But he still smiles and nods.

'I see.' He pushes a swaying banana leaf out of his way and begins to walk on. I don't think he 'sees' anything.

'But I see you all the time running up and down the yard, lifting things and doing strange exercises that they no doubt only teach you in the city. Is that also for swimming?'

'Well, yes. The more my muscles are toned and flexible, the more I can improve my speed in the water.'

'Well, it definitely sounds like this is more than just a sport to you.'

It is.

You see, I've learned that I have to compensate. I can't afford to just be ordinary. Swimming is the only reason they accept me. And although I don't want to believe it, it's probably the real reason why Musa initially became my friend.

26

The thick leaves in front of us shake. I look around me and realise I can't see the cattle any more. I look in front at Ranga, who is now swiping his way through the thick leaves, heading deep into the banana plantation. I wonder why he has chosen this particular path. Surely he doesn't take the cattle through this plantation all the time. The leaves in front of me shake again and Ranga turns back.

'What are you doing, Tumi? Please stop that. It's not funny.'

He thinks I'm doing that? Wait! What if something is about to happen?

My palms moisten, my mouth dries up, my armpits itch. The leaves shake harder this time. There's definitely something coming for us, coming for me!

Breathe, Tumi! Run, Tumi!

This is it, isn't it? This is how I die. They will never find my body! Oh goodness, what if they never look? What if I'm sold to some man across the border who will cut me into pieces because he believes I'll cure some weird disease?

The leaves shake again. Ranga steps back towards me, his fists in the air, ready to strike. I want to be ready too, but my legs won't move. One face flashes through my mind.

Bamkuru!

I breathe. I have to be ready to fight this time. I try to lift my hands and form fists but they feel heavy, iron clad, and they tremble like sun-dried leaves. My stomach grumbles instead.

Really? Hunger? Now?

The rumbling grows louder.

What sort of dying is this?

Something leaps out from behind the leaves, roaring. It's a boy! With a scowl on his face. My knees weaken. Ranga and the boy burst into laughter, and I step back, confused.

'You almost scared me, Jabu!'

'Almost? Ah, you should have seen your face.' The boy mimics Ranga's scared expression.

'You know you'll pay for that, right? I'm going to get you, mfana! Just you wait!'

'Ha! Wouldn't I like to see you finally get me this time.'

The boy turns to me and smiles.

'This one still looks like he swallowed a ghost. City boy?'

I'm calm! I don't know why my heart is beating recklessly like it's about to burst, because I'm calm. The boy walks towards me, wearing a pair of dirty trousers that barely reach his ankles and a slightly undersized T-shirt that leaves out a tiny strip of his belly. He reaches out his hand, causing me to jerk backwards in escape. It would have been useful if I could have done this when I actually thought there was something to be afraid of.

'You city boys need to relax. It was only a joke.'

'Tumi – Jabu. Jabu – Tumi. Jabu herds cattle with me sometimes. He lives just a little further than us.'

'Where did you pick this one up?' this Jabu boy asks, inspecting me with his eyes.

'He's a distant cousin. He's only here for a bit, holidays and all. You'd like him actually. Runs around the yard. Hey, Tumi, you should join Jabu here on his morning runs. He's training for the Vumba marathon. Boy-boy came second last year!'

'Yeah, I'm going for gold this year. I'm not even playing.'

I inspect him but still say nothing. His calves look toned enough.

'Doesn't talk, this city boy of yours?' Jabu says, walking in front of Ranga. They say something I cannot hear, before Ranga turns to me and says, 'Come on, let's walk faster. I don't want to lose the cattle.'

Ranga leads us out of the thick of the plantation and into the beautiful green lush of Vumba. The cattle have given up on us and are already grazing happily, tails swinging in the air. The mountains smile in the distance, with a little mist showing at the tip. This new boy, this Jabu person – who pounces on unsuspecting boys – walks next to me, whistling away in complete contentment.

I should be happy that there's someone else who doesn't look at me as though something is wrong. Someone who understands, an ally. A possible new friend, who pulls funny pranks. After all, I like pranks, sometimes. But there's something about this Jabu boy that I don't like, and it's not because he just scared me half to death. There's something about him that makes me hate him a little. It's the way he reminds me of myself. It's the way his pale skin looks exactly like mine.

'm only fourteen – well, soon to be fifteen – and I feel as though I've amassed a lifetime's worth of experience. None of it good either. I'm not sure I'll have much left to learn when I'm older.

My head is on the soft fluff of a pillow, facing skyward, and my eyes keep blinking. Last night I bumped into a few monsters and gave up on the idea of closing my eyes. The rooster is cackling, so I know morning has not stalled. Days are peeling away and I'm wondering when I will finally make it away from this place. I glance at my phone, and the little green bubble on the screen.

Yo Tumz, thought you should hear it from me first bruh. Coach chose Bongani for Captain, and it doesn't look too rosy for you coming back into the team.

My eyes stay there for a while, tracing and retracing the

words. It's enough to splinter my life, like glass delicately cracking when heated. I roll over but my eyes can't help sliding to the screen again. Bongani is now captain; the words have not changed. I feel the disappointment so deep in my gut it is almost something I can touch. There's just over a week before the try-outs.

I should sneak off to the river before anyone wakes up. I cannot just lie here as my dreams leave me. If I do nothing, it will always come back to confront me. If I do nothing, I lose it all.

'Tumi?'

I turn. Noku is half sitting on her bed, her upper body leaning against the headboard. It is dark in the room but I can make out her hand scratching her sleep-filled eyes. I go over and, to her surprise, engulf her in a big hug. I need some warmth and she is full of little bursts of it.

'Tumi, I can't breathe.'

I hadn't realised that I was holding her too tightly.

'Tumi, are you OK?'

'Yes, I'm OK. Now go back to sleep, OK?'

She rubs her eyes again and slides back under her duvet.

'Are you scared because of Ambuya?'

It takes me a little by surprise and I nod before I can take it back.

'I've seen you looking. Is it her scars?' she whispers. I can see fear tickle at her big eyes. She squeezes my hand

and whispers again. 'But Daddy said she got her scars doing something brave, Tumi. It's not true?'

I stare at her, afraid to say anything.

'Don't be scared.' I squeeze her hand back. 'Don't be scared, because I won't let anyone hurt you. Now, go back to sleep. Don't be scared, OK? Everything is all right.' She holds my hand for a while as I sit with her, and as soon as her grip relaxes and she begins snoring, I reach for my swimming trunks and tiptoe out of the house.

28

The breeze is a biting chill, and it's no better by the river. As I stand on the bank, I start to think that perhaps I have lost it. What am I doing? The water looks so deep I'm afraid that if I drown they might never find me.

Why are you really doing this, Tumi? Will they consider how you froze yourself to death so you can be one of them?

I dip one foot in, and the cold seizes me. There are goosebumps on every part of my body. I don't want to do this, but I know what it will mean if I don't. I will sit on the bench and the only thing they will see about me is the colour of my skin. I think of Bongani and Liam, and my mind immediately remembers Bongani's post on Instagram.

Nah, Tumi, you've got to do this, bruh. Pull yourself together!

I'm reminding myself what's at stake as I set the timer on my phone and slide into my swimming trunks. My eyes scan for places I can dive from, and where to go up to. From the Msasa tree where I'm standing to whatever tree that is ahead. It looks like it might be about two hundred metres. The morning is still quiet, apart from the crickets gossiping. I think of the team. I think of Mkoma. I think of myself.

Breathe, Tumi. Focus!

I bend my knees, point my hands above me, then take a deep breath. I can do this! My body breaks through the surface and I can feel the cold like sharp spears driving into my skin. I come up for air, propelling myself against the flow of the current. I can hardly feel my arms as I push myself forward. It's harder swimming against the current. I'm already tired. The lap feels never-ending. My legs drag as I climb out of the river and hurry back to my phone to see how long it has taken me.

3 minutes, 08 seconds.

Slowest I've ever been, but it's definitely different swimming in the river, and I have to climb out and run back to check the time. There are goosebumps on my arms and thighs. I rub myself warm and jog a little to bring the warmth back. My eyes are fixed on the current of the river. But I know I need to get my time down to 1 minute 40 seconds in an actual pool to make the nationals, but I don't know what that means I need to aim for here – maybe 2 minutes 20. Lifting alone won't get me there.

C'mon, Tumi! You got this!

Knees bent, hands pointed, deep breath, splash.

My mind is still and my legs are lighter. This time the water feels as though it is giving way to my body, easing me forward. My breathing is tempered, although a little more rushed than usual. I suppose it's the cold or the current. As I dunk my head for the final time, I can see the Msasa tree again. I pull myself out of the water and reach for my phone.

3 minutes 02 seconds.

That's better than before. But the target is still 2 minutes 20 or even faster than that. I brace myself again.

Knees bent, hands pointed, deep breath, splash!

On my way up for air, I think I see a figure out of the corner of my eye. And Bamkuru's voice swings through and lands a punch!

We should have burned you like we did your kind in the past.

Everything goes still for a moment, and I can feel my body flowing as though it's one with the water. When I come back to myself, I panic, realising the current is sweeping me downriver. It is almost as though I've forgotten how to swim. I try to move but the screams come back. I cannot tell if they're coming out of me as the river gulps me down its throat, or if they're just in my head. My hands are blocks of ice, unable to paddle. My nose is burning as though someone is pouring acid inside.

And as I open my eyes, I see a pair of hands like mine

reach out just in time and pull my gasping body out of the water.

'What the hell you doing, city boy? Don't you know people don't swim here for a reason?'

29

I t is evening now. The night is already still, and we are sitting around the fire in the kitchen hut. Ranga has just excused himself for bed. I am sitting with Ambuya and Noku, who is insisting that Ambuya plaits her hair.

'I haven't done this in a long time, mzukuru, and it is late. Why don't we find someone to do it for you tomorrow?'

'No, Ambuya, I want you to do it,' Noku insists, batting her brown eyes.

Ambuya looks at her and smiles.

'Very well, mzukuru. Get your comb from the main house and let me see what I can do.'

Noku springs up towards the main house, skipping with joy on her way.

When she is back, Ambuya sits her on a mat on the floor and tucks her between her knees. I watch her as she parts Noku's thick hair in the middle before gently brushing it out. I watch them for a while until Noku begins to doze off, probably enjoying all the brushing.

Ambuya looks at me. 'You know, my mother used to do the same for me till her hands wouldn't allow. She used to love it. Even during the war, when things were out of their normal, she would make time for it. It is one of the fondest memories I have of her.'

She pauses and smiles to herself, now beginning to plait the first cornrow on Noku's head. I watch her, quiet and anticipating. I don't interrupt, because I know the story is coming.

30

Ambuya's story

A few weeks had passed since the bas had humiliated Matthew on the veranda. Baba had not said anything about it to me. I suspected he had discussed it with Amai though, because of the way she frowned when I mentioned that I had not seen Matthew in a while.

'Tilt your head,' Amai said as she kneaded my thick hair with oil. I closed my eyes and enjoyed her humming voice as she caressed the strands of my hair, running her fingers through the tresses and rubbing the oil into my scalp. It had been a long while since she had done this. When I was younger, she used to sit me tightly between her knees and slowly brush the knots out of my hair before braiding it into thin cornrows.

I always loved the gentle rippling of my hair as she combed through its thick tousled coils. I loved the smell of the oil and the tease of sleep that lingered at the edge of my eyes as I relished in the comfort of having my hair taken care of. But regardless of all this goodness, a little discomfort still sat in my stomach. I took deep breaths and told myself at the end of each one that I would have the courage to speak up. But of course every time the words rose up and made it to the tip of my tongue, I would lose my nerve and feel them fizzle out like melting sugar.

Amai continued on, massaging my head and humming a tune. I kept my eyes closed with the weight of the sunlight balancing on my eyelids. I could hear Baba's dog panting from where he sat in the shade, close by. He always did that, as though he was tired of sitting. Baba had gone to the farm even though it was a Saturday. I was only home because the Rogerses had gone to town for the day. It had been four days now and no one knew where Farai was.

'Your hair is growing longer, Thandie. *Hee*, I'll give you the mirror in a minute and you'll see for yourself! So beautiful!'

Her lips touched my almost oily forehead. I opened my eyes.

'Look in the mirror and see. Whose child is this? *Hee?* Who bore this beautiful child?'

She handed me a small piece of a mirror that had broken many moons back. I looked at myself and smiled. I watched her reflection as she slid a flower in the thick of my hair and smiled too.

'Black skin and thick hair. I couldn't have done a better job!'

I chuckled.

'You should always stand proud like your hair, Thandie. You see how it defies gravity and refuses to be bullied? Yes! We should have learned from it and not have been so easily bullied off our own land.'

I turned my head and looked back at her. Amai hardly ever spoke like that. She was always cautious and neutral.

'Never mind me. Go inside and wipe the oil off your forehead. Look at us talking about hair when our children are dying. You should have seen what I saw there at the clinic. This war must end!'

She stood up, shaking her head and grabbing all of the bottles and combs around us. We had received news earlier that morning that a bus from the mission school had been blown up by a landmine. Children going to a singing competition, caught in the web of war and spat out as though they didn't matter. Amai had gone straight to the clinic as soon as she had heard and had promised to go back later on.

'Poor Nurse Edwards. In her condition, it is such a hard thing to be dealing with.'

I swallowed. I knew what would happen next. She would head into the house, change and go back to the mission clinic to see if she could do anything at all to help, even if it meant simply praying with the other women.

We had been told that some of the students had been

taken by the ambulance to the general hospital in Umtali. Others could not wait for the ambulance to come back for them, so the villagers had organised carts to take them to the clinic or had minor wounds and were waiting there to be tended to. I held my breath as I watched her move slowly towards the kitchen hut.

'Amai ...'

The words came out before I was ready. Amai paused by the door and looked at me, her eyebrows lifted. I cleared my throat and breathed in all the calm I could.

'Can I go with you to the clinic? I could be of use.'

She narrowed her eyes and sighed. 'I don't think I'll go any more. My joints feel heavy. I might have overdone it with your hair. I think I'll stay home and rest awhile. I might go tomorrow.'

Her voice had grown a little quiet. I stayed silent for a while, shifting from one leg to another.

'Maybe I should go in your place then? Since you said Nurse Edwards might be short of help?'

Her brow furrowed and she watched me without blinking for a while.

'Kunei – what is there exactly – Thandiwe? Why do you want to go there? Since when do you have a heart for what the missionaries do?'

'Ahh, but you said it yourself, Amai. It was children in that bus, and I just want to help, do something useful.'

Amai clicked her tongue and continued into the kitchen hut in silence. My heart sank and my chin with it.

'Tisvikewo!' I turned behind me, and then back at Amai again, my eyes begging for permission before the visitor got any closer.

'VaGuhwa, please sit down. Thandiwe, fetch some water for our guest and put that pot on the fire, please.'

'Oh, have I caught you preparing dinner already? I will stay. You know how the elders say it is rude to refuse your neighbour's food.'

Amai smiled. How the old man managed to time his visits so precisely, I will never know. But I grumbled in my spirit as I went around the side of the kitchen hut to fetch the water. In that sun he still wore his coffee suit, with an old light blue shirt tucked in inside it.

'Mai Thandie, it's been long. How are you? How are you feeling these days?'

'Oh, it's all pains of old age, VaGuhwa, nothing to be avoided. And you? How are you?'

'I am doing well. It's just those children who have hurt our hearts. All blasted by the landmine.'

'Yes, it's so sad, isn't it? I heard three of them died. Their poor parents, I can't imagine.'

'It didn't look good at all when I passed the clinic just now. Everyone is trying their best to help. I even saw that boy – what's his name, the Rogers boy?'

Amai's eyes whizzed past me although she made sure they didn't stay long.

'Matthew?' I asked, perhaps a little overly eager.

'Yes, him,' VaGuhwa replied, narrowing his eyes and watching me.

There was silence for a while, and I made sure to keep my eyes down, scolding myself for having intervened in the conversation.

'Aah, ko Mai Thandie, have you heard?' He turned around to see if anyone else was listening. 'You know that girl Chipo from the next village? You know, the one who has a white man in the city. They found her up there, close to the river, beaten to death and abandoned at the side of the road.'

His eyes brushed past me, and a hint of a smirk danced at the corners of his lips. A frosty shiver gently ran its hands down my spine.

'Oh no! That is terrible.'

'Ahh, they say she was starting to parade her dealings with the white man. Forgetting what it meant and all that. Foolish, I say it was.'

Amai looked at me. 'These children don't seem to understand that the world we live in is black and white! And where things are that defined, there is no space for anything that might even begin to look grey. We're still neck deep in the middle of a war – that hasn't changed at all.'

'Mmm.' VaGuhwa's eyes followed Amai's to me. He sat back and gulped from the metal cup of water I had handed him.

'And you, Thandiwe, how is everything?' He leaned in and turned again to check that no one was listening. 'You know, I never asked where you and your brother were heading to that night. Were those pots I saw? You know how people like to talk.'

Amai and I looked at each other while VaGuhwa sipped yet again from the metal cup.

'Thandiwe, won't you be late? Surely you should run along to the mission to help like you suggested?'

'Yes, Amai.'

'Mmm.' VaGuhwa nodded. 'They need as much help as they can get there.'

I tried to suppress the smile pushed up by the things fluttering in my stomach, in spite of what it meant. And it is like that, isn't it? Sometimes the familiar smell of trouble does that to the blood of a young woman.

But as I stood up to leave, VaGuhwa grabbed my hand and hissed into my ear, 'Don't forget, Thandiwe, this is still a war. Terrible things happen when men are at war. And although the village acts blind, don't let it fool you. It has eyes everywhere!'

31

That afternoon as I walked onto the clinic compound, I could feel the stares as they followed me.

Men and women sat in little groups, talking among themselves. A few patients from the village who were there with concerns about minor ailments sat on the bench outside waiting to be seen by the nurse. Amai had said the doctor had been called to the clinic. But he had so many villages to attend to that it could be hours before he was able to get to us. It didn't make things any better that the roads were becoming more unsafe with landmines, positioned to ambush the security forces.

At the side of the clinic, a small group of women sat around a fire, stirring cauldrons filled with mountains of sadza and vegetables. Others carried things in and out of the clinic, cleaned and prayed. It was always like that. People came together to help, even if their problems required attention. That is what intertwined the African village.

My eyes scanned around. I could see Teacher Edwards and another man carrying a stretcher into the clinic. My eyes roamed again, looking, searching.

'Thandiwe.'

I turned. Tawana was walking towards me, a smile on his face.

'Is everything all right? Is your mother all right?'

'I'm here to ... I'm here to help. Anything I can do.'

'That's very kind of you. We need all the help we can get. Nurse Edwards can use your nursing skills.'

I hesitated.

'Do you think she would let me help? You know I didn't even finish my training, Tawana. Perhaps I could help you with whatever you're doing instead?'

'Don't you worry. She'll be happy to get some help from someone with your skills. Come with me.'

I tried to be discreet, looking around again. Tawana turned back to me just in time to see it.

'Are you looking for someone?' A slight smile sat on his face, one that suggested he knew something. 'He stepped out for a moment. I'm sure he'll be back any minute now.'

I feigned confusion.

Tawana smiled and stared at me a while longer. Then his face became serious and his voice lowered. 'You need to be careful though, the two of you.'

I looked down.

'If you mean Matthew, we're friends, nothing more.'

It was true. There were no lies in that statement.

'Don't worry. I don't know anything, so I won't say anything. Come, there's Nurse Edwards.'

I followed Tawana, mind reeling and worries flying around. The need for caution kept coming back and I began to fear that there might really be something to be afraid of.

'Nurse Edwards, this is Thandiwe ...'

'Thandiwe? Oh yes, Thandiwe, of course!'

The woman stopped, slender and pale from what I gathered was exhaustion, and with a bulging belly that must have been a burden. She wiped the sweat from her brow with one hand while the other put the clipboard she was holding on the ground.

'I have been waiting to meet you. Your mother speaks so very fondly of you.'

She pulled me into a tight embrace and kissed my cheek. I pulled back, surprised. I'd never been embraced by a Missus before.

'Where is your mother? I hope she's all right. She had said she would come back.'

'She's all right, just tired, madam.'

'Madam?' She cackled and squeezed my hand. 'Oh, none of that here! Call me Emma.'

She rubbed her belly and loosened the zambiya a little.

'And I will most certainly pass through and see your

mother tonight, once this little guy stops kicking in there!'

A much older nurse walked in, face buttoned up and weary, as though she did not want to be there.

'Nurse Edwards, we need you in the next room.'

At the same moment, like a haunting ghost, Farai appeared and stood by the door, signalling for Tawana.

'Walk with me, Thandiwe,' said Nurse Edwards. 'I hear you did some nurse training?'

I lingered a little, wanting to hear what Farai had to say.

'Your white man, give him this. It is urgent,' was all I managed to glean. And in that moment, before I could hear any more, Nurse Edwards turned back to me at my lack of response.

'Yes, mada— Emma, but I didn't manage to finish. I had a few months still to go when I left,' I said, walking quickly to keep up with her.

'All right, I see,' she said, stopping by one of the beds. She signalled for me to help her prop up the patient, an old frail man with a tube stuck in his nose and another one in his arm.

'Good afternoon, sekuru.'

The old man smiled at the nurse, while I watched her speaking my language naturally as though it was hers too. And found myself somewhat relaxed by it.

'This is Thandiwe. She'll be helping me take care of you today. Won't you, Thandie?' Nurse Edwards said, turning to me. I smiled, but then noticed her eyes lingering on the stubbornness of my hair as it yet again defied gravity. My hands immediately ran over it, in an attempt to convince it to lie down, to hide.

'I'm sorry about the hair. I can look for something to cover it up with.'

'Heavens! Why? I certainly don't mind. Do you, sekuru?' she asked, turning to the old man, who only shrugged.

'You know what I wish though? That mine was even half as full and proud as yours.'

I looked at her in surprise, almost waiting for her disgust to set in. But it didn't.

'Now –' she peered over to the other room – 'can I trust you to finish with sekuru here, and then tend to that poor boy with the broken leg over there? There's a few like him who were on the bus this morning. It's all so terrible, isn't it? I'll ask one of the girls to come and help you so you won't be by yourself. I'm going to see if I can call the doctor again and urge him to hurry so he can help some of our boys who have burn wounds. Is that all right with you, Thandie?'

I nodded.

'You, my dear, are a godsend,' she said as she took my hands in hers. 'All right then. It's a full house today so we'd best get started.'

32

I began to worry because I had not seen Matthew for a week.
*What had really changed, Thandiwe? What did you
expect?* I asked myself.

'Thandiwe, you better not be daydreaming again. People
will start coming any minute now!'

I carried the huge clay pot of beer outside. VaGuhwa
was already out there whispering something to Baba, who
seemed rather preoccupied with the meat he and the other
men were butchering. I felt as though I was still waiting to
hear that he had sold us out.

The war had grown fiercer, and Baba had wanted to host
a small gathering to cheer people's spirits. 'Slaughter one
of the cows and invite the village,' he had said to Farai and
the other boys.

Amai hadn't been pleased about it because that meant
giving away more meat. But she hadn't fought it. Two more
of the mission's children had died from their injuries in

the landmine accident. Then three girls from a homestead a few kilometres from ours had returned home screaming and crying; they had been raped by the security forces on their way to fetch water. An old man had been beaten by the comrades, accused of selling out to the white man. It was all hate, painted in different faces and hunting us all down. I imagine that even though Amai was reluctant to host the gathering, she understood that everyone needed a pinch of joy.

Farai headed to me with a dish full of pieces of meat. I watched him as he placed the dish down and sat next to me.

'You seem in happy spirits, Farai.'

'Do you not see all this meat? When last did you eat meat, Thandie? Look, Baba's dog is busy there with the bones, forgetting to bite strangers.'

We both chuckled. Baba had been right. We had been in need of a bit of joy.

I rinsed the pieces of meat in some water before throwing them into the cauldron.

'Do you know how many people are coming?'

'With the way you're stewing that beef, it might turn out to be the whole village.'

He was right. People had already started to fill the compound. Two of the village boys now banged on the ngoma under the bowing tree, sending everyone, young and old, on their feet dancing.

'You know what you must do, don't you?' Farai suddenly said, leaning in towards me, his voice quiet. I looked towards the cauldron with the meat I had already cooked and quietly scooped out enough to fill a dish. He shook his head and I proceeded to add more.

'We must be careful tonight. We cannot be seen, but we cannot afford not to go. Not with all this noise being a clear sign that there has been some activity involving food here.'

I nodded. 'How will I know where they are?'

He looked ahead at Amai and kept his gaze there.

'Bullet has business with you so he might come. You'll be wise to stay here tonight in case he does. Don't leave.'

Don't leave? I thought. *Where would I go?*

Throughout the evening my mind was preoccupied with it all. The comrades' dish of meat grew cold from waiting. Amai retired to the bedroom hut while Baba snored on the mat where he lay, a jug of beer spilt by his side. I sat there on the log, peering and turning like a possessed owl. Waiting.

Waiting to see if the comrade would come. Waiting to find out what he wanted. Waiting to hear what business he could possibly have with me. And as I lifted my head, my eyes caught a movement a little far off, behind the kitchen hut, a figure signalling for me to come. I turned around to see if anyone was watching. My heart fluttered and fear sat right on my neck.

My legs trembled at every step, but I tried to hurry

nonetheless. As I reached there, my mouth opened in surprise.

'Matthew? You need to stop coming here! You're going to get yourself killed!'

'I had to see you.'

I dragged him further into the trees. His skin was warm as though he had been in the sun and he smelled of dried tea and the fresh squeeze of lemons.

'What are you doing here? Don't you know it is not safe?'

'We don't have much time. I have a surprise for you. Come.'

His whispers sounded like hisses floating on top of the pounding drum. Those things, mzukuru, those uninvited things fluttered once more, bumping into each other and causing chaos in my stomach. And as they did, I remembered my brother's warnings and stepped back.

'You should go. If the comrades ... It is not safe tonight. You should go.'

'Thandiwe, hey, look at me. Look at me,' he said, lifting my chin. 'I won't let anything happen to you, OK? Nothing will happen.'

You know, mzukuru, they say temptation is glittery and shiny. Perhaps that is why even the wide-awake walk so freely into it.

I walked on, fears shrilling and heart pounding wildly, like the drum I was leaving behind. But I kept going, in spite of all my questions, doubts and fears. My eyes shifted to Matthew's hand, then to his fingers that had somehow slid into mine. I blinked twice, surprised that I had let him take hold of my hand and wondering why I was not pulling away. But still, we walked hand in hand, in silence, following the narrow path in the trees towards the river.

'We're here.'

I looked at him and chuckled.

'Matthew, your surprise is the river? You might be a little disappointed, but I've already seen it.'

He smiled softly. 'Here, sit on this. Any minute now.'

He took his jacket off and laid it on the ground. I sat down beside him, parked for a moment in comfortable silence.

'Look,' he said, pointing to the moon. My eyes bulged as I watched the moon slowly peeling out of its shell, revealing a new blood-coloured skin I'd never seen before. I gasped in disbelief.

'No! I've heard of it, but didn't believe it really happens. Isn't it rare?'

I remembered reading about it somewhere. That the lunar eclipse was uncommon and you could make it through this whole life without seeing one.

'But how did you know it would happen today?'

'I have my sources.'

I smiled and looked back up. It plays like a film in my

head now, the laughing that followed, the playful mood. They say that about death – that when it arrives, sometimes it mocks you with moments of strength and agility before it claims its debt and snuffs out the blaze of life. They say it gives you time to see what you're leaving behind.

'So have you thought about it?'

I looked at him, confused.

'Are you going to go back and finish your nurse training? I heard that you were an absolute natural at the clinic, and God knows they need more help there if you decide you want to stay here.'

I smiled, breathing deeply at the dead dreams resurfacing.

'I don't think that's possible any more. I'm needed here, at the farmhouse, remember? It's not the same with Amai unwell.'

'But you're only a few months from completing your training. And you've wanted to do this for as long as I can remember. You even used to pretend to be a nurse when we were younger, remember?'

'That was a child's dream, Matthew. I have a new life now, I suppose, and it only does me better to accept it. Besides, there's so much to do, with all the work at the farmhouse, taking care of Amai and the children, cooking for the comrades. It's really a never-ending list.'

He blinked and I could see the confusion.

'I mean, there's a lot I'm expected to do. I don't think I would have time for –'

'What do you mean, cooking for the comrades? Are they forcing you to do that?'

My hand flew to my mouth as if I could shove the words back in. But, I thought, this was Matthew.

'You won't tell anyone, will you, Matthew?'

'Are they forcing you, Thandiwe? Oh, those bastards! We can tell Phillip! He works with the colonel at the security forces now. He will be able to help.'

I remembered the coldness in Phillip's eyes the last time I had seen him. The snarl, the disgust. Why would he help me? And how exactly? Even though I did not appreciate all the chickens we were killing to feed the comrades, I supported the cause. I was not a sell-out!

You know what they say, mzukuru, evil has a loud laugh when it roars.

'I am doing my part.'

I said it as calmly as I could, praying that if the words hit his ears a little more softly, he would accept them and we could move on.

'Wait, so you're working with them? Willingly?'

'Them? Who is them, Matthew?'

'I can't believe you would do something like this, to associate yourself with those people!'

'Those people? Am I now *those* people? Was I *those*

people when you came to find me at my father's homestead?'

'You're not like them though, Thandiwe, don't you see? Whatever they've told you or threatened you with, I can help. Let me help.'

My eyes caught the intention in his. It was as though he had teased a flame in a bucket full of paraffin. Anger I didn't know I had simmered and bubbled to the surface the same way Amai's okra did when she added soda to it. Of course the comrades had to be fed! They couldn't fight if they were hungry! My hand slowly turned into a fist as I stood there, trembling with rage.

He turned to leave and I grabbed him by the sleeve of his shirt.

'No, Matthew. No! *Those people?* Those people are my people. Those people are me! Fighting for me! Did you really think I would be rooting for the whites?'

I looked at him the way a cat eyes a lizard, ready to pounce as soon as it slides off the rocks.

'The whites?' He seemed surprised, like it was the first time he was hearing of it.

'People are dying, Thandiwe! This is a bloody war – it isn't some stupid game of making fun of my aunt any more.'

I knew it even then: we were balancing on a tightrope that had already caught fire. And yet, even with all this knowledge, the words still spilled out of me because my anger made more sense.

'And I guess in a war, people pick sides, don't they, Matthew?'

I waited for him to say something, to make right our wrongs, as his eyes sparkled in the milky light of the moon.

'I suppose you're right. And I guess if you're helping the terrorists, it means you must be one of them.'

My stomach lurched. That word again.

Don't mind the tears of an old woman, mzukuru. It's the sting of my memories and the poison of regret that I wish I could wipe away. Because that night we said more than we should have. And with every word we entered into a new world we could not yet see. A world we later passed on to you. It was those words we said to each other, they were what tugged in the real war.

33

Tumi

I am thinking of Ambuya's tales from last night and trying to imagine this place as it was in her stories. I want to see if it makes sense. I breathe in and look in front at Jabu, who is still going, running up the incline as though it is nothing. I am now starting to regret that I agreed to this. I am not tired, but my chest is burning and I have a deep desire to be lifting something instead. I pull out my phone and pant as I run behind him.

'Man, we need to take a break,' I yell. My phone says we've been at it for seven kilometres. And iPhones don't lie.

'We're not there yet.'

Not where? Death?

I am starting to resent him a little.

Just because he saved my life yesterday doesn't mean he gets to run it now. Thing is, I can lift for a whole hour or even two without complaining. But cardio out of the water isn't my thing. It's simply monotonous.

'Nah, Jabu bruh, we have to stop.'

He turns back and looks at me, his face shiny with sweat. I am standing with my hands rested on my knees, craving water. He jogs down towards me and pats me on the back.

'I thought you said you wanted to win. This doesn't look like it, city boy.'

Honestly, do I have a sign on my forehead encouraging this whole nickname business?

'Come on, let's go, mfana. We're almost there.'

'Nah fam, I'm tired. I need a break.' I'm a little annoyed. Not because of any of the stuff from before. I mean, this Jabu boy . . . I mean, Jabu, he is good people. But I'm annoyed because his forehead is that shiny and yet he still wants to keep going. I sit down at the edge of the main road that leads to the wealthy side of Vumba with all the resorts.

'You're the one with all the fancy equipment there in the city, and yet you can't keep up with a farm-boy? Look at you, panting like you're dying.'

I ignore him and wipe the sweat off my brow.

'It's this noise you listen to that's tiring you, I bet,' he says pointing to my headphones.

'Man, stop hating on my music.'

'Let me listen to one song. Maybe I'll like it,' he says, stretching out his hand. I slide the headphones off my head and hand them to him, then select something from Stormzy's album on my phone. There's no going wrong with

Stormzy. If he doesn't like it, there's no hope for him.

I watch his face, expressionless for a while. Then it gradually twists before he chuckles, shaking his head.

'What sort of music is this, mfana? I can't even hear anything with all that noise he's making. Play another song. Maybe I'll like something else.'

'Ay, this is not an evangelical church, bruh. It's either you like it, or you don't. There's no repentance here!'

He laughs and hands me back my headphones.

'You've got to get up though. First rule of running: you never sit down, otherwise you won't want to get up. We can walk the rest of the way if it's better for you, but we definitely can't sit down.'

I roll my eyes, but take his hand as he offers it and pulls me up. We walk slowly up the incline. The sun is starting to come out, and the fog is clearing. As we get to the top, I see a tea estate, and an old farmhouse in the middle. My eyes search for the Msasa tree in the driveway that Ambuya mentioned. I'm not sure if I'm trying to see if her story is true or if I'm just curious.

'Who lives there?'

'What, the tea estate?' Jabu asks.

I nod.

'Some workers, I think. It belongs to some big company that makes tea there in the city. Why do you ask?'

'No reason,' I say.

'And is there a mission school somewhere here?'

'Mission school? Here?' he says, repeating the words like I haven't heard that I said them. 'Oh, that old place? They don't use it as a school any more. I think it belongs to some organisation or something. Wasn't it in the eighties or nineties when it was a school?'

I don't know if I should be relieved but I am.

'Why are you asking all this?'

'History stuff. Just trying to get a picture of it all.'

He watches me for a minute as though he is waiting for the real truth. Then he shrugs. I keep walking on beside him.

'Mfana, this is me,' he says, pointing to a little path forged alongside the road into the trees. 'I certainly can't keep up with this do-you-know-Vumba-well quiz.'

'Are you running again tomorrow?' I ask.

'Only if you won't slow me down. How much longer before your swimming thing?'

People really have got to stop calling it a swimming thing!

I think of the team, of Bongani. I haven't heard anything more from Musa. I tried calling him yesterday but he texted back to say he was tied up. Wished me luck though, as though to say I'll be needing luck at the national try-outs. Man, I need to be ready.

'Only five days. Well, four, actually because my brother

comes to pick me up before the fifth day.'

He nods towards the river.

'Any more drowning stunts before you go? Yesterday's performance was quite entertaining.'

'Ehh, listen to this nonsense! You interrupted me there yesterday, son. I was busy slaying it.'

He laughs, kicking back his head.

'Look at you laughing, Jabu, but can you even float? Busy there spitting insults!'

'Ahh, I'm not the one claiming to be a fish, ka! Even if I can't float, at least I won't be doing this,' he says, acting as though he's drowning. 'But listen though, mfana. Since your time is running out, why don't we do a short run tomorrow and then pass through the river? Maybe I can see if you're really a Kirsty or just a wannabe. These waters need experienced folk like me.'

'Ay! Listen to this farm-boy. Challenge accepted! Me, I don't play in the water though. Don't say I didn't warn you!'

We laugh as he walks away, and I am left smiling. Because for real, he's good people this Jabu boy . . . this Jabu.

34

Evening has come and the television is buzzing on that one boring channel. Ranga is in the kitchen, and Ambuya is sitting opposite me on the other sofa with Noku. No matter how many times I check my messages, there's nothing from Musa. Only an email from the school's official sports account to say I've been kicked off the team. Something about missing too many days of practice and inconveniencing the rest of the team. I didn't read the rest of the email. There's no need to because I already got the message. I'm on my own, and I'm going to have to make it on my own.

I glance at Noku, who is now trying to teach Ambuya some game she no doubt learned at nursery. I smile as the old woman is repeatedly told the game has to start over because she's done something wrong.

'No, Ambuya, put your hands like this. You aren't listening,' she says, laughing and shuffling the old woman's hands. I'm smiling as I look at Ambuya. My eyes drift to the poem hanging on the wall and though I glide over the words, I linger on the picture stuck there in the corner of the frame. The picture where Ambuya is standing next to a young white man. I think I know who it is now.

Ranga brings in the mats and lays them on the coffee table in front of us.

'But, Ambuya, I want Nando's,' Noku starts to whine.

'Eh, mzukuru wangu, there's no Nando's here for miles. Just you wait though – this will taste way better than your Nando's.'

Ranga smiles at Noku as he sets down plates of steaming sadza with stew and fried spinach. Noku glances at Ambuya again and becomes possessed with an unending series of yawns. She curls up on the sofa next to the old woman.

'I'm so sleepy now though, Ambuya, pun intended,' she says, sending me into a fit of laughter. The one time she had heard Mkoma use the term, he had told her it meant he was dead serious, the same way she is now about not eating that sadza. Ambuya chuckles as she watches Noku, whose eyes are open only a little to see if her story is being bought.

'Eat only a few morsels, my mzukuru, and then you can sleep.'

'Ahh, Ambuya, but I'm already dreaming now. Daddy says people shouldn't eat if they're sleeping,' she says, faking a snore. Of all the times to take heed of Mkoma's instructions!

'It's not even a lot of food, Noku, look,' Ambuya says, lifting her plate. It's pointless. She should already know that she's not winning this one. Especially because she doesn't have Mkoma's deep voice to scare the little thing.

'People can choke and die if they eat while they're sleeping, Ambuya. You don't want me to die, do you?'

Ambuya laughs, shaking her head. Till this day, I haven't met anyone who has won against Noku. She's a heavyweight professional, is what she is. And Ambuya knows what defeat looks like. We all do.

'What about some rice? I think there's a little rice left over from yesterday, no?' she says.

Noku perks up. 'Well? Am I eating or what? I'm a small-small child, feed me oo-oo abeg before I go collapse and die!' Her accent slides in, sending us all into bursts of laughter. Ambuya's eyes are teary with merriment. For the first time her scars don't really scare me. They're there, a part of her, the same way her arms are a part of her. I think of her story, and my eyes glide up again towards the picture on top. The scars are there in it too, something I hadn't noticed before.

'Ambuya?' I start. She smiles at me and I hesitate. Everyone is looking at me now and I don't know that it's appropriate to ask about the scars.

'How does a war start?' I manage. I don't know where that question came from, but it worked, because now she is smiling softly at me. Her phone rings and she glances at it before she answers me.

'Well, mzukuru,' she says, 'I imagine all wars start the minute we invent the words "us" and "them".'

She picks up the phone and I watch the expression on her face slowly change.

Her eyes bulge, her lips quiver and she turns toward me.

'No,' she gasps.

I have seen fear before, but never painted with long strokes and drawn thickly within the wrinkles of an old woman's face. And although I can feel my heart beginning to pound, all I can hear screeching in my head are her words: *all wars start when we invent the words 'us' and 'them'.*

35

Ambuya's story

You know, mzukuru, there's something they say about silence. That it can be a source of strength. Maybe it can, but what they don't tell you is that silence can burn, holding you hostage as it corrodes everything inside. It can be the soft, dying embers of a fire which, if left untended, can set a whole house ablaze. And that day, it was the kind of silence that took turns to stare us in the face. The kind that gnaws at you like a hungry rat. A silence so loud you can hear nothing.

I stood by the mantel, feeling the weight of his stare boring into me. We both brewed in that silence. And then finally, fighting my pride and everything that came with it, I walked to the table and sat next to him.

'Are you still upset then, Matthew? About the other night.'

'I'm not upset.' His expression remained neutral.

'Then what is wrong?'

'Nothing's wrong,' he said.

Now, you're still too young, mzukuru. You haven't learned that to ask a person if anything is wrong and be told that it's nothing is a polite way of being told 'You know, I'm doing absolutely everything I can not to punch you in the teeth for a reason you should have realised but clearly haven't yet.'

I watched him sipping his tea, going on as though 'nothing' was wrong.

The door to the bas's office creaked and both Matthew and I turned. I immediately stood up, knowing that I could not be at the Missus's table, sitting casually next to Matthew as though we were equal. Wednesdays were meant to be peaceful days. Routinely, Matthew and Baba loaded the truck with sacks of tea and Matthew would drive off to town. The Missus always went to visit friends in Umtali, dropped there by the bas as he went to play cards. Then it would be just me, cleaning, cooking, thinking, mostly thinking. But since Phillip had moved into the farmhouse, unpredictability had become part of the game.

I nervously wiped the glass window of the cabinet next to the mantel. But even though I had made it back to the mantel by the time Phillip walked out of the office, my heart still shook at the sight of the old man. Hand over his chest, holding a thick yellow envelope, head bowed slightly and eyes looking down and avoiding me, and that same coffee suit. He lifted his head slightly and our eyes met briefly.

'VaGuhwa,' I whispered, bobbing in respect. He nodded to acknowledge it and immediately looked away.

'You can leave, boy, and don't spend that all on beer now,' Phillip said, drawing out a chair next to Matthew. My heart shivered, mzukuru, as though there was a cold wind blowing in. Did Phillip know? I wondered. What had the old man told him?

'Cousin, what do you have planned for the day?' he asked.

'I was hoping you would come with me to Umtali to drop off the sacks of tea,' Matthew answered.

I continued to polish the mantel, watching their reflections in the glass window of the cabinet.

'Umtali, eh?' Phillip said, watching me. He stood up, walked to the mantel where I was and reached into the bottom cupboard, where the bas kept all the strong drinks. He held a bottle of whisky in one hand and brushed my arm with the other as he pulled out two glasses.

'Cousin, a drink?' he asked, his eyes still watching me the way the leopard watches a kudu just before it pounces. And although I stayed there polishing and wiping, I was afraid, mzukuru. Afraid of the truth, because it is exactly as they say, that only the truth will set you ... well, off to an early grave.

Matthew seemed oblivious to all that was happening. I saw him shake his head, and my eyes tried not to be obvious as they peeked at Phillip, who was inspecting the bottle in his hand.

'Have you been taking some of my whisky, girlie? The bottle is almost empty,' he said, standing so close behind me that I could smell the last cigarette he had smoked.

Matthew's head lifted.

'No, bas.'

'Don't say no when the alcohol is missing now.'

'I didn't take it, bas.'

'This one is a troublemaker, isn't she, Matthew?' he said, gripping my hand. I let out a little squeal, with my back pushed against the mantel and trying as hard as I could to refuse to be scared. A knock on the front door came just in time, and this time both Phillip and Matthew turned. I tried to calm my breathing.

'Bas, the bags are ready,' Baba's voice called from the veranda. My heart drummed, and in confusion I prayed that Baba would come closer to the door so he could see, yet also hoping to stay out of his sight because I knew what would be done to him if he intervened.

'Perhaps we should attend to that, cousin?' Matthew asked, watching Phillip, who paid no attention as he pressed on my arm.

'I'll need help with the bags, Phillip.'

He smirked and let go of me, laughing through his nose.

He knows. My God, he knows!

The voices of the three men – Baba, Phillip and Matthew – could be heard from outside. And although I could not see anything from the kitchen where I was, I knew that they were loading the sacks full of dried tea into the truck. The voices disappeared, and I peered through the kitchen window at Baba, returning to the estate. My stomach churned and I wondered if I could call him. But what good would that do?

The sound of footsteps returned to the house. I halted, waiting for it, whatever it was.

'You! In the truck! You're coming with us!' Phillip demanded.

My eyes went to Matthew.

'Phillip, maybe we should leave her behind. After all, maybe she's been given things to do in the house.'

'You remember what Uncle spoke to us about, don't you, Matthew? Blood or water?' Phillip's voice softened.

'I remember well, but she needs permission from the registrar, and it takes a while to process. If we go with her, they will arrest her for violation of the segregation laws; you know this.'

'Don't worry so much, cousin,' he said, ruffling Matthew's hair as though he were a small boy. 'Isn't she with me? Look at me. Am I not the law?' His fingers rubbed the emblem of the security forces on his breast pocket.

'I guess,' Matthew said, nodding, apologies dancing in his eyes.

'Now that that's sorted, why don't you get in the truck, eh, girlie?' he said with a smirk.

And again, mzukuru, I was afraid. I see you wondering now, not knowing that in those days people like us could not roam the streets without a pass from the registrar. Not understanding that after we had built the cities with our sweat, slaved to raise the towns that sat on our land, *they* looked at us and decided that that contribution was invalidated by the paint the womb had given us.

'You should smile more, girlie,' Phillip said as I passed him, heading for the truck. 'You almost look as though something has been stolen from you.'

Of course he would say that; it was typical of a thief.

36

I stood outside the back door of a little restaurant in Main Street, deep in the heart of the city of Umtali. It had been a while since I had been this exposed to privilege. But even when I had been in Salisbury, I'd never been allowed to wander to the heart of the city. Phillip had said nothing when they had left to go inside, except that I was to stand there by the door and wait. Matthew had only watched me in silence. He seemed to be stuck in a dilemma. I hadn't heard what his uncle had said to him about blood and water, but I didn't need to be any kind of genius to figure it out.

I peeped through the back door of the little restaurant to see if Matthew and Phillip were on their way out. A middle-aged woman sat inside at the far end, fanning herself with a bottle of cola in front of her. I smiled nervously at her and she looked away. The men had been in there for about twenty minutes, although it was beginning to feel like an eternity.

A man passed, with a little boy young enough to be his grandson. When the little boy saw me, he smiled and waved, but as soon as the man saw, he whisked the little boy into his arms, his hand covering his grandson's nose. I shook my head. Even anger could not come out. Only colour, and yet a grown man feared he might breathe it onto his own skin.

My eyes drifted to the sign hanging slightly above my head with its letters big and bold:

EUROPEANS ONLY, DOGS AND AFRICANS NOT ALLOWED.

I remember seeing the white van with two threatening blue stripes as it drove from the road to the kerb where I stood. I remember how my heart jolted within me, scampering in all directions and looking for a place to run to. I remember breathing as softly as I could, fearing that even my breath was criminal.

Five men descended from the car, one holding a leash to a panting German shepherd with glimmering amber eyes that gave away that he was looking for someone to devour. I was asked once how I came to be prayerful. I am sure God laughs about it – the girl who breathed in and whispered a little prayer as she watched vultures strut towards her, in pressed khaki uniforms and brown shoes.

'What are you doing here, girlie?' one of the men asked.

The dog sniffed at me, and the officer with the leash yanked at it, pulling it back.

'I'm waiting for Mr Rog— I'm waiting for my bas, sir.'

'You know you're not supposed to be here, don't you?'

'Yes, sir.'

'What is your name?' another officer asked. I froze.

'Ros— Thandiwe, bas. I mean, officer ... er, sir.' I could feel the dog's breath kissing my skin and my nerves melting into shivers.

'Let's see your pass then.'

My armpits stung and I peered back into the restaurant again.

'I ...' I swallowed as I watched that middle-aged lady now standing up, moving towards us.

'My bas, sir ... he said ... My bas, he has it, sir.'

'That's the thing with you bloody kaffirs! Always ungrateful, never respecting the law.'

'Officer, oh, I'm so glad you came. I was so worried. This is who I spoke to you about on the phone? She has been standing here suspiciously for hours. I was so afraid that she might throw a bomb in here. You know, you can never be too careful with these Africans.'

I looked at the woman, confused.

'You did well to ring us, ma'am. We don't want a repeat of what happened last week.'

She nodded, satisfied with herself. And in that moment

I remembered how Baba had mentioned something about a bomb going off in one of the suburbs in Umtali. How the security forces had then set a curfew, for 'everyone's' safety. It was ironic, mzukuru, that after years of bloodshed, they had only now noticed that people were unsafe, when the war had tired of being hidden in the Msasa trees of the reserves and had strutted to their carefully trimmed hedges.

I watched as one of the officers consoled the woman, who was seemingly distraught and shaken by it all. And although I only knew he was speaking because his lips moved, his words escaped me as I hung on to myself, praying. One of the five men unhooked a pair of handcuffs that jingled on his belt.

'Officer, my bas, he's in there . . .' I tried, my heart speeding up. The other men laughed and I held my breath, afraid that maybe all the anger and fear would merge into each other and erupt. I stepped back as the man reached for my arms. The dog pulled at its leash, snarling and barking and showing its teeth.

Before I had gone to Salisbury for my training, Baba and Amai had sat me down. 'You never run if the security forces stop you, you hear, Thandiwe?' Baba had hissed, and Amai had pulled his arm to calm him down. 'You do as you're told. You remember that we have no one on our side. You must remember that we have not taken back the land yet.' That had been the end of the conversation.

I took another step back as the dog barked, jerking in my direction, hungry for a bite. I had given up on Matthew and Phillip, given in to the idea that this was why they had brought me here. And although I am old now, mzukuru, and my memory sometimes fails me, I can never forget how I thought to myself, *You're alone, Thandiwe. There is no one here who will stand for you.*

It must have been the very moment when my distinct desire to remain alive overrode all of Baba and Amai's teachings. Because, at that moment, the brakes on my feet broke and I charged past the unsuspecting officers. I'm not even sure where I thought I was going, or how far I thought I would get. But I ran, as fast as my legs would oblige, speeding away. I could hear the loud barking sounds of the dog and the mad fury of chasing feet behind me. But even then, I ran.

And without having gone far, I found myself face to face with the ground. My right cheek pressed on the tarmac and I remember wailing as the face of that raging dog came close to mine. I don't remember it exactly, but I remember my screams as the dog's teeth punched through the skin of my jaw, chewing at me like a piece of biltong. And my tears, I remember them too.

One of the officers twisted my arms behind me and I winced at the click of the cuffs. And as I lay there on the ground, I thought mercy had smiled at me at the sight of Phillip exiting the restaurant with a frown on his face, trotting in our direction.

'What's happening here?'

'Bas Phillip, please tell them I'm with you,' I struggled to say, blood filling my mouth and pain thrashing on my jaw.

'What's happened? What has she done, officers?'

One of the policemen whose knees were not in my ribs smiled as he saw Phillip, a smile that spoke of recognition and a possible friendship.

'Phillip? I should have known you'd have a hand in it if trouble was around.'

'George! I see they finally gave you handcuffs!' Carefree laughter rippled from him, coated in confidence that things like this could never happen to him.

'She belongs to you, Phillip?'

'It depends. What did she do?'

'Well, scared that poor lady there half to death threatening to bomb the place. Girlie here has no papers too, nothing. She says she's with you. But you know, after those attacks last week, if we just let them walk around as they please, it'll only create more problems.'

Although I could not see very clearly, I could see that one of the officers was standing slightly away from the rest of them, trapped in a precarious uneasiness that drew my eyes to him. I watched as he tried his best to make sure that his eyes didn't break any laws and mix with mine. At first, I thought my sight was simply offending to him, but something about his expression when he eventually looked at me urged pity within me. His eyes seemed to bear fear and beg forgiveness. As though he too was a little hare pinned into a corner, just like me.

'Oh no, we certainly can't have that happen again! What do you propose we do then, George?'

'Unless you're willing to come to the station with us so that we can get your support of her in the books, I'm afraid we're going to have to lock her up until the real Mr Rogers comes to get her, if he wants her back.'

'Oh, so old man Rogers is the real Mr Rogers, you mean?' Phillip said, laughing.

The other officer's voice went quiet and he leaned in closer to Phillip as though he was afraid the others would hear.

'Also . . . bringing in another potential terrorist will really go a long way towards that promotion they've been promising me. You know how it works.'

Phillip cackled and I almost believed he would say it, that he would sell me to them.

I heard Matthew before I saw him, hurrying down the street towards us.

'Phillip? What is going on?' he asked as soon as he reached us. 'Why is Thandie in cuffs?'

'Disturbing the peace, Matthew. Girlie here was apparently threatening to bomb that poor woman's tea shop,' Phillip said, waving a limp hand at the cafe. The other officers nodded in agreement.

'What? That doesn't sound –'

'Can I talk to you for a minute, cousin?' Phillip said, gently pulling Matthew aside. He placed his arm on Matthew's shoulder, and for a while, as the officer held me there in cuffs, all I could see were the two men's backs. After a few moments, they returned.

'All right, George, we should head back to the farm before it gets late. The real Mr Rogers will come for the girl, won't he, Matthew?'

My eyes scoured Matthew's, begging for him to say something. But his were a silent pool of fearful existence. The weight of blood over water had never been so clear to me. He looked down, and I almost believed that, although he chose it, it still tore him apart. You know, mzukuru, it can feel something like death, to be rejected in your own home.

PART THREE

Dark and jagged scars

37

Ambuya's story

When I was a little girl, probably only four or five, I would watch Baba water the gum trees that lined up along the bas's driveway, creating a sort of avenue that led to the farmhouse. At least twice a week, Baba would carry a bucket back and forth from the tap at the back of the house and water the trees before returning to the fields. Each and every one of them he would shower with water until the thick muddy scent rose and danced around my nose.

Now, behind the gum trees, a big Msasa tree drank the little trickle of water that the gum trees didn't drink. Yet it still grew, its big long hands reaching out to shade the gum trees. And every time I watched Baba, I would wonder about that tree and why he never bothered with it.

Then one day playing in the mud, I noticed the splinters that spread generously around its trunk and the several branches that lay on the ground. The big tree had gone, almost overnight. Only a thick stump remained. And in my horror I ran to Baba and asked him where the Msasa tree had gone.

'Some trees are only for firewood, Thandiwe, my girl,' he had said, sweat trickling from the sides of his face and a large pail in his hand.

I cried that day, an agonised cry that left my poor father in shock, having to answer something he probably had never thought about. How could it be that some trees were allowed to grow only so that they could be burned? Who determined it?

As I sat in the car the day I was released from the cell, I thought of those questions. I tried not to look at Teacher Edwards, because I had anger spilling out of me, the way water does from a full bottle. I know after two days in the cell, I must have been grateful that he had come to get me. I know it because it was the reasonable thing to be – grateful. But you see, mzukuru, I don't remember it.

'We'll need to get that stitched up. It doesn't look good at all.'

I leaned my head on the window and watched the many gum trees outside.

'Don't worry. Nurse Edwards will clean it up for you and get you fixed up.'

I could see him out of the corner of my eye, turning to see if I was still awake.

'Then we'll get some food in you. Definitely. And water.'

I closed my eyes and their faces came to me. All of the faces that had watched as the dog mauled my jaw. All of them who had been in the car to the station, who had been in the investigating room, along the corridors to my cell.

Teacher Edwards increased the volume of the car radio as the news started to play.

This is the Rhodesia Broadcasting Corporation and the time is six o'clock ... The security forces have issued a communique. Here is the text of the communique: security forces headquarters announced today that ... ten terrorists and an African man running with a terrorist gang have been killed by security forces and quantities of war materials have been seized ... Elsewhere, a European man who surprised a gang of terrorists in the act of destroying a tractor was fired at and sustained a foot wound. He has been evacuated to the hospital ...

My head jerked towards Teacher Edwards as the unexpected click from his tongue landed on my ears.

'This is exactly the problem – they keep justifying these murders! How long shall we keep this up? Denying people their dignity and yet acting surprised when they stand up to get it back. I am so tired of this.' He breathed out deeply and immediately switched off the radio. Seeing my shock, he lowered his voice.

'I'm sorry, Thandiwe,' he said, his eyes darting between me and the road.

But as the shock wore off, laughter broke out of me. And as it unwound, it gradually rippled out of him as well. And although the skin on my cheeks stung and my swollen eye pulsated, I allowed it all to roll out. Long and hearty. Continuing until the laughter turned to deep sobs. I buried my face in my hands and tried to catch the tears that flowed from my eyes. Teacher Edwards reached for my shoulder and squeezed it.

'I pray it'll be all right. I pray God avenges this for you and makes this evil stop.'

38

Teacher Edwards brought the car to a halt in front of the clinic. An older nurse watched us before hurrying over.

'Where's Nurse Edwards? She'll need to take a look at –' Teacher Edwards said, stepping out of the truck before the nurse interrupted him.

'You'll need to leave immediately, Mr Edwards. You'll need to follow her. Oh, it's all so terrible, so very terrible. You must go at once!'

'What's happened? Slow down, Mary. Tell me what's happened.'

'It's Tawana.'

My heart stood still. In that same moment, I caught sight of the nurse's face as the distraction of my injuries slammed her over the head.

'Oh heavens, child! What's happened to you? Have the comrades done this too?' she asked, causing Teacher

Edwards to look at me again as though the broken flesh was a new thing he was seeing.

'What happened to Tawana? Please …' I struggled to say.

'It's all so terrible. Some village boys found him left in a wheelbarrow in front of his house with a note nailed through his ear. I … I … I think it was the comrades. I don't know, Mr Edwards.'

'Where's Nurse Edwards now?'

'She left just a few minutes ago when the boys came. She took Nurse Brenda with her.'

'Left for where? Tawana's quarters?'

'Yes, yes! Mr Edwards, you must follow them immediately so you can bring him with the truck. Nurse Edwards didn't look too good either. She cannot wheel a grown man back, just her and Nurse Brenda, and I still have patients in the clinic.'

By the time she finished speaking Teacher Edwards was already back in the car. I had instinctively rushed back in too.

'Should she be going with you? Should I not take a look at that?' the nurse said, her expression puzzled.

Teacher Edwards looked at me, perhaps considering whether or not to instruct me to stay. I'm sure it was the look on my face that sent it all away. He revved the car madly as he reversed from where he had parked and turned quickly towards Tawana's quarters.

* * *

Tawana's house was not far from the clinic, but as I flinched from the sight of his battered body I understood why the nurse had insisted Teacher Edwards go with the car. I looked down when I saw him, ashamed that my little tattered jaw and my swollen eye had moved me to such agony. There lay a man, every inch of his body painted with bruising and swelling so bad that I had to remind myself that indeed he was a man. A living one, we all hoped.

As soon as we walked in, Nurse Edwards rushed to her husband and then stared at me in horror when she saw my face.

'What have they done to her? Why won't this war end, Patrick?' She sobbed in his arms as though it were up to him. 'It's all so bad, Patrick. Really, really bad . . .' she kept repeating before she pulled herself together and returned to Tawana's side.

'What happened to him?' I think I must have whispered, because it seemed no one heard me.

In that moment, watching Tawana as he lay there with only his chest slightly moving, what played most in my mind was how he had always hated to keep still. I remembered how he had caused Amai grief, so that she was always running after him and telling him to sit down when he was young and staying with us after his father died. But now he lay there bound by stillness, almost as though he were a corpse.

Nurse Edwards sat at his side, stitching his arm. I watched it all, drinking in the horror of it. The piercing and looping of the needle as it went in and out of his skin, the constant and gentle dabs from another nurse whom I guessed must be Nurse Brenda, carefully tending to the other wrecked side of the man's body. I winced, although I doubt he felt any of the stings of that needle. I imagine it was the kind of pain that the body is overwhelmed by and can't process because it is everywhere.

'What happened?' I whispered again, louder this time.

'We suspect that they sent for him last night.' Nurse Edwards paused for a moment, pulling the needle towards her and gently securing the stitch on Tawana's skin.

'They must have told him they had a message for him to take to us at the mission. The note we found on him ...'

My eyes followed hers to Tawana's ear, which had a dark hole punched in the middle.

'... the note said the comrades needed to eat. They said disallowing the boys to take food from the storeroom was a bad idea,' she said, handing a piece of paper to Teacher Edwards.

'Patrick, what are we going to do? Surely you're not still thinking of meeting them tomorrow? They're going to kill you.' She wiped her eyes with the hand that didn't hold the needle.

Teacher Edwards moved behind her and pressed her

shoulder. 'Nothing is going to happen, Emma. Don't worry yourself.'

We all looked at him, and although he tried to look firm and sure of what he had just said, he did not sound convinced.

'You're meeting the comrades?' My voice was tiny, picturing the horror of what had happened to Tawana, picturing the pain I felt, whipped up and multiplied.

Teacher Edwards was quiet for a while. 'They've sent for me,' he said softly, as though he was afraid anyone else might hear. 'We've spent days thinking of it, wondering what they could want. I wasn't afraid before, but now ...' He looked at Tawana, his brow twisting.

'Anyway, I'm to meet with them tomorrow. I don't know when exactly or where. All they did was leave a note for me at the clinic a few days ago.'

'First it was the children, now Tawana? This war isn't ending any time soon, and to be honest I'm not sure I want to see how it ends. I've seen enough!' Nurse Brenda said, wringing bloody water from the rag she was using into a small dish. I realised I recognised her as the weary older woman I had seen briefly at the clinic the other day, and she wore the same look today. Tired, angry, bitter. 'We have to leave this place. We can't continue on like this.'

'We can't just leave, Brenda. How can you even suggest it?' Nurse Edwards intervened.

I stood in the middle of whatever windstorm was unfolding, watching them and somehow convinced that I was responsible for it all. How could I not be when my brother was there fighting with the comrades and I was carrying cauldrons at night to feed them?

'Tell me though, Emma, what exactly are we still achieving here? You said it yourself – the comrades might kill Patrick if he goes to meet them. And will they not kill him – or worse, all of us – if he doesn't?'

Silence screamed.

She went on. 'I honestly think that at this point, all we're doing is endangering lives, including our own. How can we help anyone if we're dead? Look at Tawana lying there almost dead, and he's one of theirs! What do you think they'll do to us?'

Nurse Edwards sighed, looked at her quiet husband, then back at Tawana. The needle between her fingers paused, and I could see the slight tremble of her hand as fear crept through her.

'Besides, you cannot just think of yourself!' Nurse Brenda's voice rose a little higher as her finger pointed at Nurse Edwards's bulging belly.

'Remember when we came, Brenda? When they told us of this little village deep in Rhodesia where the Lord's work had to be done?' Nurse Edwards started, her voice calmer than her trembling hands, now resuming her stitching.

'Remember the commitment we made when we left in England? We are still bound by that. We came here for the people, and I believe this with all my heart – that we have really become a part of them, and them a part of us. They still need a school. They still need a clinic and, God help us, but I think we must stay to continue providing those.'

'A part of them? Have you lost your mind? We aren't a part of them!'

I looked down.

'Open your eyes, Emma! We're only here because they need us for medicine and books. We're not a part of them!'

'And so what if that's the only reason? Heavens, have you already forgotten? Does the commitment we made to help everyone who needs help, regardless of who they are, not matter any more? I hate the killing too, I hate the death, Brenda, of course I do! God knows I hate it as much as you do, but we are here to heal, and we will do that as best we can even if that's the only reason we're here.'

'I'm sorry, Emma, but we have done our part. I've done my part. More than what was required of us, if you ask me! If there's still work to be done, then let someone else come and finish it!'

'If this is how you feel, then Patrick can speak to headquarters in London and arrange for you to go back home, but we're staying. Our work is not finished.' She looked at Teacher Edwards, who stood there like I did, quiet, with his hand over his mouth and his brow slightly furrowed in thought.

'With that kind of talk, you're only inviting death, I tell you!' she said, before wringing into a bucket nearby the bloody water from the rag she had been using to wipe Tawana.

A quiet whistle from the wind floated in and brought a chill to her words. I thought of the day at the bas's veranda and I looked at Teacher Edwards. If it came to it, did he believe enough to die for this? Did she?

39

As I stood there, I found myself immersed in confusion. There were wounds on my face that caused a boiling inside me because of how my kind were treated. But there were wounds on Tawana that slowly corroded my insides at how hate had sneaked up on men who thought they had a cause. The three missionaries fell silent, staring at Tawana.

'Darling, we should move him into the car and get him to the clinic immediately. We've given him a sedative which has made him stable enough for us to do that now, but he needs treatment as quickly as possible. The doctor is due to come this evening, according to the schedule, and I must make sure he sees Tawana first.'

Teacher Edwards stood there for a minute longer watching Tawana's breathing, before stepping out of the room and heading to the truck.

'We're going to have to leave these rags to soak, otherwise

they'll stink out the whole room. Thandiwe, my dear, could you please fetch a bowl of water? I think he has a tap out at the back there,' she said, pointing outside.

I nodded and went outside. I watched the water slowly trickle into the bucket. I thought of everything they had said in there, and everything I had heard Baba say, everything I had experienced. My head felt swollen, full of emotion. As I looked up to the tap, my heart almost lurched out of my throat at the sight of Matthew standing there in front of me.

'Where did you ... ?'

'Thandie,' he said, moving closer to me.

'Matthew, what are you doing here?' I breathed, stepping back a little.

'I'm so glad to see you, to know you're all right! I've been worried sick. I tried to get my uncle to come fetch you, but he wouldn't hear of it. Thank God for Mr Edwards who insisted on going as soon as he heard. Your parents were so worried ...'

I blinked, staring at him, hearing the words but not taking them in.

Remembering everything from that day: the men in uniform, the dog, Phillip.

'You said ... you said nothing while they took me away, Matthew.'

'You shouldn't try to speak; your jaw doesn't look good.'

It was as though he couldn't hear what I was saying. My gaze followed his right hand as it gently took mine, and the other reached out tenderly for my jaw. His eyes drooped, as though filled with sadness, and I could see them running up and down my face, searching.

Gently, I pulled my hand away and stepped back again. 'Why didn't you say something, Matthew?' It was fainter than a whisper, but I was determined to sound strong. It was an angry strong, I thought, one that showed I was still in control. Yet all I could hear in my voice was a thin and fragile thread that sounded like it was ready to break.

'What did you want me to say? What could I have said that would have changed anything? I spoke to Phillip and he –'

'I don't know!' I shouted, then swallowed, trying to muffle the volume of my voice. 'You could have told them that you were my bas, Matthew! That I was with you. They would have heard you.'

As he reached out again, this time trying to embrace me, I shook my head, quickly wiped the tears from my eyes and stepped further from him. A space existed between us, and we both stood there listening to the water overflow from the bucket.

'Thandie ...'

'You could have said anything, Matthew.' My words bumped into each other. 'Anything at all. Even if it wouldn't have changed their minds, even if it wouldn't have changed anything, they would have known that someone who looked like them, one of them, they would have known you disapproved of what they were doing. They would have known that I wasn't – am not! – a terrorist!'

He looked away.

'You're looking away?' I said, wiping my eyes again and moving close to him, searching his face.

He avoided my eyes. 'I don't understand, you know. I don't understand why you're supporting the comrades, Thandie. Did you see what they did to Tawana in there, to those children at the mission? How can you support people like that? What cause is that?'

'What about the people Phillip and the rest of the security forces are killing? Look at me, at this!'

My voice trembled as I reached for my jaw. I wiped the tears again but with my arm this time.

Matthew moved in and held my shoulders down. I looked at him, startled, feeling the slight tremble of his hands. But it was the tears forming in his eyes that assured me he would not hurt me. 'You must know how much I hate what they did to you.'

'But you stood there and watched. *You!* You stood there. And watched, Matthew! You just ... stood there!'

'I tried to help, Thandiwe. I tried.' He paused and sighed, then his voice quietened down. 'But those men were obeying the law! Doing their jobs and trying to make sure everyone was safe! You have to understand how –'

'Safe against who? Against me, Matthew? You think I had a bomb there with me? You believe it?'

'Of course not.' He scratched his beard. 'But, Thandiwe –'

I raised my hand to stop him from speaking.

'You should have never come here to our country, all of you. You should have stayed there, wherever it is the wind blew you from.'

'That is not fair! You know very well that this is home for me as much as it is for you. I was born here!'

'If that's true, why am I the only one who has a swollen eye right now? From walking without permission in a part of this home you say is ours. There are two countries in Rhodesia. One where *you* walk free, and one where I dare not even imagine that I'm afforded the same right. That, Matthew, is *our* home.'

His eyes narrowed and for a minute I thought he might cry.

'You know, Matthew,' I breathed, 'you can defend them all you like, but hate, no matter what dress you put it in, will always stubbornly wiggle its tail and remain hate!'

We stared at each other, allowing pride to cross its legs and scoff at us.

'I guess the question now is, what does it make you then – when you watch and do nothing while they treat our dignity like something that is theirs to take?'

I knew I'd hurt him. But I watched, letting the words crash on his head. We were already marked for different sides, and we had chosen them long ago. After all, blood *was* thicker than water, and in a war, people did choose sides.

'Hey, you two, we've got Tawana in the truck. Thandiwe, we'll need to get your jaw looked at immediately, so you should come with us. Matthew, you don't mind staying behind and locking up, do you?'

I'm sure we both heard Teacher Edwards, but all we did was stand there, drowning in our choices.

40

Tumi

Ambuya has just told me what Mkoma told her on the phone. She didn't want to, but I think after last time she decided she'd rather not have me drawing my own conclusions. Now everyone is looking at me.

They're all watching to find out what I'll do. I feel as though I'm watching me too. I should have known that the day wouldn't end as well as it started. It had been the first time in days that I'd slept till morning. I hadn't let fear whisper in my ear the whole night. I had even laughed with Jabu about running earlier this morning. And now . . .

Jabu.

'What about Jabu?' I ask quietly, staring at Ambuya as though it's up to her. 'Is he safe?'

I try to unsee the worry that flashes on Ranga's face.

'Nothing is going to happen to anyone, mzukuru, least of all Jabu. Don't worry.'

Ambuya says that like she knows it for sure. I nod,

perhaps only to console her that I am not worrying too much. But inside I'm freaking out.

Mkoma is coming, so everything will be all right.

'When will Mkoma get here?'

Ambuya looks at me and sighs. Her eyes are soft and the same worry lines that I'm used to seeing on Mkoma's forehead are there on hers, though hers are mixed with age.

'Your brother said he'd just got off the phone with the prison. Something was wrong with the engine of the plane that he was flying, so they've had to make a stop in Ethiopia to get it serviced. He might only get here tomorrow night or the day after.'

I nod.

'Don't worry, mzukuru. Nothing will happen.' She's said it too many times and it doesn't sound true any more. 'Nothing will happen. We'll all be fine.' She is speaking very softly the way you do when a child has just fallen asleep.

Ranga is quiet, just observing. Noku is lying on the sofa, dozing in peaceful oblivion. I chew the inside of my cheek and think.

How the hell did this happen?

'Did the prison tell Mkoma where Bamkuru went after they released him?'

Ambuya shakes her head, then shifts Noku on the sofa so her head won't slide off the armrest. She looks at me again.

'I won't lie to you, mzukuru. I think we should be prepared in case he comes here. I've sent a message to one of the policemen at the station. He's the son of a friend of mine. But I'll need to go there in the morning to make a formal report. Tonight, perhaps Ranga should sleep in your room, so that you're not alone. I'll take Noku with me.'

She pauses and attempts a smile. 'But don't worry, mzukuru, nothing will happen.'

t's dawn now, and my eyes are heavy again because I have been tossing and turning the whole night. Waiting. Trying not to wait. I dread that he'll appear out of nowhere and that this time he won't leave till the job is done. I roll over and glance at my phone. Three days till the try-outs.

Ranga mutters something in his sleep. It's odd to see him sleeping there, but still somersaulting the same way Noku usually does. I wonder if there's something about that bed that makes people feel as though they ought to be jumping through hoops in their sleep.

I'm envious that he is snoring away like a kettle boiling. He's meant to be here in case something happens, but I don't even know if he'd wake up. I get up from my bed and head to the window. The fog is floating above the trees today, as though someone is hazing them with a smoke machine. The window is painted with dew and there is sadness in the clouds as though they are about to cry.

I think of Jabu, something I didn't imagine I would say. I pray he isn't waiting for me out there, thinking I'll join him for the morning run. With Bamkuru out of his cell, I'm not safe outside. Jabu isn't safe either, but he doesn't know it. Another worry waltzes in.

If anything happens to him, it would be because of me, wouldn't it?

'Mfana, you all right?' Ranga asks, stretching and sitting up in his bed. I nod, but we both know I'm not. He rubs his eyes and looks at me for a while, yawning. I look back outside, watching the fog cascade through the trees. Little droplets come from the sky and tap at the window.

'You don't look like you've slept at all.'

I watch the drizzle in silence, hoping Jabu emerges so I can warn him. But I'm too chicken to go out and look for him. I bite my bottom lip, thinking, then turn back to Ranga.

'Do you think we ought to warn Jabu?'

'Don't stress yourself, man. Nothing is going to happen.'

I look back outside as the memories wash in like a wave. It's easy for Ranga to say that. Because he wasn't there when it happened. He didn't breathe that choking smell of chloroform. He didn't hear Maiguru's crying and begging. He didn't try to wriggle out of those men's grip and free himself. He didn't feel the screams, loud and disturbing, all the way down from within my belly. He wasn't there, so he can't know!

'Nothing is going to happen,' I repeat after him, rolling the words over in my mouth with my tongue and tasting them to see if I can find any truth there. Half praying that they can at least try to sound true.

42

Then it's morning and the rain is still pouring and we're sitting in the kitchen hut sharing folk tales, waiting for Ambuya to finish roasting the peanuts on the fire.

'They taste better when they roast on the flame,' she tells us. And when it comes to politics of the belly, I must give it to her: the old woman knows her trade.

'Take some, but be careful not to burn,' she says, looking at me and Jabu who is now here, sitting beside me, safe and laughing. Ranga reaches out to the pan first, scooping the hot nuts. Noku gets up from the other side, where she is petting the cat. By the way it is lying down on the mat and letting her stroke it, it seems to have surrendered.

Ambuya stretches forward from where she is sitting, trying to peer outside where the skies are now darkening. The drizzle is still falling, but a little lighter now.

'Maybe you boys should walk Jabu home – it's getting

dark and I don't want his parents to worry.'

Jabu reaches for his umbrella and stands up.

'Ahh, Ambuya, I can go by myself. It's raining outside.'

'We can walk with you,' I say, getting up before anyone decides it's a bad idea. Ranga nods, shoving the handful of nuts into his mouth.

'Can I go too, Ambuya?' Noku asks, tucking the poor miaowing cat under her arm.

'No, mzukuru, you'll stay with me, helping me roast these peanuts, no?'

Noku nods and goes over to Ambuya, while the boys and I head out, all crowded under one umbrella. The thunder roars and we all walk a little faster. The sky is closing up, darkening even more. Just as we reach the gate of Ambuya's homestead, Ranga turns to me.

'It's getting late, Tumi. I don't think it's safe for you both to be outside so why don't you head back home and I'll take Jabu home.'

I think on it for a while. The truth is I'm scared to be outside this late with Bamkuru being out and all, but I'm also worried about Jabu. 'Nah, I'll come with you guys.'

'Mfana, don't you think it's wiser that you go back? Just think about it for a second. If your uncle comes through, your grandmother and niece will be all alone at home, exposed,' Jabu says.

We all know it's a bunch of nonsense, but I nod and head

back, walking as fast as I can and turning every chance I get, even though I'm a safe distance from the kitchen hut, just to make sure I'm not being followed.

Everything is going to be all right, I remind myself. *Tomorrow Mkoma will get here, and we'll head to the try-outs in Bulawayo. I'll win the race, get into the team and I'll have my life back. And everything will be all right.*

43

Ambuya's story

I can see in your eyes that you are still afraid, mzukuru, still rattled by what happened earlier. I know how it feels to have fear tail you like a dog, barking whenever you forget it.

I had that feeling the week I came back home from the station. The war kept pushing through the trees and into our homes. Reports kept crawling through: more children without fathers, more girls raped, my brother Farai still not back home.

The swelling around my eye had gone down. Only a dark ring was left there as testimony of what had happened. I gently ran my finger along my jaw, feeling the twine that had been used to stitch it at the mission clinic. The wound was healing, but the skin along my jaw was still drying from the tear. I caught Chido, one of the older children I had taken with me to the river to do some laundry, watching me, and I quickly looked away. I wondered what Matthew would think when he saw me. I wondered if he would want to see me, if I let my hair out and allowed the wind to sweep through my afro the way he likes it. As I thought it, it angered me. How could I care like that? Had I forgotten what he had done?

Chido and I knelt on the granite that extended out of the river, me washing the heavier materials and her washing the blouses and shirts. My hands did the work, brushing against each other with the clothes between them, the foam from the soap seeping into the river. She hummed a song, something they had taught her from the service at the mission. The pile of clothes we had brought to the river continued to shrink as piece by piece we passed them through our hands and into the dish to be rinsed.

The humming stopped abruptly and I lifted my head to see why. I immediately crawled in front of the child and knelt upright.

'Comrades,' I said, turning to see if anyone else was coming. It was only us at the river, as though the rest of the village had known that the comrades would come. I looked at Chido, whose eyes were wide with fear.

'Did the white man do that to your face?'

I thought of Matthew and suddenly I could not speak. Instead I watched them both. The older comrade, who had a razor mark on his cheek, was in camouflage, with a broken bit of shrub tucked into the top of his beret the way they did those days to hide among the trees, escaping the eye of the security forces. A bayonet hung from his shoulder and he stood with one leg slightly forward as if supporting the rest of his body. The other one was about my age. I remember the toothpick in his mouth, swirling back and forth while his eyes swung between me and the child. A leafy branch was also tucked behind the beret that he wore, and his boots were worn and muddy.

'Come,' the one with the razor mark ordered, beginning to move back into the trees.

'Comrades, we have done nothing wrong,' I pleaded.

He paused and looked at me.

The other comrade chuckled, toothpick still swirling. 'Are you refusing?' he asked.

I looked behind me at the child, shaking like field grass in November.

'Comrades, I have a child with me,' I pleaded.

The one with the scarred cheek peered behind me.

'Bullet wants to see you, nothing else. Now come,' he said, turning and walking back into the trees. The other comrade stayed watching for a second, blinking lazily before bobbing his head towards his companion, making sure we would follow. I got up, hand clasped tightly around Chido's little hand.

'Thandie, what about the clothes?' she whispered.

'Leave them,' I said, yanking her hand towards me and following behind the two men.

There is a cave, mzukuru, close to the foot of the mountain just after the river. It is held hostage by monkeys now. But as we walked through the trees I could see a little smoke coming from the cave. I had never been there before, not even when I served the comrades. They always moved around, blending with the trees and hiding like chameleons. As we entered, I saw that a few of them were sitting close to the fire, roasting some meat, while the others congregated around a map, pointing and whispering.

'Bullet, I have your girl,' the comrade with the scar announced, making the rest of them turn and stare at us. I had not seen Bullet in weeks, yet when he stood and walked towards the fire and the entrance of the cave, I recognised the deadly look in his eyes. A tattoo now covered his left arm, and he had grown a little leaner since last I saw him.

'And so, we meet again,' he said, walking towards me.

I gripped the child's hand tighter.

'What happened to your face? The white man?'

I looked down, thinking of my reflection that I had seen in the water earlier. He reached out and slowly ran the back of his hand across my face. I feared everything. That VaGuhwa had said something to the comrades and they thought I was involved with Phillip's activities at the farm. That they were simply displeased that I still worked there. That they'd heard something about me and Matthew. Or perhaps that they thought I had told the officers something about them when I had been taken to the investigation room.

'I heard they caught you in Umtali. What did you tell them?'

'Nothing, comrade,' is all I managed. Chido fidgeted, and by the wince she tried to mask, I knew I was holding her too tight. I loosened my grip and prayed that my heart would stop thudding in my ears.

'Your brother, you know where he is?' Bullet said, turning his back to me and reaching for a piece of meat on a skewer turning by the fire.

My brow furrowed and I shook my head. 'I thought he came and joined you.' Why was he asking me about Farai? What had happened to him?

'Bingo here says you do know. Don't you, Bingo?'

A short, sheepish comrade whom I assumed had to be Bingo looked at me and smiled.

'Sure do,' he replied sharply, showing missing teeth that I thought had been knocked out fairly recently.

'So then, Thandiwe, let me ask you again. Do you know where your brother is? Because Bingo here says you do.'

I looked behind at Chido who sniffed, trying not to sob aloud.

My insides turned in fear. 'Comrades, please. The child is frightened now,' I pleaded.

Bullet circled around us, his boots striking the hard,

rocky ground of the cave. My heart jumped at every beat.

'You know what we do to sell-outs, Bingo?'

'No, comrade, tell me,' Bingo said, smirking.

'Let me ask Thandiwe here. What do we do to sell-outs, Thandiwe?'

'Comrade, I know nothing. Please!'

There was an excitement in Bullet's eyes. One that feasted on the fear in mine. And I wondered to myself whether it was still the cause he so passionately fought for. Or if the war had scrambled his mind and convinced him that the power that intoxicated him was now the new cause.

The comrades over by the map had resumed their muttering, pointing and speaking.

'Bullet, I think we have something.' One of the comrades held up a radio receiver.

I watched Bullet strut over and listen. There were showers of static as though the signal had been interrupted.

'The signal is a bit weak but it sounds like one of the forces' officers speaking. We think he's giving orders, maybe the next hit? Maybe a location?' another comrade explained to the serious-faced Bullet, while a third tuned the radio, searching again for the signal.

'Find that signal again. I want to know what those fools are up to!' Bullet hissed, towering over them. Just then the radio caught the signal again and a voice I recognised came through the waves. I frowned in confusion. Phillip?

Bullet turned a knob, increasing the volume.

'. . . the package been suspended? Over,' said Phillip's voice.

A brief crackle followed before another voice, seemingly far away, intercepted.

'The package has been dropped on site, sir. Over.'

One of the comrades passed the receiver to Bullet, who held it a while longer, waiting to hear more. But there was radio silence.

'Find out what that package is, Bingo! I want to know what they're planning! The rest of you, get ready to move!' Bullet snarled, before his eyes glided to me. 'You know he's one of them now, your brother? I hear he fights for the white man like he is one of theirs.'

I stared at him quietly, my mind reeling, wondering what Farai possibly could have done.

'Tell him, when you see him, that the comrades always have the last word.'

He nodded to another comrade standing close to us, who grabbed both our arms and led us out of the cave. My heart shuddered as we marched, moving quickly through the trees. A short-lived relief flared within me as the comrade dumped us close to the river, near where we had left our clothes. I watched the comrade go back into the trees and disappear, and as my head turned, the child broke into a loud shrill scream.

It was the feet I saw first, dusty ashen feet swinging. And as I looked up, my knees gave way. It was the same brown suit with cream stripes but creased this time. The shirt he had worn was now pulled up and bunched awkwardly in his armpits. A rope clung tightly around his neck, wound up on the branch where whoever had done this had tied it. The package had been suspended.

44

We somehow got home, shaken, Chido sobbing and her hand clenched tightly in mine. I walked on, fighting to make it to the kitchen hut. It felt as though I was held together poorly, like with old tape. It was the first time, mzukuru, the first time that I had ever seen the lifeless, dull eyes of a dead man. A dead man in a suit they had bought for him! A suit he had gotten for selling out his kind. And now the security forces had somehow found a reason to kill him because they could, because there was no one to stop them, no one to question them.

As we walked onto the homestead, all that greeted us was silence, as though word of the horror had reached home before we did. The sun had begun to retire and Baba's dog already sat by the door of the kitchen hut.

'Stop sobbing! People will hear!' I hissed at Chido as I pulled her along, heading into the kitchen hut.

I could hear Amai's voice as we approached.

'. . . if not for your useless theories. Now look what's happened.'

'How could I possibly have arranged this, Mai Thandiwe? How could I have known? And anyway, is this not the reason we should keep fighting?'

'Fighting for what? I have had it with you feeding my children to –'

'Baba,' I started. They both went quiet.

'Why is she crying? What happened, Thandiwe?' Amai asked, moving towards Chido, who broke out into hearty sobs and threw herself into Amai's arms.

'What happened?' she asked again.

'They've killed VaGuhwa,' I spat out, my voice trembling at the sound of the news coming out into the open.

Amai and Baba exchanged glances.

'Who told you that?' Baba asked.

'We saw him close to the river, hung there like a sack of manure.'

Amai turned to see if there was anyone outside before pushing the door closed. Her voice was quieter than a whisper.

'I think it's what he was saying yesterday. Remember what I was telling you, Baba Thandie?'

'I heard Phillip order –'

'Shh!' Horror was painted over Amai's face. Her hands had begun to tremble. 'You know nothing. You saw nothing.

You heard nothing. This is how you stay alive, you hear me?' she hissed, now holding my hands in hers.

'Mai Thandiwe, take the child to the bedroom hut where the others are and try to have her calm down,' Baba said quietly.

Amai nodded and headed out.

He looked at me. 'You do as your mother said, you hear me?'

I nodded in silence. My eyes then glided to the sheet of paper still in his hand and I questioned him with my eyes. He sighed, signalling for me to come sit next to him on the ledge. He handed me the letter and my eyes jumped from word to word.

'It can't be true! Is it true, Baba?'

If I had not seen it for myself, I never would have believed it. The comrades were right?

'But can they force him to work for them?'

'You forget, my child, the world we live in. There is no choice for the African man; there are only orders to be followed.'

I swallowed. So many questions ran through my mind. How had Farai lost his platoon? How had the security forces captured him and forced him to work for them? Why did his letter insist he was all right?

'Baba . . .' I hesitated. 'Do you think we will see him again?'

Baba sat there for a while, thinking, then stood up and walked out of the kitchen hut. It was in that moment that I knew to prepare my heart and stay watchful for news, for it was possible that we might never see my brother again.

And, mzukuru, it was a feeling that stayed with me even after the men dumped VaGuhwa's body in a shallow grave. I remember standing there thinking of the comrades, praying that they would not come and punish us for Farai's involvement with the forces. Praying that we would not all end up in a shallow grave like VaGuhwa, branded sell-outs and without anyone to mourn us.

I kept wondering how they had captured Farai. How they had convinced him to turn his back on his platoon, on his people, on the cause.

My heart beats now, mzukuru, as I remember all the danger that crawled around us like cockroaches hunting for crumbs in Amai's kitchen.

45

Tumi

I listen to Ranga snore through the night. I am afraid that if I close my eyes I will see Bamkuru's face in my nightmares. Not that anything stops him ruining my peace of mind even when I am awake. My head is packed with worry. I cannot help but fear for Jabu, alone out there where Bamkuru is lurking.

'Ranga,' I whisper loudly.

He groans and I wait to see if he'll wake up, but when he doesn't, I call him again. He pushes past the sleep to open his eyes.

'What?' he says, panicking and looking around the room, perhaps to see if Bamkuru has come.

'We should go find Jabu,' I whisper.

He yawns and sits up. 'It's late. We'll see him in the morning. Besides, Ambuya spoke to the police about Bamkuru, remember?'

I think about this for a while, not convinced. Ambuya

did speak to the police, but I am sure that whoever the police are, they are at home, sleeping. I am afraid that there is no one watching, keeping Jabu safe. I feel as though I am responsible for him.

I glance at my phone and stare at the early-morning hours dancing on my clock. Two days until the try-outs, but I'm not sure how to fit that worry in with the others.

'He's going to wait for me at the river, bruh, I know it. We were supposed to run today.'

'Why would he though? He's not dumb enough to do that. We told him, didn't we, that Bamkuru might come?'

I shrug. This would be much easier if Jabu had a phone so we could call and warn him. But this is the village – not everyone can afford one.

Ranga mumbles to himself then clicks his tongue. 'Fine, let's go. Why must you be all fancy, wanting to run up and down mountains? He-ee, look at me, I swim. He-ee, I run marathons!' he says, as he pushes his feet into some old shoes under his bed. I know he is complaining because he is grieving his sleep, but I don't for a second doubt that he wants to come. I can see it in the way he hurries to put on his shoes.

I grab my running shoes and sit on the bed. I'm not sure if I've said it before, but I'm afraid.

I think Ranga can tell, because he is staring at me in silence, waiting for when I am ready. The house is silent and I can hear myself breathing. Outside there is a mist masking everything. The darkness is there, waiting for us to enter into it.

46

Ranga and I walk very close to each other, afraid that if we leave too much distance something might grab and take us. Ranga is in front, walking slowly as though he is testing the ground to make sure it doesn't swallow him. He turns back and hisses, 'This is a terrible idea, man. We should have told Ambuya.'

'You said everything would be all right though.' What I don't admit is that I agree with him.

'Ah! Me? When did I say that?' he says. A branch swishes in front of us and we both freeze. A monkey swings past and we almost hug in relief.

'Bruh, you said it, when we were walking Jabu home in the rain – you said everything would be fine,' I remind him. He must remember it, for the both of us. Perhaps everything really will be all right if at least one of us believes it.

'Eh, me, I was just saying what people say in those situations. I'm not God. How am I supposed to know if things will be all right? I'm just a boy also, I don't know anything,' he says, crouching as he moves forward.

I stop and go over his words in my head before bursting out in a laugh that startles him.

He looks at me, confused.

'You're just a boy?' I say, laughing, almost forgetting that I'm more afraid than he is. I watch him as he thinks back on what he said and lets out a little laugh as well.

'Man, I just want to get out of here.' He continues to edge forward. We are in the thick of trees, halfway to Jabu's house.

We carry on walking.

'This is ridiculous. We should have told Ambuya,' Ranga says again. I look behind us to make sure we're not being followed. The sun is slowly beginning to lift its eyelids. I can tell from the light that is pouring into the morning, revealing the colour of the banana trees that circle Jabu's family's homestead.

'That's it,' Ranga says, pointing and picking up speed. I hurry after him.

There is silence when we reach the homestead, as though there is no one there. I follow Ranga as he heads to the back of the huts towards the kraal.

'The cattle are still here. Hopefully he's still sleeping,' he says, moving to one of the huts in the middle where he knows that Jabu and his brothers sleep. I stand aside as I watch him push the door forward and tiptoe inside. After a minute, Ranga steps out with one of Jabu's older brothers and I find myself holding my shredded hopes in my hands.

'Jabu left a little while ago. He went running,' the boy says, wiping sleep from his eyes.

Ranga and I look at each other. There is a sickening in my stomach.

'How long ago?' I ask.

'I don't know exactly, but maybe an hour or two. What's happening? Why are you looking for him so early?' The brother heads to the back to open the kraal. Ranga and I follow him in silence, as though he'll suddenly produce Jabu.

'My uncle –' I stop there.

Jabu's brother frowns in confusion, waiting for me to continue, but the words are jammed in my throat.

'What are you two doing here?' Jabu's panting voice emerges from the other side of the kraal. Ranga and I look at each other in relief. Jabu is soaked in sweat and his brow is shiny. I cannot wipe the grin off my face.

'See? I told you, didn't I, mfana? That everything would be all right,' Ranga says, beaming just as much as I am.

47

As the three of us continue back to Ambuya's, my phone flashes and I see a green bubble with a message from Mkoma, saying he is now driving here from Harare. Judging by the time stamp, he should be here in a couple of hours. I can't wait to leave this place and make headlines at the try-outs. The whole St Catherine's team, all of them, won't know what's hit them.

Jabu is yapping away, as always, walking backwards in front of me up the slope from his house through the banana leaves, towards the main road where we've been jogging lately. Right now it seems absurd that I was once so worried that I couldn't sleep through the night. But even so, I am really relieved he is all right, that everyone is. We are teasing each other and laughing as we walk up the hill when the banana leaves move, somewhere on my far right.

'What was that?' I say, withdrawing my laughter from the rest. I don't think the others hear me because they march on, tagging and teasing as they continue. My eyes search among the banana leaves and, though I don't see anything, a shiver spreads through my spine as I hear a crack somewhere close.

'Guys, do you hear that?' This time my voice is plump with urgency.

The boys quieten for a second, but after nothing comes out, they soon start again, chatting away as we continue up the incline. I have a sick feeling inside me, as though we're being watched. I keep turning my head, trying to convince myself that I have made it all up and there is nothing.

'We should walk faster. There's something in there,' I say, pointing to the thicket of banana trees ahead of us. Ranga and Jabu listen for a while. I can see the fear seeping into Ranga's eyes. Only Jabu seems completely unsold as he bends down and picks up a long stick lying on the ground.

'See? Nothing here,' he says, poking at the banana leaves. 'You two need to stop with this panicking. It's beginning to drive me crazy.' He continues on past the thicket.

Ranga turns to me and shrugs. And although I am following them now, there is a quickening in my heart that convinces me that something is about to go down.

There is movement again in the trees behind us, and before I can turn to see what it is, I freeze at the piercing screams coming from Jabu. Two men are now standing in front of us. One has in his hand a machete, and the other one ...

I can't breathe.

The other one ...

My knees weaken and my heart thuds harder. I can hear the chickens clucking in my head again and suddenly it is as though I am right back there in the sack with the cabbages.

'Bamkuru,' I say under my breath, trying to repel the word out of existence.

'There you are. I've been eager to see you again,' he says, his face dark and his voice thick. 'My, my. There's two of you now, I see. The ancestors will surely bless us for cleansing double the filth off the earth.'

Run! my head screams, but I am shaking and can't move.

Jabu tries to bolt, pushing past the two men, but before he can go far, the man with the machete grabs hold of him, and his arm locks around Jabu's neck.

'You didn't think you could escape me, now, did you?' the man says, his grip tightening.

Bamkuru begins to approach me, but without a word Ranga and I exchange a glance, and as though we have said everything we need to know, we both charge towards the two men, kicking, biting, punching.

I pick up a fallen branch and manage to scrape at Bamkuru's eye, leaving him yelping as he falls to his knees. Ranga's punches force the man with the machete to release

Jabu from his grip. They struggle for a while, the man now gripping Jabu's hand in his while the poor boy tries to free himself and avoid the swinging blade.

'Run!' Ranga screams. This time I don't freeze. Instead I push all my strength into my feet and run as fast as I can, following Ranga, who is sprinting ahead of me. There are screams floating all around me, ringing in my ears. I don't know if my memories are wailing again, or if the others are screaming behind me. I manage a quick a glance behind me and see Jabu catching up. We run till we can see Ambuya's homestead. Until our breath is stolen and all we can do is gasp. And as we reach the main house, rushing to get in, my mind is calm for a moment at the anticipation of safety. It is then that I realise that the screams can't have been from my head. Because although I feel calmer, there is a whimpering somewhere behind me. When I turn back again to check on Jabu, my body shakes wildly like a dead leaf. There is blood everywhere on his shirt, and he looks as though his legs might just give way beneath him.

48

There is a feeling that I had the first few months after the police found me stuffed in a sack like a vegetable. A belief that I was locked out of my body, forced to watch it being devoured by fear and anger, yet unable to control or stop it. Unable to move, as though my legs had sunk in wet concrete. Much like now, as I watch Ranga hold Jabu with his brother and father, trying to help him into the neighbour's car; Ambuya pacing all about the yard, hand over her ear as she talks to the police, and blood covering her shirt from where she tried to stop the bleeding from Jabu's hand; and Mkoma . . .

Mkoma's here!

I watch his confused and perplexed face as he drives into the yard, into this mess. I don't think he sees me standing here by the bowing tree, because I see the panic on his face as his eyes take in the blood on Ambuya's shirt, and then his gaze slides to Jabu's back as he gets into the car.

'Tumirai!' he shouts, jumping out of the car before he's barely even turned it off and running towards Jabu. My heart is pumping fast, but knowing that he's here now sends a little courage seeping back inside me.

'Mkoma,' I shout, finally managing to drag myself towards him, though I think my shout sounds more like a whisper. When his eyes find me, he pulls me into a bear hug and I can feel the relief as he breathes it out on me. But even though he's realised it wasn't me who got hurt, there is still horror drawn onto his face. I watch it worsen as his eyes fall again on Ambuya, who is now coming over in her stained shirt, and my brother looks as if he might either retch or faint.

'Ambuya, what happened? Are you all right?'

'I am all right, mzukuru. It's Jabu who has been hurt,' she says, pointing to the car. There is sadness in her eyes and I think I know just how she feels.

Mkoma glances at the wincing Jabu and then back at me. Jabu is trying so hard to be strong, although the pain is flushed red on his face. Yet regardless of the occasional whimper, I'm impressed at how he keeps trying to reassure everyone, especially his father, that there is nothing to worry about and that he is fine.

'Did Bamkuru do this?' Mkoma asks through his teeth, and Ambuya nods.

'I'm afraid we have to go now. My boy needs help,' Jabu's

father says with a little impatience in his voice.

'Yes, we should get him seen to immediately. I will come with you.' She turns to Mkoma. 'Mzukuru, the police are on their way and they will need to speak to someone when they get here. Can I leave you with Tumirai and Noku? She is still asleep in my bedroom.'

'Yes, Ambuya, of course. Go with them. We will take care of things here. Keep us informed,' Mkoma answers her.

As the car starts, I look down. I should probably have asked to go too, probably should have insisted that I had to, because Jabu is my friend. But my legs are shaking, my heart is pounding and the only place I feel safe is here with Mkoma.

The car drives out of the yard and a torrent of shame washes over me. How could I be such a coward? What right do I have not to be hurt when this happened because Bamkuru was looking for me?

'Tumi? Are you all right? You look like you are about . . .'

Before he can finish, I am bent over the bushes close to the bowing tree retching away. Sometimes the truth doesn't set you free. Sometimes it is a large banner reminding you just how messed up things are because of you.

49

Two officers are roaming around the yard, looking everywhere as though something will spit out information about where Bamkuru has gone. And a third officer is with Mkoma, writing something down, leaning on the car for support.

My hands are still trembling, and I jerk every time a leaf rattles, afraid that Bamkuru will emerge out of nowhere and finish the job.

Noku also seems unsettled. I don't blame her. She woke up to police roaming around everywhere and me with blood on my shirt. She didn't know it wasn't from me. I'm surprised she didn't cry, because if I'm being honest, I want to cry right now. Her little body is curled up next to me with her head in my lap, and we are both quiet as we watch Mkoma.

The officer with the clipboard strolls over to me and I feel dread spreading through me like a deadly virus.

'Tumirai, do you mind if I ask you a few more questions?' he asks.

I look at Mkoma. I'm not very keen on reliving this. It feels a lot like the time with the chickens and cabbages.

'Where did you say you were when your uncle found you?'

I look again at Mkoma as though he has the answers. He nods, telling me it's all right to speak.

'We, umm, we were coming from Jabu's house.'

'Right,' he says. 'And was it him you saw hacking at Jabu's hand or the other man?'

It flashes in my head. Not the hacking, because I didn't see it myself. But the moment I realised that his three fingers were dangling there on his hand almost as though they would just fall off. I am still ashamed at how I just stood there, how even after he had been put in the car, I was too afraid to ask to go with them.

'Did you see the hacking yourself?' the officer asks again.

I shake my head.

'But can you describe the other man?'

The man flashes in my head and my heart shivers.

'Mkoma, can we go now?'

Mkoma comes over to me and presses my shoulder. 'It's OK, Tumi. Just tell him whatever you remember, and we'll be on our way.'

I nod and try to describe what I can while the officer scribbles.

'We think this man who was with your uncle is from across the border. That's the problem, because here in this country –'

'No! Don't say that's the problem, when it's you who released from prison the man who tried to do this very thing before. *You*, the police, are the problem! Because what we're talking about here is as good as attempted murder, and yet *you* let a man walk after only serving three years for the same crime!'

Mkoma's voice is beginning to rise a little, and I can see on the officer's face that he is not happy about it.

'We only do what we're instructed to do, sir. We aren't the ones who sentence people.'

'You can't even do anything! Because the men who did this are missing, aren't they? Perhaps we should offer you a bribe since that's the language you understand. Maybe then you might actually catch the man!'

'It's not going to help anyone if you start shouting and insulting us like this,' one of the other officers says, walking towards us. 'We're only here to try and help you.'

'No, ka, that's what I'm refusing. Don't tell me you're trying to help us, when this is your *job*! You're not doing us a favour here, my friend.'

'Sir, please calm down,' the officer tells him.

For a brief moment I almost want to chuckle. I must give him this – Mkoma is quite entertaining when he's upset. I wonder if he knows.

'Calm down? When murderers are getting free passes from the prisons?' He looks at me and orders, 'Ay, Tumi, get your bags, and Noku's as well.' He turns back to the police. 'We're leaving. Because clearly the police have nothing to give but apologies. Isn't that right, officer?'

50

The furrow lines are back on Mkoma's face. And when I glance at the mirror, this time I see them on mine too. Noku is asleep in her car seat, so still I have to put my hand on her chest to see if she's still breathing. Mkoma has just got off the phone with Ambuya. She says they've taken Jabu to the hospital in Mutare and he is still in surgery. They're trying to reattach his fingers. I see it play again in my mind: the banana leaves, the screams, the running and the blood-soaked T-shirt clinging to Jabu.

I really hope he's going to be all right.

Trees whizz past us as the car speeds forward. I stare at my phone for a while, rereading the message that Musa sent a little while back.

Tumi, good luck for tomorrow if you make it to the try-outs, man.

I hate it when people say good luck. It almost makes me feel as though I really am in need of it. But maybe he's being genuine and doesn't mean it like that. And if Musa does mean I need luck, maybe he's right. I don't feel at my best any more, and my training doesn't feel like it went anywhere. I can't afford to lose this after how far I've come, but it somehow feels wrong to be worrying about swimming while Jabu's lying on an operating table, fighting for his life. I look at Mkoma in the rear-view mirror and he still looks worried.

'Do you think they'll get him?' I say.

'I really hope so,' Mkoma answers quietly. 'Are you ready for your race tomorrow?' He changes the subject.

I nod and look out of the window. I shouldn't be continuing on as though my friend didn't just get hacked with a machete. It's really messed up.

'You better be,' he says, his voice lifting a little bit. I look at the rear-view. I can see he's trying to cheer me up, but it doesn't erase the bags under his eyes, and I feel so bad about it all.

'Because I took a whole day off just to watch you. And Saru is coming too.' There's a slight smile on his face. 'And of course you know Noku will be cheering too in the stands, won't you, my girl?'

His eyes shift to Noku, who's just woken up, sitting quietly in her car seat for once, stroking the cat in her lap.

I'm still shocked that she managed to convince Mkoma that the cat would die if she left it. 'You know how boys are, Daddy. He'll just be there thinking I'm coming back, and when I don't, he'll starve to death,' she'd insisted, and he'd been too defeated to argue with her. She should probably be a lawyer with that kind of determination.

'I'll be screaming loudly on top of my lungs for you, Tumi,' she says, mouth wide open, showing her missing teeth as she demonstrates. Both Mkoma and I smile at the light Noku brings.

'Mkoma, do you really think it wasn't my fault what happened?' The question spills out of me.

Mkoma's right hand remains on the steering wheel while he reaches back to squeeze my knee with the other one.

'Hey, listen to me. This was not your fault, OK, Tumirai? Bamkuru is a … He's … They'll get him,' he says finally. 'And this time they'll lock him up for good, do you hear me?' I nod because I know it's what he wants. But I'm not sure I believe him.

The car begins to slow down and I crane my neck, trying to see why.

'Daddy, why are we stopping?' Noku asks, also trying to see what's happening.

'Looks like there's been an accident,' he says, indicating to stop at the side of the road. I push forward so I can see better. All I can make out is the back of a car pushed into the face of a big truck. There are a few people trying to help, some on their phones, perhaps calling the police, and others heading towards the three paramedics who arrived just as we pulled up.

'Noku, stay here, all right? I'll be right back,' he says, pushing open his door. I step out of the car too, and follow Mkoma to where a small crowd has now gathered.

'How can we help? I have first-aid training,' Mkoma says to one of the paramedics.

'We're trying to get these two men out of the car without injuring them further. If you would please stand aside, sir, that would be the most helpful,' one of the paramedics answers, as they start manoeuvring the driver of the crushed car out through the window as gently as they can.

As I move closer to the collision, I can see metal crumpled up. The smaller car looks like it took most of the heat, and I wonder how they're going to take out the passengers. The driver of the big truck is sitting on the side of the road with his leg bleeding. There is another paramedic tending to the man, who looks shaken.

'They came out of nowhere, you know. They came out of nowhere and tried to overtake that car,' he said, pointing to another car I had not noticed, now smashed into a tree.

'The man was driving as though he was crazy. Just came speeding from nowhere,' he repeated.

'Try to keep calm, sir, the police are on their way,' the paramedic reassures him.

'Get some gauze from the ambulance, please!' another paramedic calls to Mkoma as they manage to get the first man out of the car. I stand a short distance away, shocked by all the blood, my thoughts rushing to Jabu.

'Hold his arm so we can make sure the metal doesn't shred through his chest.' He beckons to another driver who has stopped.

I walk slowly to the other side of the collision, taking long breaths so the sight of it all doesn't knock me over. Flashes of the blood staining Jabu's T-shirt flood my mind and I think I might puke. I watch as the two paramedics carefully bring the man to the stretcher.

'This one's lost a lot of blood!' the paramedic shouts. 'Get me a bag, Doug! We need to load him into the ambulance and head out!'

The stretcher passes by me and my heart catches fire. I think I see Mkoma walking from the other side of the road towards me, but as he reaches me, I dash to the bushes close by and hurl.

'Are you all right, Tumi?' Mkoma asks, his face knitted in worry lines. 'It's all a lot, I know. I shouldn't have let you come out of the car,' he says, rubbing my back. I take deep breaths, fighting to calm myself down.

'Mkoma,' I manage to whisper. 'It's him!'

51

I have never liked the smell of hospitals, because of how nervous they make me. They smell like strong detergent and bitter medicine, and I am convinced that if misery had a scent, it would stink like that.

I sit on the bench in the waiting area next to Jabu's oldest brother, who seems perturbed.

'I'm going to go outside for some air,' he says, his voice soft. I watch him head towards the door where Noku is, playing on the veranda with Ambuya and the cat. They wouldn't let Noku bring the animal inside, and she kept insisting in her occasional accent, 'No, Daddy, I'm not going anywhere oo-oo without Sah Lionel.'

Sir Lionel – such a weird name for a cat.

As Mkoma appears back from the bathroom where he'd gone, I watch him as the doctor stops. The doctor's lips are moving very quickly and he keeps glancing at his clipboard. I can't read the expression on Mkoma's face, but

I can tell from the way he has now folded his arms that he doesn't like whatever he's being told. My heart skips a little because I don't know if it's news about Jabu or Bamkuru.

Mkoma calls to Ambuya and in no time they are both walking towards me with the doctor. I sit up and wait to hear what has to be said.

'As I was telling your grandson here, Mr Mpofu has suffered a severe loss of blood. Now, routinely we would do a blood transfusion to replace the lost blood so we can tend to his other injuries, but there's a complication. The type of blood he needs is quite rare and we do not have any in stock. As a result, we have not yet been able to give him any blood. We have been trying to communicate with other hospitals close by as well as with the national blood service to see if anything can be done, but it isn't looking very good.'

'Perhaps you can test my blood, doctor? I'm his mother. I probably have the same blood as him,' Ambuya intervenes.

Mkoma shakes his head and sighs. The furrow lines are there again on his forehead.

'Of course. If possible, I would like to get you all tested, depending of course on whether you are willing to donate. But as his family, chances are definitely good that he would have the same blood type as at least one of you.'

We look at each other in silence.

'Ambuya, I understand you have to volunteer, but I'm

afraid I can't let Tumi, or even myself, do this. We can't forget what just happened.'

Ambuya takes Mkoma's hand in hers and presses it, trying to smile. 'No one will hold it against you, mzukuru. Least of all me.'

The doctor watches us for a while and then scribbles something on his clipboard.

'Very well. I won't force you to test against your will. A nurse will come and take you to the testing room, Ambuya, and we will determine what has to happen after that. I will keep you updated,' the doctor says as he begins to leave.

I chew the inside of my cheek and I can feel my heart pulsating in my ears.

'I want to do it,' I blurt out loud enough for the doctor to hear me.

All the grown-ups are staring at me, emotions all mixed.

I take a deep breath in and repeat myself. 'I want my blood to be tested.'

I don't know why I said it, but I am not taking it back.

52

glance over at the far right of the waiting area, where Mkoma is. He keeps nodding his head as though whoever is at the other end of the phone call will see it. It's been an hour since Ambuya and I got our blood tested. Mkoma wasn't pleased at first, but I can see him fighting with himself and trying to be supportive.

Ranga has gone with Jabu's brother and father to find something to eat. Jabu's doctor came to say that they were taking him into surgery to try and reattach the fingers and it would be a while until they were done. I've been mumbling prayers ever since.

I look up at the TV fixed into the wall. There's a game show and I try to pay attention to distract myself. It doesn't work, and before I know it I am scrolling down my Instagram feed. The team is already in Bulawayo by the look of it, posting every picture with some cocky hashtag. I rub my forehead and watch as Mkoma dumps himself into the armchair beside me.

'You know you don't have to do this, right?' he asks me.

I nod, eyes still fixed on my phone.

'Tumirai,' he says, reaching out for my shoulder. My eyes slide to him. 'You *really* don't have to do this. You owe Bamkuru nothing. They will eventually find another donor for him, and even if they don't, that is not your problem.'

'It's only blood, Mkoma,' I say quietly, trying to dismiss the conversation, but feeling as though if he says it one more time, I might just agree with him. If I'm being real, I'm not sure it is just blood, because it's Bamkuru's life I'm trying to save. And when I think about it, like really think about it, I shudder at my craziness, because he's done some really messed-up stuff to me. But it's funny how life works. How even though he denies me as his family, it turns out I am the only one with the blood type that he needs.

'What about the try-outs? If we don't set off tonight, we won't make it in time for you to register before the race tomorrow.'

I'm not going to lie. I desperately want to walk out of here and not turn back. I want that spot in the national team so bad my heart is tearing apart just thinking about it. But there's a small part of me that is stronger than the rest. And that small part is keeping me here.

'No one is going to judge you for choosing swimming, Tumirai,' Mkoma says, his voice a little stronger than before.

'Mkoma, please.' I try to keep my voice from shaking. 'I have to do this.'

I can't let Bamkuru keep holding power over me. And somehow I have a feeling that giving him my blood will take some of that power from him.

Mkoma sighs and leans back in the armchair, possibly tired of arguing.

'Mkoma, do you think after the surgery Jabu will be able to use his hand normally again?' I ask.

'I don't know, Tumi, but I really hope so.'

I chew on my cheeks and the dilemma sets in. How can I call myself Jabu's friend, and then go ahead and give blood to the man who tried to kill him?

Ambuya walks towards us, holding Noku's hand. She smiles as she sits on the other side of me, and we all just park there in silence for a while.

One of the nurses walks in and something about her makes me think of a younger Ambuya. In my head I can see her wearing the same uniform.

'Tumi,' the nurse says, smiling when she reaches us. 'You can come with me now and we'll get set up.'

I look at Ambuya first, then at Mkoma, as though I'm trying to get his approval.

Tumi, what are you doing? Bamkuru doesn't deserve this!

'Are you ready, Tumi?' the nurse asks.

I look at Mkoma again, who squeezes my hand.

'Yes, I'm ready,' I say.

'I will come with you and keep you company, mzukuru,' Ambuya says as she gets up with me. I smile because I'm grateful for the distraction that the next part of her story will give me.

To be honest, even though I'm still fighting within myself about all this, I've decided I'm going to go through with it.

53

Ambuya's story

A few weeks after we had buried VaGuhwa, I stood by the side of the road, staring at the wounded man Tawana had called me to attend to.

'There's a man who's been shot! Thandiwe, please, Nurse Edwards has asked for you to come quickly,' he had almost shouted from the gate of the farmhouse. Matthew, who had been working on the bas's truck, took his attention away from under the bonnet and insisted he was coming with us.

And as I watched the deep red that soaked the wounded man's torn shirt, I deeply longed to tell Nurse Edwards, to tell them all, that I knew nothing about nursing. I had not finished my training. Had they forgotten?

'Thandiwe, hurry and press your hands on his side before he bleeds out,' Nurse Edwards ordered, eyes focused on the man lying on the grass. I nervously knelt down beside him, opposite Nurse Edwards.

'Press your hands here, Thandie,' she repeated, pointing to the mess of red under his shirt. 'You must hurry, otherwise we will lose him. He won't let me touch him,' she said with an urgency in her voice. My eyes stayed on the man's face for a while, then I nodded and pressed one hand on top of the other, over the gaping wound.

'I'll be damned if I let him die without doing everything we can for him,' Nurse Edwards said, tearing a strip of cloth from her sleeve and handing it to me to help stop the bleeding. 'But we must get him out of here. Bring the wheelbarrow closer, Matthew,' she ordered him.

Tawana looked up at the buzzing helicopter in the distance. I tried to keep my heart steady, not pressing too hard with my palms and paining the man's torn skin. I repeated it in my head so I would not forget, even though I could hear Nurse Edwards spitting out the instructions clearly.

Wipe. Press down with his shirt to stop the bleeding. Feel for the pulse, but don't remove pressure.

'Move him into the wheelbarrow,' Nurse Edwards barked at Matthew, who now just stood there.

He also looked up at the helicopter in the distance. He scratched his head. 'Maybe we should leave if he's not going to make it? What if they find us with him? Won't they think we were helping him with whatever it is that got him into this state?'

We all looked at Matthew, trying to understand what he had said.

'You want us to leave a man to die on the side of the road? You want us to stand up and walk away?' Nurse Edwards asked, puzzled.

I continued to press on the man's wound as he groaned, sweating beads of pain.

Tawana moved closer. 'Help me carry him, Matthew. We're not letting this man die,' he said, ignoring Matthew's hesitation.

The man screamed as though something had burned him, his eyes filling with anger as they alighted on Matthew.

'It's no use. He won't let me touch him anyway,' Matthew said. I looked up uneasily at the helicopter that seemed so close to us now, though we were partially hidden under the trees. If the forces found me here with a comrade, they would not let me out of the cell this time. And yet if the comrades found me with Matthew, it would be the end for us all.

Nurse Edwards winced and tried to conceal her slight panting.

'Are you all right, Nurse Edwards?' I asked, watching her.

'We need to decide how to get this man into this wheelbarrow,' she continued as though she had not heard me. Tawana leaned in and put his arm under the man's back, signalling me to help him lift his weight.

The man screamed again and winced as he pushed Tawana off him with every bit of strength he had in him. 'We should never have let you go. Now look at you, running around for the enemy!' he spat at Tawana, now trying to stand up.

I frowned in confusion, as Tawana and Nurse Edwards exchanged a glance.

'Tawana, what is he talking about?' Matthew asked, his face tight.

Tawana ignored Matthew and continued to try to convince the man.

'Comrade, we have to get you to the clinic or you'll die here. We're wasting time.'

'Tawana?' Matthew's voice trembled. 'Have you forgotten how they almost killed you? What is going on here? Have you brought them here, Thandiwe?'

'Me? How could I possibly have brought this man here? Was I not at the house with you all day?' I said, anger seeping into me and pushing my hands harder on the man's wound, not feeling Nurse Edwards yank at my arm to remind me to calm down.

Matthew was still looking at me. 'This is all your fault. They have become accustomed to coming here, because they know they'll get help.'

'Are they monkeys that you should speak of them as though they return because they're given food?'

'They might as well be!' he shouted, his voice carrying above the buzzing of the helicopter.

'Just leave, Matthew! Leave and do nothing like you always do!'

My words struck him like venom from a snake, but he wasn't finished.

'You need to bloody stop acting like everything in this damn world is about you and your skin. I am getting tired of –'

'Tired? What do you know about being tired? Don't you dare judge how I fight death for the dignity of my life, while you stand there in the shelter of your privilege! Because you have no idea, Matthew! None! You have no idea about oppression, no idea what it feels like –'

'Shut up, the both of you! Have some respect for the man! He is dying!' Tawana burst out. We looked at him, embarrassed that we had demanded an audience to watch our world catch fire.

Tawana's eyes were calm as he sat next to the dying comrade. Matthew and I watched in silence as his lips moved in prayer, words hidden in the breath of the trees. Nurse Edwards sat there, rocking lightly. Tawana's eyes slowly shifted to me, then to Matthew.

We all watched as the comrade drank in his last sights of the world, pieces he would carry with him, before he left us. We sat there for a minute longer before Nurse Edwards pulled herself up and waddled like a duck that has had too much to eat, heading for the wheelbarrow we had brought from Bas Rogers's. Once she had sat down, she panted steadily and looked at Matthew.

'You'd better push this thing to the clinic as fast as you can. I'm not telling this baby she was born in a wheelbarrow!'

54

Dark stretched its hands towards us, reaching out and teasing our shadows. A small group of people formed outside, some standing and some seated, all waiting for the little Edwards to arrive. Tawana sat by the bench close to the clinic entrance with one of his crutches resting by his feet and Matthew by his side. I sat with Amai under the tree, nodding at something one of the women was saying, yet also preoccupied by all the dead bodies I had seen, and hoping that Nurse Edwards wouldn't become one of them.

It felt like hours before Teacher Edwards stepped out, collecting all the gazes and attention and making the small group of men and women quieten down.

'Thank you, everyone, for being here. Your support is immeasurable, especially in this unstable time.' He paused. 'We hadn't known ... The doctor says that Nurse Edwards is carrying twins.'

The crowd whispered among themselves, mostly exclamations of joy.

'But there are some complications.' He paused again and scratched his head. 'We have one of the babies out, a boy. He's a little weak so the doctor has put him in an incubator. We're now hoping that Mrs Edwards and the other baby will be all right.'

The men and women gathered there took turns to embrace him and pass on encouraging words. I followed suit and mumbled something I thought might lift his spirits.

'Can we see the boy, Teacher Edwards?' Amai and another friend of hers from the village asked after the others had returned to sit under the trees.

'They're not letting anyone in, but I can have a word with the nurses,' he said, leading us inside to one of the inner wards. Four incubators stood in the room, all but one beside a bed containing a dozing mother. We walked on behind Teacher Edwards, following him to the lone little incubator in the corner of the room. A nurse with a chart in her hand stood scribbling something. As we approached, she put down the chart and came to meet us.

'We just want to take a peek at the baby, nurse. I hope that's no trouble.'

'That's perfectly fine, Mr Edwards. But I'm afraid there are too many of you. Baby can't have too many visitors at the moment. Perhaps just two of your guests could see him?'

I nodded and excused myself, whispering to Amai that she should go on without me.

I leaned against the wall close to the big open window outside which Matthew and Tawana were sitting. There were just a desk and some chairs in the room with me, and in the ward nearby I could see a few patients sleeping in the beds.

Teacher Edwards's voice trailed in my direction as he walked out of the ward, still speaking to the nurse inside. '... out soon, I hope.' He sounded full of stress.

'Stay strong, my friend. We're all here praying,' came Tawana's voice. I could see part of his reflection shining on the open frame of the window.

'Tell me about something lighter perhaps. What have you boys been up to?'

I watched Teacher Edwards turn sideways to face Tawana and Matthew.

Tawana chuckled, looking at Matthew. 'It's this one who's still in denial,' he said, nudging him.

'He still thinks it'll all go away, eh?' Teacher Edwards chuckled.

I frowned, unable to decipher what it was they were talking about.

'Oh, are we doing this again then? You two ganging up on me?' Matthew's voice intervened.

'Because you're acting like a little boy – isn't that right, Mr Edwards?'

'I couldn't have said it any better myself,' he answered, and the two men laughed.

I kept my silence and drew in closer.

'I'm sure you heard our little brawl the other day, Mr Edwards? It's no use. Whatever I say, she despises me and blames everything on me.' Matthew fell silent.

I leaned back. Were they talking about me?

I pressed my body closer to the wall and tried to remain hidden.

'And from your little performance today, I might as well say the same about you, don't you think?' Tawana asked lightly.

'You don't understand, there's just such ill will between us now. There's too much to forgive. Perhaps things that can't be forgiven. It feels as though we're trapped in our opposing positions.'

There was a brief silence. My eyes followed Tawana's reflection as he leaned in further to face Teacher Edwards.

'I saw one of the comrades who beat me up today,' he said.

I frowned again, wondering why he had changed subject.

'Yes, I heard. But from what I heard, it was more than you just seeing him,' Teacher Edwards answered softly.

Matthew spoke up. 'Still can't believe you tried to help a man who almost killed you. You didn't forget about that back there, did you?'

Tawana's face became serious. 'When we first saw him, Nurse Edwards and I –' his voice became hoarse as though refusing to come out of his throat – 'when I saw him lying there, blood gushing out of the tatters of his skin, and him trying to muffle his groaning pain so the flying helicopters wouldn't hear, as if they could . . .'

He breathed some of the heaviness in his throat away.

'When I saw him there, I grabbed Nurse Edwards's hand and hissed that she should not leave me alone with him, because I was sure of it, sure that if she did, I would choke him to death with my bare hands.'

'Yet you still insisted we save him.' Matthew shook his head.

'Because in spite of all I felt in that moment, I had to choose. I had to choose whether or not to be imprisoned by my anger. I had to choose whether to let it control and torture me, to be the thing that defines me. And only God knows how I made my choice, because nothing in me wanted to.'

'So you're biting it all down?'

'I am feeling it all and choosing with every fibre of strength I can manage, not to let it lead me. The way I imagine it is that one day you'll look at yourself in the mirror and will have to answer for the man you've created. We will all have to. This hate must end here, even though my pain disagrees with me and my insides still burn with rage. But if we're not careful, we'll keep brewing this war, and watch it devour us all.'

Silence.

Nurse Brenda emerged from nowhere and whispered something to Teacher Edwards, who quietly excused himself and headed back inside with her. I couldn't hear everything they were saying, but I managed to catch some of the words that flew between them.

'. . . my cousin who is in Umtali . . . agreed for me to stay with her . . . return back home to England . . . won't press you about this . . . safer for us all if we leave.'

'. . . suppose you're right, Brenda . . . might have to relocate . . . see if things will improve . . .'

I don't know why I lingered there. It was as though I felt the words building up in Tawana and needed to hear them. And sure enough he spoke again, this time to Matthew.

'You need to sit down and listen to each other, both of you. It is all I can hope for you, my friend. I have no answers, but I do know you cannot mend what you ignore, nor can you heal wounds you refuse to acknowledge exist.'

I stood there a while before allowing my back to slide down the wall, leaving me sitting on the floor with salty tears on my lips.

In that moment, the sound of screaming filled the air as a young boy sprinted towards one of the teachers in the small group waiting outside. I immediately got to my feet and hurried over. The boy was panting, a note held in his hand. Tawana reached out, took it from him and quickly scanned it, one hand holding the paper and the other covering his mouth. He looked up at the small group of men and women who had now crowded around him.

'The comrades say the missionaries have five days to leave the mission ... otherwise death is coming their way.'

Silence! A paralysing silence that ran its fingers down all our spines. A silence so threatening that the poor nurse who dashed outside to bring us the good news of Nurse Edwards's second baby was only met by a stillness that stared her in the face.

55

The morning after Teacher Edwards's babies were born, I stood by the Missus's stove, exhausted. I had not gotten a wink of sleep, thinking of what Tawana had said to Matthew, and of the bad news the young boy had brought for the missionaries.

As I reached out to turn the pan of chicken on the Missus's stove, the loud chugging sound of the bas's engine choked as the car drove in. I hovered by the kitchen doorway, listening for footsteps and eyeing the sizzling pan to make sure the food didn't burn. For a moment, only the wind whistled through the front door. Then finally the bas's voice punched through the silence. I could hear the traces of alcohol in it as he ordered someone to leave him alone. I peered out just in time to see him topple on the veranda stairs and cuss while he sat there, stranded. After briefly hesitating, I skittered towards him to see if I could help. The Missus stood a little way behind him, seemingly annoyed.

'Bas, are you all right?'

'Oh, he's all right. Too drunk to walk – that's all that's wrong with him. Been drinking the whole damn bottle!'

He looked up at her and scowled.

'I bloody bruised my knee here.' He paused, burped, then continued, 'Because this wife of mine kept pulling me. Always nagging! Nag, nag, nag,' he said, now trying to focus on his wagging finger.

The Missus breathed out an exasperated sigh.

'Well, don't just stand there, girlie! Didn't they say you're a nurse? Well . . . fix my knee then, won't you?'

I knelt beside him and looked up to the Missus, who only rolled her eyes and walked past me. I hesitated for a while before eventually untying the dhuku from my head and tying it tightly around the bas's knee. Feeling the wind push against my hair, I quickly tried to smooth back my voluminous hair, nervously peering to see if the Missus had seen me.

The bas pushed me aside and struggled to get up. 'Bloody useless, all the women here. Fussing over hair all the time,' he said, staggering into the house.

By the time I came back to the veranda with the table mats, the Missus and Bas Rogers were already sitting outside. The Missus sat on the right like she always did, a magazine on her lap and her knitting needles clicking against each other as she pulled the wool over them. She paused for a second, watching me dish out the food, before snipping a piece of the wool off with the shiny pair of silver shears that had been by her foot.

To her clear displeasure, the bas was humming loudly, swaying and laughing to himself in the chair.

Her eyes rose to my head and my heart skipped. I quickly looked around to see whether the bas had tossed my dhuku somewhere close, but I could not find it and she did not say anything.

As my eyes wandered, they picked up the sight of Matthew and Phillip walking towards the veranda from the tea plantation, in shirts bleached by the sun and with their hair playing loosely to the tune of the wind. At the sight of him I could only stand and stare, remembering what Tawana had said.

'Aunt April.' Phillip leaned in to kiss her cheek. I watched him from the other side of the table, his body relaxed and that smile on his face.

'Look at the both of you! Have you been rolling in mud? Honestly, between you two and your uncle, you're going to drive me into an early grave. Rosie, get a broom and sweep this mess off the veranda, will you? And you'd both better clean up before you come and have your lunch.'

As I walked through the corridor to the kitchen, my ears picked out Matthew's cackle in the background, and I pictured him going over to greet his aunt with a kiss.

I picked up the broom and got ready to return to the

veranda. But as I marched out of the kitchen, there he was, his dirty feet trudging in and stopping mine completely. For a minute, frozen awkwardly in time, we simply stared at each other in silence. I shuffled my feet and looked down.

'We should find time . . .' He cleared his throat and scratched the edge of his right eyebrow. 'Um . . . we should talk.'

I remained quiet.

'I don't mean now. I mean, it doesn't have to be today even, but I think we should talk.'

I pursed my lips.

'I mean, if you want to. I'm not forcing you or anything like that.' The tips of his ears now matched the flush flooding his cheeks.

'I heard what Tawana said to you yesterday,' I blurted.

He stared at me, blinking quickly. 'And he was right. I shouldn't have said all those terrible things.' He moved closer so that I could smell the leafy aroma of tea leaves, mixed with the strong musky scent of sweat on his shirt. 'This fighting between us must stop, mustn't it, Thandie?'

He took my hand in his and lifted my chin with his other hand, his fingers brushing over the jagged scar along my jaw and forcing me to look at him.

'Yes, the fighting must stop,' I echoed, though I doubted whether just saying those words could erase the distance between us.

He smiled, and before I knew it, he had pulled me into his chest and wrapped his arms around me. His right hand slid to the small of my back. I could not stop focusing on the thinness of his lips as his face slowly pulled in towards mine.

'Matthew, you should come see how –' Phillip, laughing, entered the kitchen. I watched his forehead crease like clothes that have been left un-ironed.

I took a step back, and Matthew slowly let go of me.

'Cousin,' he said uneasily, moving towards the kitchen door, but Phillip quietly turned around and exited the room, leaving us both standing just where we had been when we first began wading through the ocean between us.

56

The Missus rang her little bell and I hurried outside to clear the table. Bas Rogers had slid back into sleep, clutching a bottle of beer. The Missus had resumed her knitting. Matthew sat on the ledge, eyes focused in the distance as though deep in thought. And Phillip watched me as he sipped at the water in his hand.

The Missus turned to Matthew. 'Why don't you help your uncle inside, darling? He might as well lie down properly.'

'And bring the chessboard on your way out, cousin. It's a perfect afternoon to test your strategy,' Phillip said lazily.

I watched Matthew out of the corner of my eye as he got up and walked past me. My heart lurched as he neared me, and proceeded on to his uncle's side. The bas grunted at Matthew's touch and grumbled as he led him into the house.

'Aunt April . . .' As soon as Matthew and the bas had gone inside, Phillip pulled out a cigarette from his breast pocket and placed it between his lips. 'Isn't girlie here meant to cover her hair or something of the sort?'

I swallowed, and began walking back into the house. The chair screeched and I froze as he moved in front of me.

'Well, there's a hair in my water, Aunt April,' he said, and his eyes locked with mine.

I glanced at the glass on the table and then at the Missus.

'But, madam, I only took off my dhuku to wrap it around the bas's knee,' I tried to explain.

'No need to explain, Rosie, I didn't ask you to speak,' she said, forming the wool into intricate knots with her knitting needles.

Phillip stepped closer and grabbed my arm. The Missus stopped knitting and her eyes danced between Phillip and me. My heart tore at the roughness of his grip. It was on this very spot that the bas had lodged his hand over my throat.

'Bas, please . . .' I whispered.

'Come sit down,' he ordered.

'Bas Phillip, please, I'm begging you,' I pleaded, my voice thickening with tears, trying to free myself of him. Without warning, he sent a forceful slap to my jagged cheek with the back of his hand and I fell to the ground.

The Missus stood up, and her knitting fell off her lap.

The skin that had started to heal along my jawline cracked under the heat of a thousand fires.

'I said! Sit! Down!' Phillip hissed.

I sat, my whole body trembling. I feared he might actually kill me.

'Aunt April, pass me that,' he ordered, his index finger pointing at her silver knitting shears, still by her foot.

'Phillip . . . please . . .' I shifted, getting ready to stand up.

'Don't you try me, girlie,' he threatened, hoisting his hand in the air, ready to strike. I was so afraid, mzukuru, that I think my teeth might have chattered. The blades of the shears shone as they swung in Phillip's hand.

If I had not seen it for myself, I might never have believed it. A chunk of hair collapsed dead onto the ground, and my eyes followed it as its lightness was carried off by the breeze. My body stayed there, numb, and unable to utter a single word. I felt pain, mzukuru, almost as though he had shredded my flesh.

'Phillip!'

I opened my eyes and it was then that I realised that I was crying.

Matthew stood there, face pale and staring at us both.

'Phillip, what do you think you are doing?' He pushed him away from me.

'You will not fight with your cousin over this scum!' the Missus ordered.

Tugging and struggling ensued between the two men, blows flying in all directions. Then from nowhere there was a loud bang, and little white pieces of the ceiling rained on the ground. We all stared at the rifle the Missus was holding as she stood by the main door, her hands trembling.

'I will not have this fighting in my house! What has got into you both?' she demanded.

'Aunt April!' Phillip gasped, rushing to her.

'Thandiwe, are you all right?' Matthew asked, sliding over to me.

I must have heard the words coming out of his mouth, but I could not speak. You know, mzukuru, they say of Samson that when the Philistines cut his hair, strength seeped out of his skull, pouring like fresh honey from a comb. They say it robbed him bare, taking everything from him like a begrudged lover. I felt it then, the light wash of the breeze as it caressed its fingers through my patchy head and blew away my strength.

And I'm told that before I left I stared into Phillip's eyes and smiled. How I wish he had known before he had done it that hair can trigger a war bloodier than the gun. Because really, mzukuru, true wisdom lies in never thinking that you are entitled to touch a woman's hair.

57

There is a thing they say about dead things – that they are hard to let go. They say it is the grief that ties you to them, and makes you scared of losing what you've already lost. As I walked off the veranda towards the gum trees, tears salty on my lips, my hands held up the hem of my skirt containing the broken tufts of my hair and would not let go. I see the questions in your eyes, mzukuru, wondering where I was going with it, and what I thought I would do. And I can only plead insanity, because all I know is that I grieved for that loss.

'You run after her, you turn your back on your whole family, Matthew! For good!' I could hear Phillip screaming from behind me.

Then were feet thudding hurriedly behind me and the shout of my name: 'Thandiwe, wait!' he insisted, now standing in front of me.

'Let me through, Matthew.'

I tightened my grip on the hem and lifted my head high. I had lost so much already. I would not be ridiculed for whatever it was I was doing now.

'Let me through!'

'You're upset!'

I pulled my head back with my eyebrows raised. 'Upset? Don't you dare tell me what I am! You don't know a thing!'

'I am risking everything by being here with you, Thandiwe. You could at least –'

'Risking everything? Must I now kneel down in gratitude? Because clearly I'm now indebted to you for this kindness, Matthew. You honestly think you're doing me a favour by coming here? Look at what they did, because you smiled at me!'

He looked down.

'We were only fooling ourselves, thinking we could forget our places and begin again. There is no mending this. *This* –' I said, choking down the tears – 'is what they think I deserve!'

I expected him to walk away, but instead he stared into my eyes.

'I meant what I said earlier. The fighting must stop.'

He frowned for a moment as though deep in thought. 'Would you like us to bury it?'

'What?' I clicked my tongue in annoyance and tried pushing past him.

'You already have it there in your skirt, so we could bury it.'

I stayed silent, not knowing what to say.

'Come,' he said, leading me along a path that started a little distance after the big Msasa tree, meandering into the thick of the woods. I followed him, hands still clutching my hem. I could feel my mood lighten as I watched him dig a small hole in the ground, and I wanted to cackle at the absurdity.

'Do you want to say something?' he asked after he was done.

I looked at him, still baffled.

'Well?' he asked with a seriousness on his face that made me melt inside. I shrugged and let go of the hem, watching the tufts slowly unroll into the little hole he had dug.

He watched too, then cleared his throat. 'Well, I'd like to say that this hair was a true thing of beauty.' My eyes welled up as his turned and stayed on me. 'But you, even without it, are still a work of art. The most beautiful thing I've ever seen.'

I looked down, thinking of my patchy head and mangled jaw. He scooped up the loose earth he had dug and swept it back into the hole, spreading it over the hair and patting it down before standing up and looking at me again. We stood there awkwardly for a while, not knowing how to proceed.

'You should go back to the house before your cousin

sends an army looking for you. I don't have any more hair to shave on my head.'

He looked at me, smiled and drew closer to me.

'He'll have to shave mine then. I'm sure he'll enjoy that too.'

I could feel the light touch of his breath on my face as he spoke. I gave a light chuckle. The reality of what had happened writhed inside my being. And then it came like a purging. Sudden gushes of violent sobs that erupted out of me. He pulled me into his chest and held me so tightly I thought I would break.

'I'm sorry,' he whispered into my ear. As his cheek lingered on my face, I could feel the dampness that sat between us, and I knew then that we were both crying.

58

Two days had passed since Phillip had cut my hair and Amai had carefully shaved off the remaining tufts. All I could think of now was how in anger I had run to Bullet and told him that the bas and Phillip were hiding guns in the bas's barn. I had wanted the Rogerses to pay for what they had done to me. But even so, guilt crawled all over me like fire-ants, and I hadn't told Matthew what I'd done.

'It feels like the end,' I said, as we walked side by side up the small hill close to the river.

Matthew answered softly. 'If it's the end, then it's a beautiful one.' He paused. 'Thandiwe,' he said hesitantly, 'don't get upset . . .'

I frowned.

'I'm leaving tomorrow night.'

'Leaving? What do you mean, you're leaving? Leaving to where? For how long?'

'I'm going to Mozambique. There's a job that a friend of mine has arranged for me at one of the mission schools there, and I feel I should take it. You know how things are with my family at the moment, and I don't think I can –'

'Tomorrow?'

'I'm going to meet him close to the mission and we'll make our way from there. I didn't want to go like last time, without you knowing.' He squeezed my hand.

A lump sat in my throat and I could not say anything.

Then, as if I'd been waiting for it, gunshots sounded on the horizon, making us both duck for safety. A blaze of orange flames rose in the distance. My heart pounded, remembering what I had done.

'It's the farm! Quick, we have to go!' Matthew shouted.

I felt regret descend on me like a cold shower and prayed no one had gotten hurt as I watched the barn flare up wildly like tinder. I could tell from the denseness of the smoke that all the bags of dried tea leaves that were waiting to go to market must have caught fire. By the time we reached the barn, scores of men and women from the village were hurrying with buckets of water, passing them in a chain. My heart pounded at the sight of the Missus sobbing on the veranda. A little further from the house, Nurse Edwards tended to the bas, dabbing at what looked like a burnt arm.

The bas got up. 'I'm going to help put out the fire.' He moved away from Nurse Edwards.

'Oh, I'm glad you're here,' Nurse Edwards said when she saw me. 'There are other people injured.'

I stared at her, wondering where she had left her babies, and whether she herself had fully recovered.

'Nurse Edwards, shouldn't you be resting? You shouldn't be here.'

'There's no time to spare. There's a boy I saw earlier who's burned his foot. Look – there he is. You wouldn't mind helping him, would you, Thandiwe?' she said, gathering up all her dressings and ointments.

I glanced over to the other side, where the boy was carrying a heavy pail of water, limping closer to the flames.

I grabbed what I could from Nurse Edwards's little bag of medicines before rushing towards him.

'You can't be walking on that leg.'

'The fire will spread if I don't help,' the boy protested.

I coughed as a wave of smoke hit my nose. The tea estate was now full of people working together to try to put the fire out.

'They've almost got it,' I said, ordering the boy to sit down.

'I saw them, you know,' he said, giving in and groaning as he sat. 'I saw two of them in camouflage, and one of them threw the petrol bomb into the barn through one of the high windows. I was on my way from the estate with Bas Phillip.'

I flinched at his name, and tended to his leg quietly, afraid to let the guilt slip out through my mouth. What would Matthew say if he found out?

'I think they wanted to burn it all down, from the look of things. Next time they will make sure it can't be snuffed out.'

Fear crept over me at his words.

'Did you see their faces?' I asked as calmly as I could.

He said nothing but let out a whimper as I rotated his leg to check for other burns.

I understood. Anything he said could have labelled him a sell-out, and during those days when identities were hidden in the shadows of the war, you could not easily trust anyone.

'You'll be fine. It's only a little swollen.'

The boy nodded and tried getting up so he could leave. As I tried to convince him to rest for longer, my eyes spotted Phillip behind the Msasa tree, hidden from everyone else by the shadows. My heart began to thud at the sight of a tallish figure towering over him with what looked to me like a bayonet pointed at him. I knew who it was, and I knew what he would do.

I hesitated, fighting with myself over whether I should step in. Just looking at him, the rage rose within me, pushing out and making the hairs on my arms all stand on end. But it frightened me that his life was in the balance and I had put it there. I took a few steps in the direction of the Msasa tree, urging myself to run there and stop the comrade. But as I considered it, I remembered everything Phillip had done.

He had to pay. I wanted him to! For everything he had done to me, to my people.

And then Tawana's words burst over me, mzukuru, and I stood there, knowing that if I turned a blind eye, I would be brewing war just as he had said. Phillip had become my mirror, mirror, on the wall. And I wanted to be better, mzukuru.

The choice stared me right in the eyes. And although I hated it, I found myself sprinting towards the tree screaming, 'Bullet – no! Let him go!'

59

Bullet's face showed no remorse, a toothpick swivelling at the corner of his mouth, as he pointed the barrel of his bayonet at Phillip.

He glanced at me. 'You came for the closing ceremony, eh, Thandiwe? I'll make sure I give you a good one.'

Phillip looked up at me, his face painted with fear.

'Comrade, let him go.'

'Let him go?' Bullet was perplexed.

'Please let me go. I won't even report you,' Phillip begged.

Bullet looked at me and burst out laughing. 'Oh yes, because even though you are there on the ground praying for my mercy, you still think you're the law, don't you, *master*? I should be quaking now, shouldn't I, *master*?' he said, kicking Phillip and now aiming the thing right between his eyes.

'Comrade, please, let him go,' I pleaded.

'Oh, so you have become like your brother now, have

you?' Bullet said, his bayonet swinging slightly towards me. 'You have forgotten how the white man has stolen our land and claimed it for himself. How he has made African bodies rot, laid there scattered in trenches of blood in the woods, while he sips tea in his home as though he does not see it! You have forgotten how badly we want freedom.'

I watched his feet move closer to me, but his weapon didn't leave Phillip.

'I should have believed them when they said not to trust you. After all, don't you cook for the white man and tend to his needs too? You think we don't know how you run around for him? Now look at you, begging for his life. Pathetic!'

'Comrade,' I tried again, hitting the back of my hands against my palms.

'I thought you understood, Thandiwe. I thought we were on the same page. *These* people –' he poked Phillip in the chest with the point of the bayonet – 'come here and steal our land, order us around, piss on our culture and our values, and now they are stockpiling guns to finish us off in the trees!' he said, kicking Phillip in his side. 'The guns were not in the barn! Tell me where you hid them!'

'Bullet, please,' I tried again, shocked to find my trembling hand forcing the barrel of his gun downwards.

'What are you doing?' Bullet shouted. I stood in front of him, both hands pressing on the gun, stopping him from firing it. And while we tussled, Phillip got up and scurried away, leaving me face to face with the beast that had now awoken in Bullet.

'You have chosen the wrong side of this war. Now look how your white man has left you alone to pay for it!' he hissed, standing over my fallen body. 'You disappoint me, Thandiwe.'

I watched as he spat out the toothpick. In horror I listened to the sound as he unbuckled his belt. A fear that preys on women took hold of me, and I remember how I slammed my eyes shut and curled tight into a ball. It was the second time I had ever prayed, hoping that if there was a God, he would not laugh and look away.

And I tell you no lie, mzukuru, but just like a miracle, when I opened my eyes Tawana and Matthew were kneeling next to me, with Phillip standing a short distance from them. I remember standing up, weeping with joy and relief, and throwing myself into Matthew's arms. An immense sense of relief washed over me and I pulled his head towards mine. His lips were soft and warm when I kissed him, and I remember in that moment being completely unaware and blinded to everyone else around us.

60

Tumi

I am watching Ambuya as she sits on the armchair close
to me. She is silent now, with worry lines that look like
Mkoma's. I watch her for a while, thinking that perhaps
she is trying to remember more of what happened next. The
story cannot be over.

'Ambuya?' I urge. I want to hear more. Her story has kept
me so calm through all this. There's a tube hooked to my
arm and a bag hung somewhere on the stretcher chair but I
had almost forgotten that I have a needle sticking into me.
I mean, I'm not scared of needles or anything, but listening
to the sound of Ambuya's voice, living in the world she built
with her words, has kept me distracted.

'Ambuya?' I say again, hoping she will continue her tale.

'I think perhaps I have told you enough, mzukuru.'

'But, Ambuya, you said the story would help me.'

*I mean, it's true, she did say that. But it's also not cool
to leave me hanging.*

Ambuya smiles. 'I did say that. And I believe you have already heard what I wanted you to hear. You're a smart boy after all. But, mzukuru, war is a painful thing, and perhaps memories of such pain should not be passed on to littl'uns like you. I have already told you too much.'

'I just want to know how the story ends,' I try for the last time. Ambuya doesn't say anything.

After a while the nurse comes in, pushing a trolley. 'How are we doing in here?' she asks.

'Not bad,' I mumble.

She fumbles with the blood bag, then looks at me.

'I think we have enough,' she says, getting ready to take the needle out. She dabs antiseptic on my arm and sticks a band-aid on it. I've been asking every nurse that comes through here if they know how Jabu's doing, but there hasn't been much news. It's been three hours now since his doctor said they were taking him into surgery, and I've had no more information.

I try again.

'Have you heard anything about Jabu, my friend? How is he?' There is an anger in my voice when I say it this time, because everything that happened to him floods back into my mind.

The nurse looks at me and smiles. 'He is out of surgery now. The doctors managed to save his fingers, but he's in an induced coma. We're going to have to monitor him to see how he responds before we can know for sure.'

'What of my son? How is he, nurse, do you know?' Ambuya asks.

I don't know why it angers me that she cares about Bamkuru after everything he's done, but it does.

'The doctors are doing everything they can,' the nurse says.

That doesn't mean much, I don't think. All those medical dramas I've watched teach you that it's best not to get anyone's hopes up. Though in this case, I don't really know what my hopes are.

'Once I have more news, I'll let you both know. I'm sure he'll be very grateful to know that you helped him.'

I scoff and look away. I was sure before why I insisted on doing this blood-donation thing. After all, my real hope for recovery is for Jabu. But I can't stop myself from thinking that when I look at myself in the mirror, one of the actions I answer for can't be that I let Bamkuru die.

61

I am standing at the door staring at the bed where Bamkuru is. One hand is chained to the bed and there is a tube in his nose. More tubes are hooked up to his hand. A policeman has been stationed outside. But the way Bamkuru looks now, I doubt he's about to try to run again.

I should be terrified, watching him sleeping there. I should be cowering and hiding behind Ambuya, who is standing next to me. But even though I did him a solid and donated some blood, I'm still hella angry.

Mkoma couldn't come in. He said he had to stay with Noku and her cat, but I think his truth is that he needs time. If I'm being real, I think I need it too.

'You don't have to go in, mzukuru. It will not change anything. You have already done more than anyone could ever ask of you,' Ambuya says, placing her hand on my shoulder.

I say nothing but keep staring at Bamkuru. I hope there's

someone praying for him right now because after all he did to Jabu and me, I feel as though I might just leap in and tear his throat out.

'If you decide you want to go in, you shouldn't expect anything from him when he wakes up,' Ambuya says.

'But I saved his life.'

'I know.' She squeezes my shoulder. 'I know, mzukuru. But you're going to have to forgive him as well; it's the only way you can be free.'

The only way I can be free? Mandem doesn't deserve my forgiveness. Heck, I shouldn't have felt I had to be the bigger man and give him my blood. I definitely don't feel like the bigger man right now, that's for sure!

'I've given him my blood. That is way more than he deserves. I cannot just forget all that he did, turn a blind eye and pretend it didn't happen. If anything, he owes me –'

Ambuya turns me to face her. 'Feel every shred of that anger. Don't suppress it. Feel it and let it flow through you, but after that, you forgive him, you hear?' Her voice is firm now. 'Because if you don't, you will be trapped in this prison.'

I grit my teeth. 'He doesn't deserve it.'

'You're absolutely right, he doesn't,' she says. 'But you deserve peace, my mzukuru. Forgive him for yourself: even though it hurts now, let each piece of this go. No matter how little, no matter how slowly, let the pieces go, mzukuru.

And forgive yourself too, because you are not God and you have no right not to.'

How can I possibly forgive myself? It is because of me that Jabu got hurt. It should have been me. I shouldn't be standing here.

62

I am heaving, buried in Ambuya's chest, feeling the anger and the tears come out all at once. After a while, I step back and collect myself. A nurse comes from the corridor and we give way, following her into the room. She unhooks a transparent bag with yellowish liquid from under the bed, replaces it with a fresh one and walks off with the other one.

Bamkuru fidgets, and my heart beats wildly as I watch his eyes open. I step back a little. He tries to move his hand and realises that it's restrained. I feel a strange satisfaction from it.

'How did I get here?' he asks with a grogginess in his voice.

I look at Ambuya.

'You tried to kill me,' I blurt.

Ambuya slides her hand in mine and holds it tight. There is a silence for a while and, even though I know he won't, I can feel myself waiting for him to beg for my forgiveness.

Bamkuru tries to sit up but the combination of the medication and the tubes push his body back down.

'You were in an accident,' Ambuya says.

'And you came here for what? Revenge?' he asks.

The nurse comes back in, and as soon as she sees Bamkuru awake, she smiles.

'Look who's up,' she says. 'You're a lucky man, Mr Mpofu. If not for Tumirai here who just donated some blood to you, we could be telling a different story.'

I know she thinks he'll thank me. But I can see from the stare in his eyes that he is disgusted by it.

'You gave me cursed blood?' he says, trying to rip out one of the tubes in his arm as if it'll magically drain out the blood already flowing in his veins.

I look away because seeing him do that somehow fills me with shame.

'How dare you!' Ambuya hisses, heading over to the bed.

The nurse rushes over and holds her back. 'Perhaps you should leave for a while,' she says, and then turns and tries to calm Bamkuru, who is panting. Ambuya is close to tears and I have a lump in my throat.

'Please,' the nurse asks again. 'It is not good for him to be like this.'

Ambuya clicks her tongue and heads out. I linger a moment, observing Bamkuru.

'Can I say goodbye to him before I leave?' I ask the nurse, trying to seem as innocent as I can.

'Very quickly, Tumi. I don't want him to get more upset,' she says, giving way for me to come close to the bed. I strut over to his bedside and pretend to embrace him before I leave. He tries to fight me, but he is too weak. I check out of the corner of my eye that the nurse is far enough away not to hear.

'Bamkuru . . .' I whisper into his ear, my heart beating madly and a bubble of fury lodged in my throat.

I want to tell him that I hope that when they take him back to prison, and every time he thinks of the outside, he remembers how my blood that he despises so much saved his life. I want to tell him that I hope he remembers this moment, and how in spite of everything he did, I fought with everything in me to forgive him and that I am now free of him. But instead I pull every good thing in me and whisper in his ear, 'I will be praying for you.'

t's been three days since we left the hospital, and one day since the trials started. Ambuya has texted a few times but every time I try asking her about what happened next in her story, she ghosts me. Musa tried calling me this morning, but I was too defeated to pick up. I just watched it ring. Now, about three or so hours later, there's a text from him and one from the coach.

Tumz, I'm worried about you fam. Holla at your boy.

Tumi, this is Coach Ngoni. We haven't heard from you, is everything all right at home?

I haven't responded yet. It all feels too fresh, and I think I need a minute before I can respond. Besides, my mind's been occupied by other things.

Jabu got moved to a private hospital in Harare and today

we're going to see him there. I think Mkoma felt bad about everything. He said organising the move was the least he could do to help. He even coordinated a successful go-fund-me page so that people could contribute to the bill. And I'm so glad people came through, because everything has just been so hard on Jabu and his family.

They woke him up two days ago, the day after we left the hospital, and his brother called when we got home to say we could come visit. So yesterday Mkoma drove me over. I was worried about seeing Bamkuru, but Mkoma said they transferred him to the prison a day after we left. I'm hoping this time he stays there.

I was a bit uneasy at first because I didn't know how Jabu would react when he saw me. But he tried to hug me with his good hand and even made a joke. His mother, who was sitting by his bed, didn't seem like she held anything against me either.

When I started to apologise she said, 'It is the devil's work, mwanangu. It is not your fault.' Although I'm not quite sure how it all adds up, because that particular devil was my uncle and I gave him my blood.

I mean, I'm still working on this letting-go-of-the-little-pieces thing. My head's got it coded like a Rubik's Cube. Some days I think I've got it down, then on others the rage floods back in and I feel as though I have to begin all over again. Ambuya says my fight to let the pieces go will have many rounds. She says it's because pain has a way of convincing you to keep it. So I'll try.

Speaking of Ambuya, I'm still curious about how her story ends. I've been standing here in Mkoma's bedroom, staring at his wardrobe and trying to decide whether to go looking for the letters again. I'm thinking that if I look at the last ones, I might be able to get a sense of what happened. What's kept me glued to this spot so far is her reluctance to share any more of it with me. I don't know if the story gets any worse, and that scares me a little.

As I struggle in my conundrum, Mkoma steps in. I turn, knowing I shouldn't be here thinking about going through his stuff like this. By the frown on his face, it doesn't look very good for me right now.

'What are you doing in here?' he asks calmly.

I follow as his eyes go to the wardrobe but I say nothing.

'Ambuya told me you had one of my letters,' he says, loosening his tie and placing his briefcase on the bed. I'm not sure if I should say anything. I'm already waiting for the 'it's wrong to go through people's things' lecture.

'What did you think of it all?'

That's not normal going according to the script.

'She didn't tell me all of it,' I mumble.

'She stopped before the end?' he asks, sitting on the bed and taking off his socks.

I nod.

'She doesn't like talking about the end, I've learned. At some point when I was in the States, the letters stopped coming for a while. I wrote to her several times, worried that something had happened to her, but she just sent a short note saying she couldn't bring herself to tell me any more. When she eventually sent the last one, she said she had had to ask one of the children staying with her to post it for her because she couldn't.'

'Why does she get stuck on the ending?'

Mkoma leans back on the bed, his body supported by his hands. 'I think it's difficult for her, Tumi. I think it's like reliving it, and she feels guilty for everything that happened. I don't know.'

Guilty? What happens at the end?

Mkoma gets up and heads to the wardrobe. I watch as he hangs his blazer and moves his hangers so they are aligned again.

He turns and looks at me.

'She told you till the part she leaves home?'

'Nah, she stopped after everything that happened during the fire at the Rogerses' farm. Just got all silent and wouldn't say anything else. She said I'd heard enough.'

Mkoma laughs and reaches up for the box.

'She told me to give you the last pages of her diary.'

My heart starts to beat and I really don't know why.

'But are you sure you want to know though, Tumirai?'

Heck, how am I supposed to be sure of that?

But I find myself nodding. Mkoma nods back and rummages through the box. I watch him as he pulls out the letter marked number ten. He pauses, looking at me for a while.

'Endings are such beasts to tackle,' he says, handing me the letter. 'But tackling beasts is what makes us stronger, no?'

Mkoma is being all kinds of philosophical right now, and I don't know what it means. But I nod because I want to get to the part where I start reading the letter.

'But she wrote you your own letter,' he says, pulling a folded note from his pocket before handing me the diary entry with Ambuya's story.

There is a picture placed inside the folded letter. One of Ambuya standing next to some white dude. The same guy in the picture she has in her living room. I know it's Ambuya, not only because of the scars, but because in this picture she's much older. Only a little younger than she looks now.

'She asked me to read it first to make sure it wouldn't be too much for you.' He hesitates. 'It's not an easy read, Tumi, I won't lie to you. Here's what I think: if you're really going to read it, then maybe you should sit down, wait till you're in the right mind for it. That is really the best advice I can give you.'

At that I swallow.

What the hell happens at the end?

64

It's late now, and we're back from the hospital after seeing Jabu. He was a bit drowsier today, but the doctor said it's normal because of the medication they gave him for the pain. Said it means it's working and he's responding well. Man, I just can't wait for him to get out of hospital.

My phone is ringing again, and I stare at the caller ID, trying to decide if I should pick up or not. I press the green button and bring it to my ear.

'Tumi! You've had me really worried.'

'Hi, Musa,' I say a little warily, waiting for the judgement, for him to gloat.

'Dude, what happened to you? You never came through. Are you good?'

'I'm cool, bruh. Just some stuff happened at home and I couldn't make it.'

'Right. Well, the whole team was talking about how we wished you were here.'

I hesitate.

'Did ... did you get in?'

'Yeah, man, we made it in the team relay. But it's not the same without you, you know.'

'Congratulations, Musa, I mean it.'

And I really do.

'Tumi, bruh, are you really all right?'

'Kind of,' I say. 'Listen, I have to go. Tell the team I said congrats! I'm really proud of all of y'all.'

After I hang up, I stare at my phone for a while. I really am proud. I'm not scamming them. I'm a little bummed I didn't get to make it in, but the bigger part of me feels proud. The other part dreads going back to school and facing everyone. But I reckon I probably just need a minute to get over my disappointment and I'll be good.

I slide my phone into my pocket, and as I do that, I feel Ambuya's letter in there. I haven't been able to read it since Mkoma gave it to me. I keep bringing it out, then sliding it away again.

Thing is, once I read it, that's it, I can't unread it, and that is making me quite nervous. It's crazy because this morning the curiosity was gnawing at me, but now that I have the letter, I can't seem to bring myself to look.

I listen to Noku playing in the lounge with Sir Lionel, and from the TV noise in the background, I think Mkoma must be watching something on Netflix.

I have time. I take a deep breath and pull the letter out again.

My dear Tumirai,

It has been hard for me to send this. I have not meant to ignore your messages, but I have been distressed about telling you what happened. Please forgive me for it, mzukuru. I am afraid this letter will be painful to read, even more, I imagine, than everything that you have heard so far. This part of my story still comes in my nightmares, and when I started sharing with you all the events of back then, I thought by the time I reached the end it would be easy to tell. But when I began to remember it, my nightmares began to revisit me. And you have gone through so much, mzukuru, I feared, and still fear even now, that I might be sending you pain.

So, my mzukuru, if you find that the pain is surging at you, please stop reading. Put the pages aside. You can come back to them when you are feeling stronger. But like I told your brother, I think you both ought to know this story. I have kept the scars hidden for too long, because it was too hard for me to share such pain even with your father and your uncle. I have asked your brother to give you the pages of my diary that were in his last letter, and I have told him to keep watch over you.

Write to me happy things, mzukuru, so I know you are well. Come back to visit your Ambuya soon, so I can fatten you with all the good food they don't give you there in the city. You must never forget how much I love you.

With love always,
Your Ambuya

65

Ambuya's story

30 November 1976

I keep remembering it all. The day after the fire, I couldn't sleep. I kept thinking of how Matthew was going to leave and how I would never see him again. I had to stop him. I had to convince him not to go. And so I crept to the mission after Amai and Baba had gone to bed. I thought if anyone could help me talk to him, it would be Tawana. Perhaps together we could convince him not to leave home. Not to leave me.

But as I got close, I could see the lights flickering in the Edwardses' house, which was a little way from the mission school's football fields.

As I neared the thickets surrounding the football field, my body tensed.

Voices! And I knew one of them!

'Move! Move!' It was a voice I knew so well. Bullet.

'Move, comrades!' The voice yelled again.

I dropped into a crouching position so I could peep

without being seen. Bullet stood with his back towards me, and three other comrades were with him, each holding a gun.

A group of seven or eight people were being marched from the opposite side of the field, and two men who seemed to have axes pushed the group to gather in the middle of the open space, forcing them down onto their knees. I strained to see better, and a hole formed in my stomach as the scene unfolding became clear.

'No,' I whispered.

'We have the goods secured, Bullet. Comrade Bingo has them tied up in stacks in the back. We should go now.'

'Go?' Bullet scoffed, circling the group of missionaries. I crouched there, glued to the ground and afraid to move, despite the orders screaming in my head.

Run! Search for help! Go home!

'Teacher, I thought we were getting along, all of us. But that was before you all went and picked a side.' Bullet stood facing Teacher Edwards. 'I saw you all at the estate yesterday, running around, undoing our progress. Now I'm still a little confused, teacher, because I thought you said you were neutral.'

'We were only trying to help.'

'You see, comrades,' Bullet said, turning to his companions. 'The thing with these people is that they will always help their own.'

I noticed how his eyes shone larger in the moonlight.

'I heard you like to pray,' Bullet said. 'Perhaps you should give us a taste – don't you think, boys?'

The other comrades burst into laughter, one of them hitting one of the missionaries with the butt of his weapon for no apparent reason.

'Where is your God now, huh? Is he here with you, watching? Or has he fallen asleep because it is night-time?'

'Patrick, I told you we should leave!' It sounded like Nurse Brenda crying from somewhere among the group. 'I said it, Patrick, but you never listen! I warned you!'

'Shut up!' another comrade screamed, and shoved her to the ground. It must have woken one of the babies because a sharp wailing filled the air.

'Please let them go,' Teacher Edwards pleaded, his voice shaking. 'You can do to me as you please, but please let the rest of them go. Let them take the children and go.'

Tears streamed down my face at the sound of his broken voice.

'Oh, are you afraid, teacher? Why so frightened? If the Lord really is your shepherd, then dare I say you have nothing to be afraid of, no?'

He forced Teacher Edwards's chin up with his bayonet.

'Isn't this what you teach our people, lying to them in your services?'

'Comrade, please,' Teacher Edwards implored.

'Oh! The white man begs. You ignore our pleadings every day as we beg for our own lives, for our freedom – why should we listen to yours, huh?'

'Comrade, I'm sure we can come to an understanding. Please, we have done nothing wrong.' My heart stopped at the sound of Tawana's voice.

'Someone shut this one up!' Bullet roared. My hand flew over my mouth to hold in the screams as soon as the gun went off.

Teacher Edwards began to pray, and like an uncoordinated song, the women broke into sobs and wails.

'. . . that you would forgive them even as they do this . . .' are the only words I can remember of it, and how Bullet kicked him in the mouth with his boot while he prayed on. I imagined blood flowing from his nose.

'Oh yes, you better pray, my friend . . . because you surely need a miracle tonight!'

'Please, comrades,' Teacher Edwards cried from the ground where he lay, 'I beg you to spare them. Do as you will to me, but please spare the others.'

His voice trembled in a way I had never heard from anyone.

'So gallant, teacher. Offering up your life so others may live. Your queen would be so proud of you. In fact, I will write to her personally and tell her that the man she sent to steal the land from us, pretending to spread peace while killing my kind, died a hero. She'll be pleased, don't you think?'

The comrades all laughed.

'You know what, I will humour you because you found me in a pleasant mood tonight. I will exchange the lives of your friends and family for yours. Aren't I so generous? It is me you should thank, not some God you have never met,' he said, stepping on the poor teacher and pushing his face into the ground.

'Please stop! Please leave him alone.' Nurse Edwards was harder to hear, her baby crying in earnest now.

'Shut up,' one of the comrades hissed.

'You should make sure you take pleasure in destroying our bodies!' Nurse Edwards screamed, louder now. 'It is all you will ever destroy! You won't touch our souls!'

When one of the other comrades who seemed to have lost his appetite for it all tried to talk Bullet into letting them go, I watched the bayonet thrust sharply at his head and his body crumple lifeless to the ground.

The rest is harder to write, but I still hear Nurse Edwards's screams in my terrors at night, as the comrade nearest to her hacked at her neck with his machete. Teacher Edwards cried, a groggy painful cry from the depths of his soul. And the rest of the group broke out in screams that wake me up still today.

I remember how the child kept wailing until Bullet

called to make the noise stop.

I should have turned away. I should have never seen it. The crunch of the newborn's skull under the man's boot.

After that it unrolled slowly, as if in slow motion. I know that an owl hooted, and a dog howled. Then havoc struck. Teacher Edwards got up, and one of the comrades pushed him to his knees. Behind him Nurse Brenda sobbed and one of the other missionaries broke into song. Perhaps to soften it all. Perhaps to distract them all. Or perhaps the horror made me hallucinate, because it was the same song that Amai used to sing.

I remember drawing in a long breath and holding it in at the raining of more blows, more punches, the screams of the other baby; more stomping, and the ringing of women's terror and sorrow. Then there was just the pungent smell of blood … and the silence that swept over those grounds that had now become a grave. And all I could think was, God help us. All of them, gone!

66

2 December 1976

I failed to write yesterday. I struggled to get out of bed at all.

Baba was worried and called the doctor. When he came by, he said that I am suffering from post-traumatic stress. But I feel as though I am in a hell that is boiling over. Perhaps post-traumatic stress is the kinder way to tell me that I am trapped here. That the war is now in my mind and might never leave.

But I keep telling myself that I must write it all down. I must not allow myself to forget. So, I will read this, again and again, lest I begin to forget. Because I cannot allow myself to. And there is more to tell of that night, more that I could not bring myself to write first time round.

I feel ashamed of how fast I ran, trying to escape when the smell of blood whipped my nostrils, and a wind arose, whistling strongly, and with it a sharp bow of lightning struck.

As I neared the trees close to the river, I saw that Matthew was there, standing under a tree talking to two men. For a brief moment, relief sank in when I realised he had not yet left, and I sprinted towards them, breathing heavily and shouting: 'Matthew! They're all gone, Matthew! All of them. They're gone!'

I am weeping again now as I write this. The same way I did that night as Matthew came to greet me.

'Thandie, what are you doing here? You shouldn't be here.'

There was concern in his eyes and his voice was low, as he quickly glanced behind him as though the danger behind him might hear.

'You should go – get out of here.'

I peered over his shoulder, fearing that I would see the comrades there with bayonets. But something worse stood there in the shadows, lurking and waiting.

'You need to run away from here,' he repeated, shoving me a little.

'I'm not leaving you,' I hissed, even though my stomach turned.

Behind him, Bas Rogers and Phillip began walking towards us.

'Matthew, I am not done talking to you!' the bas shouted from a little distance behind Phillip. I didn't see the gun in the bas's hand until he raised it in our direction. Though when I reflect on it now, I find myself thinking that I should have run the moment I noticed it.

'You say something happened at the mission?' Phillip asked, close now. I held my breath, afraid of what he might do, but his voice was warmer than usual.

'Thandiwe, the missionaries – you say something happened to them?' he said again.

As soon as he said it, the images poured into my brain and I could see it all again.

'Teacher Edwards, Tawana, the babies . . .' A lump formed in my throat and I inhaled a deep breath, trying to calm down.

'They've killed them all. The comrades, they killed them.'

I felt the weight of my body fold under me, but before I could fully collapse to the ground, both Phillip and Matthew had rushed to help me up. I looked at Phillip, afraid and confused, watching him as he helped steady me on my feet.

The bas, a little distance away, still stood with his handgun slightly elevated. And though I felt unease over it, at the time, it seemed to be almost insignificant.

'You should go back home, Thandiwe. It's not safe out here tonight,' Phillip said. 'I'll go to the mission and see if anyone is still there, and then I'll radio to some of the boys from the force to come and meet me there. Matthew, take the girl home.'

Matthew and I both stared at Phillip in surprise as he

left us, hurrying in the direction of the mission school.

I had expected him to drag me by the throat and throw me in the cell himself. To accuse me of having been involved with whatever had gone on at the mission. But it is possible that he felt grateful to me for earlier when he had been in the thralls of death, lying there at Bullet's mercy. That is the only way to explain it.

'We should go,' Matthew said, but I sensed an uneasiness in his voice.

'Matthew!' I squeaked, watching the bas cock the rifle in his hand and aim it at me.

Matthew and I both froze.

'Didn't I tell you, boy, to leave these bloody animals alone? You thought you could just sneak out of the house and take her with you? You thought you'd disgrace the family like that?'

My whole body trembled. Matthew mouthed something, but I couldn't tell what. My heart began to hammer as he walked slowly towards the bas.

'Uncle, put the gun down, please.'

'After all I've bloody done for you, Matthew, this is how you repay me? This is how you repay the family?' The bas's eyes stayed on me. Matthew walked slowly towards his uncle with his hands half hoisted in the air, every step calculated.

'Uncle, please, you don't have to do this. She has done nothing wrong – let her go.'

'Step back, Matthew.'

But neither of them would back down.

As soon as Matthew jumped at his uncle, trying to prevent him from shooting, I shut my eyes so tightly that I was sure my eyeballs would be squashed. I stood there, prepared for death.

Instead, a shot followed by a shrill scream pierced my ears and my hands flew to cover my mouth.

Matthew!

'What have you done?' I screamed at the bas, running to Matthew's side.

The handgun thudded as it fell from the bas's hands.

'Matthew? Matthew, speak to me,' I begged, my hands wet with blood.

Matthew groaned, trying to stay awake. 'Love is ash ...' He struggled to form words.

'Matthew, stay awake. Please!' I pleaded, using my hands to try and stop the bleeding. He coughed and held my hand tightly and all I could do was cry. I could see him trying to smile, trying to ease my pain. But my heart hammered and I could see his body slightly shake from the shiver of my body.

'Love is ash. The thing –' he paused in coughs and I began to sob – 'the thing that remains ... when the fire is spent.'

I curse myself now that I didn't know what to say to him.

As though all the words I knew had vanished, leaving me with nothing. All I could think to do was to hum that same soothing song that Amai used to hum. The same song I had heard when the horror of the missionaries had begun to spill over.

'You know though, don't you?' he said through chattering teeth. I held him in my arms, rocking us both and listening.

'You do know how sorry I am though, don't you, Thandie? For everything.' He gasped for breath.

'For this,' he said as he held my other hand tighter. I could feel him slipping from me and I began to hum again. I remember how gently I rocked him, humming Amai's song. Hoping that the end had not come. But after a while his hand loosened its grip on mine and I saw the stillness of his face, the emptiness of his eyes.

I think the trees shook as I erupted in a scream. It should have been me. I still cannot help but wish it had been.

67

Tumi

Mkoma and I are driving to school, and I'm feeling a lot of things. I stayed up most of the night yesterday thinking of the missionaries, thinking of the massacre. Thinking of how Ambuya must have felt watching that. I stopped reading after Matthew died. I couldn't bear it any more. There's a page still to go and all I could do was stuff it into one of my books. I don't know that I want to find out what else happened.

And it feels as though as soon as I closed my eyes last night, the hole in my stomach shook me awake.

It's the first day of term today, and I'll have to face everyone at school. I'm not sure if I have a place there any more. And it scares me – not as much as it did before, that's for sure, but it still has me unable to eat and stuff.

'Are you all right?' Mkoma asks as he pulls up in the parking lot. I linger for a moment, watching the other students making their way to the classrooms.

'It'll be all right,' Mkoma says, squeezing my shoulder. I look at him and nod before grabbing my bag and getting out of the car.

As soon as he drives off, I see Coach Ngoni slam his car door closed. The dread collapses on me, and I think I can walk away before he sees me.

'Hey! Tumirai! Wait,' he says, coming towards me. 'We missed you at the try-outs last week, is everything all right?'

My stomach turns.

'Yeah, coach, I had some stuff happening at home so I couldn't make it,' I say, and wait for him to remind me I'm off the team. That I'm not part of them any more.

'Yes, Musa did say something about that. I hope everything is better now?'

Everything would really be better if I was still on the team, but I nod.

'I was talking to Bongani and the other boys and we think we should start your training soon for the try-outs early next year.'

I don't say anything because I don't know if it's a pity move or not.

'The judges heard about your record at the school event last term, and I can't promise anything because the competition is ridiculous, but you might really have a shot.'

I look at him blankly.

'But of course you're going to have to work really hard

for it. Earn your way there, if you get what I mean?'

I don't know what to say. Not because I might have a shot in the solo events, but because the team cares. Whether or not I'm swimming with them in the national team this year, they still think I'm a part of them.

t's the weekend and I'm standing in Ambuya's lounge in Vumba, staring at that same picture of her and the white man. The same white man she was with in the picture she gave me. Saru and Mkoma are playing with Noku, and I can hear Ranga and Jabu talking outside. I couldn't stay out there too long because every time I look at Jabu's cast I shrivel in shame and guilt. He still doesn't seem to blame me, but I honestly don't see any way not to blame myself.

'Mama, Noku wants another guava or she might just faint and die, no pun intended,' I hear Noku say from the veranda where they all are. Jabu's laugh is the loudest. I smile as I step away from the picture. Noku randomly started referring to herself in the third person a few days ago and it's become her new thing. Between that and her occasional accent, I really think we're all in trouble.

My phone pings, and I pull it out of my pocket.

Fam hit me up for our normal routine when you back.

It's from Musa. I'm not going to lie about it, I'm disappointed that I'm not part of the national team with the rest of them. But for the first time since *it* happened, it's because my dream is to make it to the Olympics. And it really is just that. It doesn't feel like a point I have to make any more. Yesterday, during the assembly, before I knew that the principal was about to call the team on stage to congratulate them, I was dreading it because I thought I might hurl. But it wasn't even that deep. I mean, it stung a little, but I didn't feel as though my world was ending or anything.

I'm starting to learn that not everyone is going to be fond of me, and that's cool. I haven't gotten it down to a T yet, but I think whatever reason people might choose to shun me is on them. It doesn't need to shape my world. I even told Bongani yesterday after he called me 'mrungu' that I didn't like it because it was rude. I said it as politely as I could of course. And although he shrugged and walked off as though he hadn't heard me, mandem now knows I don't like it, and that's a step.

Sure boss. I'll be back home tomorrow, and I'll show you flames in the gym.

I slide my phone back into my pocket. Ambuya walks into

the room and sits quietly on the sofa close to the window.

'Your brother tells me you read my letter?' she says, watching me.

I look at her and all I can give her is a small smile.

'So you read the last pages of my story too then? What did you think?'

My imagination springs up again and I see the hacking and the shooting all in my head. I think she must see it on my face, because she stands up and walks to me.

'It wasn't the easiest read,' I say.

'Yes, I'm afraid it wasn't the easiest thing to live through either.' She is silent for a while. 'Did you read it all?'

I nod, then think. 'Actually, there's a page or so left. I have it with me,' I say, pulling it out of the pocket of my shorts. I've been meaning to read it the whole week, but I haven't been keen on finding out what it says.

'I understand. It is not something easy to digest.'

She smiles and looks at the picture of her on the wall where she is with the white man.

'You know, mzukuru, after I lost my friends, I wrote it all down and I spent years reading and rereading that trauma, because I told myself that if I didn't, I would forget it.'

She looks at me.

'For twenty years I read it every day that the Lord made, punishing myself because it shouldn't have happened to them, and if death wanted to claim life, it should have been mine. I think I must know those words by heart still.'

She moves closer to the picture.

'For those twenty years I danced a very complicated dance between guilt and shame. But you know, then I saw Phillip again, and he helped me let that piece go.'

I frown. 'Phillip?'

She pulls the picture from the wall and stares at it with a faint faraway smile.

'On the twentieth anniversary of their passing, I went to their graves there by the mission. They buried them close to the football field where they had died. And when I got there, he was there. I hadn't seen him since it happened. He had moved back to England and so when I saw him, at first I wasn't sure what to expect. But then we began to speak, and I found out that he too blamed himself.'

I have no clue where this is going, but I know I want to hear it.

'After he returned to England, we kept writing to each other. You see, mzukuru, he was the only one who understood what had happened and where it had all started. And he understood the guilt and the shame. He had been there. We started to write back and forth, each sharing our stories of Matthew, and reminding each other to live. Because any self-infliction of pain would not have been what Matthew would have wanted. Not what any of them would have wanted. None of that would have been honouring their lives, or what they had endured.

'Initially I had framed that poem to remind me of it. But after I saw Phillip, I put that picture of the two of us up there too, so I would never forget. So that it would continue to challenge me if ever I did. It took me a while, but I eventually stopped reading that diary and packed it away until your brother asked me to share the story of what had happened and who the man in the picture was.'

I want to say something to her, but I'm not really sure what.

'Go outside and be with your friend, Tumi mzukuru. It is not your fault what happened, and Jabu knows that. You need to forgive yourself.'

I am scared to look her in the eye.

'Listen to me, my child. Just because you think and feel it, doesn't mean it's true. It is not your fault. Do you hear me? Let this piece go, mzukuru.'

'I don't know how to do that,' I say.

'Do what you can for today. Go outside, sit there and laugh with your friend. Hiding in here will not undo what happened to him, and it is not honouring him in any way either. He came here to see you, so go outside and "chill". Isn't that what you youngsters say these days?'

I chuckle. It sounds so weird, coming from her.

'Gradually, my mzukuru, it will become easier to let this piece go, but you must keep trying.'

She presses my shoulder and I wipe the tears from my eyes.

'And when you can, my mzukuru, read the last page. I think it will be good for you,' she says, smiling and walking out of the room.

69

Ambuya's story

11 February 1977

When I woke up today, for the first time I could breathe. Baba took me to the mission graveyard where the missionaries were all laid to rest. I haven't been able to go there since it happened. But today when I woke up, it was all I wanted to do. Baba says it is progress, like a shoot growing up from hard ground. He says when I am stronger he will try and organise for me to go to the city in Umtali to see Matthew's grave. I pray I will feel ready to go when the time comes.

But today when I got to the mission, the morning fog cleared a little. I want to believe it meant something. Perhaps it symbolises my own fog lifting. Perhaps the heavens are acknowledging that I can breathe again, that I am starting to heal.

I still miss them though. All of them. But most of all I miss Matthew. I miss how he sometimes chuckled in the middle of his sentences when he was talking to me. How he grinned when he teased me, and the flush that coloured the tips of his ears when he laughed or was embarrassed. I miss how he was not afraid at the end. And how he cared.

But even though I cried as I sat by their graves, it didn't feel as though I was pinned down by my pain any more. It almost feels as though I am beginning to be alive again. And God knows it will be hard, but I have promised myself, promised all of them as they lay there, promised him, that I will try and be alive. Not just to exist but to live, to be alive.

I know though as I write this that I am not yet ready to move on. Because right now it still feels as though I have no right to. So I won't. And maybe that is all right too.

I am still figuring this path out. I don't yet know how long I will feel I have to do this, but for now I will still remind myself of that night every day.

At least now I know that if I owe them anything, it is life, to live it! And I shall not waste mine, for their sake. So here's to becoming alive again, one day at a time.

70

Tumi

'm smiling as I hold this last piece of Ambuya's story that she shared with us. It gives me hope that the fog will lift, just like hers did. I take a moment to myself, digesting everything I have read and heard, and I glance at the picture on the wall again. Perhaps Ambuya is right. Perhaps what I owe Jabu is life. I mean, I don't quite know how to do that yet, but I want to try.

When I eventually walk outside to the veranda, Jabu and Ranga are eating guavas and laughing at something. I sit next to them, and when Jabu looks at me I smile. He nudges me gently as though he understands.

I won't pretend I don't still feel pretty guilty. But for real, I do want to let this piece go. So, although it feels impossible right now, I'm going to give it my best shot.

'Daddy, we need to have business talks,' Noku begins. Mkoma's eyebrow is raised as he listens to her trying to convince him to take home another kitten that Ambuya got from one of her neighbours last week. She's putting all her ammo into it, the pouting and the big brown eyes, all her big guns.

'You know this kitten is a girl, right, Daddy? And you know how girls are. They need to be –'

'No, Noku, my friend. No. I've heard this speech before and we're not doing this again,' Mkoma protests.

'OK, then wait,' she says, putting the kitten down and as her occasional accent slides in, Jabu begins to laugh.

'You want a better speech, I have a better speech na, don't worry. Listen to this here na abeg. Noku just likes cats oo-oo.' She is moving her little hands around, with her head on the side the way they do in those Nollywood movies. If Mkoma's not careful, this kitten might just go home with us.

'Let Noku carry this little one back home na. She go take care of it well-well.'

'No, Saru,' Mkoma says, wiping his eyes as the laughter roars out of him. 'This has to stop, it's too much. She's lethal. She can't keep watching those movies.' His whole body rolls with laughter.

It's the first time in a long time that he's laughed like that, and that is more than I could have gotten from any swimming race. I glance at Ambuya smiling beside me and I feel warm inside. I finally understand the thing about Ambuya now, why Mkoma is so mad about her, why everyone is. She is a force, a blazing fire, melting away little sparks everywhere she goes and leaving embers that ignite a fierce volcano of memory whenever you dare forget her.

I'm sure now that she's who I want to be.

Dear Reader.

I've been thinking about this book for a couple of years now. At first it was two different stories: one of the terrible atrocities committed against people with albinism in Southern Africa, and the other of the missionaries – my dad's friends and teachers, whom I'd grown up hearing about. The latter story was told to me in the context of pre-independent Zimbabwe, which was called Rhodesia at the time: a place where my parents, grandparents, uncles and aunts were mistreated and discriminated against, although it was their home, simply because they were black and African. It was a place infested by hate and war, where native Zimbabweans fought for independence against colonial rule by the British, a place blighted by racial hate and prejudice until 1980. This war cost the Elim missionaries their lives. As much as the stories of hate disturbed me, hearing how these particular missionaries in a little village in Vumba had tried to live their lives with love inspired me – particularly because they had lived there like ordinary people who were part of a community, not saviours who needed to rescue a race of people or 'improve' them.

But as much as I wanted to write my version of this story, I also wanted to write about the atrocities that were –

and still are – committed against people with albinism in my region. Stories of children and women being kidnapped, having their limbs cut off or even being killed because of the mad belief that their bodies have supernatural powers. As a child, hearing about this always used to scare me, because my aunt has albinism and I feared that we would wake up one day and hear that she'd been taken, sold across the border. It is mind-boggling that such ignorance still exists today.

I've carried both these stories in my spirit for years, wondering how to tell them, until now, when I've woven them together so they complement each other. Because essentially the question that surfaces from both – one I hope you come face to face with as you read this story – is: will we let our misconceptions about each other, especially where colour is concerned, allow us to perpetuate hate? And if we do, when and where will it end?

I think this book contributes to an important conversation – one that has been ongoing for decades. Perhaps it is a conversation that we are in danger of getting used to because we've been hearing it for so long, but if we don't listen to each other, we become comfortable with ignoring it. I hope that, as you read this story, you remember those who have suffered, who have been persecuted and treated without dignity because of how they look, whatever colour they may be.

I hope that this book challenges you to refuse to let skin colour blind you – and that you ultimately refuse to tolerate injustice in any form.

Rutendo Tavengerwei

People with albinism still face significant discrimination and prejudice around the world. In some parts of Africa, atrocities are still being committed against them today because of a lack of awareness about their condition. If you would like to help by making a donation, or if you would like to know more, you can visit the following websites:

Under the Same Sun – www.albinism.org.uk/
Zimbabwe Albino Association – www.zimalbino.co.zw
Global Aid Missions – globalaidmissions.org

Glossary

Abeg – please
Amai – mother
Ambuya – grandmother
ay – hey
Baba – father
Bamkuru – older uncle
Bamnini – younger uncle
Bas - boss
biko – please (Igbo)
blud – very close friend
boom-gate – an entrance
bruh – friend, buddy
chitsvambe – a game, like tag
deep - profound
dhuku – head-wrap
fam – derived from the word 'family' and used to refer to
    friends or people close to you
fishbae – slang for swimmer
haa, hee, he-ee, ka – variations on 'huh'
holla – get in touch
iwe – you
kaffir – derogatory term used by colonialists to refer to
    black Africans
kaffir-boeties – derogatory term used to shame white
    people who associated with black Africans

ko - why

kunei – what is happening there

maiguru – an aunt

mandem – slang used to refer to friends or peers

matumbu – dish of cow intestines

mdara – lit. old man – also used to mean 'man' in general

mfana - kid

Mkoma – a term of respect for a big brother

mrungu – white man

Msasa tree – also known as zebrawood, a common African
tree

Mwanangu – my child

mzukuru – grandchild

na – now (Igbo)

ngoma - drum

outchea – out here

pungwe – a type of all-night rally/party that the comrades
would host to encourage morale in the villages during
the fight for Zimbabwe's independence

sadza – cooked cornmeal

sekuru - grandfather

tisvikewo – a greeting usually used when one is
announcing their arrival at someone else's house.
Much like 'Knock-knock'.

wangu – my

zambiya – a wrap tied by women around the waist in
situations where they are expected to dress modestly

Acknowledgements

I am so grateful to the many people whose support, encouragement and hard work made it possible to bring this story to life.

Firstly, my wonderful editor, Felicity Alexander, who so clearly understood my vision for this story and from the very beginning understood what it meant to me. Thank you so much for being patient with me through all the revision stages and for pushing me to make it better. I appreciate so much all your very hard work. I would not have been able to do this without you, or wanted to do it with anyone else.

I would also like to thank the rest of my team at Hot Key Books, who worked so hard to make this book the best version it could be. Special thanks go to my assistant editor, Carla Hutchinson, whose input is always so incredibly invaluable, my copy-editor Talya Baker, who always has a keen eye, to Jane Hamnett for such careful proofreading, and to cover designer Anna Morrison and Dan Newman of Perfect Bound Ltd, for doing such a wonderful job with the book design. Also, thanks to Ruth Logan, Ilaria Tarasconi and Saidah Graham in Rights and to Molly Holt, Amy

Llambias and Isobel Taylor in Publicity and Marketing. You guys are the real dream team.

A special thank-you to my friend Elloa-Wade Saleh Aboubakar, who was with me when I saw the old woman and the little boy in the train station and humoured me as I jotted down all the ideas in a frenzy, even though it almost made us miss our train home. Your excitement alone for this story was a real vibe.

To my hype-team Kamogelo Chadi, Amanda Nghona and Tumi Teko (who asked me to put her name in my book, and I said I'd think about it), you guys are some of the best cheerleaders a girl could ask for. I'm always so grateful to have you in my life.

To Tariro Mutyavaviri and Dionne Lakey, thank you for reading this book while it was still in its rough stages. Your feedback is invaluable.

My absolute gratitude also goes to my aunt Synodia Tavengerwei for sharing with me some of her experiences growing up as a person with albinism. And to Tally White who took the time to read this story and shared such invaluable insights on albinism as well. I am very grateful and will forever be.

To Andy and Heather Woodward, I'm so thrilled you were excited about this book as soon as I told you about it. Thank you so much for praying for me when I felt overwhelmed and for always encouraging me.

Thank you to my girl Olaronke Thomas, who is a real gem, and who helped me shape Noku's Nigerian voice with all those little phrases.

To Stephen Griffiths, thank you so much for writing your book *The Axe and the Tree*, which helped answer a lot of the questions I had about the actual Vumba missionaries. I will always be grateful for all your support and encouragement and for being so forthcoming.

A special shout-out to my parents, who sat down with me on multiple occasions to tell me their stories, at times of horrible things that happened pre-independence. Dad, thank you for sharing the story of your friends and teachers at Elim and emphasising the importance of living a life of love over hate. And Mom, I can't believe how many times you read this story, even when it still needed a lot of work, and still came through with wonderful insights. I love you guys, and thank you for always being my example.

My siblings. Gang gang! Yeukaishe Hope, you are always so passionate and excited about my writing, with so many insights and ideas. I absolutely treasure it. Tafadzwa, Tendai, Michael Nyasha and Heather, you are always ready to support, and I definitely would not have done any of this without you.

Lastly, to the Elim missionaries who inspired this book, thank you for living a life worthy of the calling you received. Your story touched me, and I hope it touches so many more.

Rutendo Tavengerwei

Rutendo Nomsa Tavengerwei lived and studied in Zimbabwe until the age of eighteen, when she moved to South Africa to study Law at the University of the Witwatersrand. She then completed a Masters at the World Trade Institute, and worked at the World Trade Organization in Geneva, Switzerland.

Her debut novel, HOPE IS OUR ONLY WING, was nominated for the CILIP Carnegie Medal 2019. THE COLOURS THAT BLIND is her second novel.

Also by Rutendo Tavengerwei

'Compassionate, gripping and intelligent'
Emily Barr

hope
is
our
only
wing

rutendo tavengerwei

Read on for an extract...

HOT
KEY
BOOKS

proudly. Whoever was playing knew what they were doing. She could hear the underlying tone of a hum that flowed well with the song. And in that magnificent noise floated all the memories and feelings she was trying to ignore.

Her mother hovered by her side, trying to figure out where they should go. Shamiso felt numb, staring down at her shiny new shoes and listening to the music that disturbed the air.

'Shamiso . . .' Her mother hesitated. 'Are you all right?'

'I told you before,' Shamiso muttered, biting her breath, 'I don't want to be at boarding school. Especially here!'

She watched her mother wipe her damp neck as though she had not heard her. Her blouse clung to her skin, moist from the sweat.

'There's no time to cry,' her mother said softly. 'Wipe your tears, *mwanangu*. You'll be fine.' She nodded at the administration block in front of them.

Shamiso saw the exhaustion on her mother's face as they picked up the luggage and headed for the

1 ▬ ▬ ▬ ▬ ▬ ▬ ▬

SHAMISO'S HEART BROKE into a shudder of beats. She could hear the jazzy trails of the *mbira* spiralling in the air. Her father would have loved that sound. She glanced at her mother, who stood next to her, fanning her sweaty neck. She seemed preoccupied. The music played on, painful and familiar.

When Shamiso was eight, her father had insisted that she learn how to play. The metal pellets had bruised the tips of her fingers as she plunked on them. A series of confused notes bumping into a glorious discord. The frustration had been too much for an eight-year-old, made worse by the fact that none of the other kids at school understood quite what the instrument was.

Shamiso listened as the voice of the *mbira* rose

administration block. They sat in the waiting room and looked around. The young man behind the reception desk seemed caught up in a tsunami of phone calls. The walls were lined with pictures of alumni at different events across the years. Shamiso could hear snatches of conversation from two men standing by the door.

'. . . yes, but by staying away . . . we . . . are only punishing the children,' one of the men said rather slowly. Shamiso kept her head down, concentrating on the tracks of the *mbira*.

'You are beginning to sound like that journalist . . .' the other man commented.

Shamiso raised her head. She guessed the men were teachers, but she could barely hear what they were saying. She leaned in.

'Of course . . . we . . . we have to be smart about this,' the first man continued, his voice rising in volume.

A bubble of anger formed in Shamiso's throat. She tried to keep calm. Her ears picked up the music, which was slowly forming into a song. She wondered whether she would ever have been able to play like that.

The notes poked at her brain. Her father had called

it the sound of home, the stolen guitar of nature. She closed her eyes. Memories sat vividly in her mind. His fingers dancing around on the little pellet strings, his lips pursed, the music swirling. She held her breath, scared that if she breathed out too soon she would lose him.

A sudden voice jolted her back to the present. 'Aww, first day at school, is it?'

Shamiso opened her eyes and wiped them with the back of her hand. A girl stood in front of her, holding a pile of books. Her curly hair was tied back tightly into a bun. She seemed to be headed for the staffroom.

'Newcomer or first form?' the girl asked.

'I'm new . . .' Shamiso mumbled.

'Would you look at that! We have ourselves a Brit,' the girl declared.

Shamiso gritted her teeth. The door to the staffroom suddenly opened. The cartoon on the door warned her that it was out of bounds. A teacher stood in the entrance, blocking the view as though the staffroom was some sacred destination that students were not meant to see. All Shamiso could hear was laughter as the teacher beckoned the girl inside.

'Well, don't worry, Your Majesty, it will definitely get worse. The queen doesn't come here for tea, I'm afraid,' the girl said in her best imitation of what she thought was an English accent before following the teacher inside.

Shamiso fought the urge to call after her. She had hardly been in this country long and she was already certain she did not like it at all.

Thank you for choosing a Hot Key book.

If you want to know more about our authors and what we publish, you can find us online.

You can start at our website

www.hotkeybooks.com

And you can also find us on:

We hope to see you soon!